THE FREEDOM WEAVER

a novel

RW HAGUE

Other Books By RW Hague

Surviving Midas

Escaping Midas

Killing Midas

find more from RW Hague

www.rwhague.com

THE FREEDOM WEAVER

RW HAGUE

HISTORICAL FICTION

To The Twitter Folks...

Nice Try.

CHAPTER ONE

The yarn danced, ducked, and dangled on and off the ends of the slender, bone knitting needles as Marta stared at the table before her. Before sitting at my table, all that had been present was the yarn, but now a blanket covered her lap. Her long locks, tied with a string and resting on her shoulder, bounced off her sage-green frock in time with her movements. Her blue eyes caught in the candlelight as she saw me looking at her, and she smiled as if knowing what was on my mind. I doubt she guessed correctly.

The pale yellow candle burned to a nub on the pewter stand, and Kai stood to fetch another from the cupboard. The candle, which stood the length of my arm, appeared the size of a twig in his hand, but most things dwarfed in Kai's presence. After melting the base with the nub, he pressed it into the pewter stand. His arm rippled and his veins popped as if what he did required great force. Better suited for the field than the house, Kai performed most actions in this manner. It was his strength for which I had purchased him.

Once the candle was lit, Kai sat carving a point into a stick with his knife while I drafted my next tapestry, a map of a town in what the Romans called Gaul two hundred years ago. My proprietor, a wealthy landowner, called it Austrasia. For now, that is. With so many feuding factions present in the world, duchies and countries changed names and shifted borders like the tides.

The customer had sent me leaves, berries, nuts, and other products of his land to add to the inspiration of the craft, but all it did was stain the tabletop as the berries rotted and the leaves dried to powder. I crinkled the parchment into a ball and tossed it into the corner. "Where the devil are they?"

Kai looked up at me, and I, being deaf, read his lips, "They'll be here soon, Zayim."

I downed the remaining wine in my goblet and stood, running my hands through my hair. My loom stood in the corner, and I considered working on the half-finished tapestry to distract myself – and to compete with Marta's competent fingers—but the colors and threads had no appeal.

I picked up the bottle of wine, and Kai placed his thick hand over my goblet. "That will be three, Zayim, and you haven't eaten any supper."

Marta paused in her knitting, her lips folding inward as she suppressed a grin. I met Kai's eye in a match I was determined to win. "Are you my nursemaid or my bodyguard?"

With a roll of the eyes, he removed his hand, and I allowed a smirk of triumph. But I poured only half a cup and carried it about as I paced. My companions continued their activities as I willed the guest to appear.

"Marta, you should go home," I declared suddenly. "I would hate for rumors to start concerning your late night here."

She and Kai exchanged a look as if knowing a fact that I did not. "Zayim, you are worried about my reputation?" Marta asked. "I spend most of my nights in your company. What reputation is there to defend?"

My mouth popped open. I had never so much as held the woman's hand yet there were rumors? Our friendship was well-known, of course, but no romance existed, at least on my end. Although I knew she wished it would.

Kai took a sip of wine as he studied me. I wish he had told me about the whispers.

"I…uh…am sorry—" I stammered.

She swiped her hand in dismissal. "It's better they think that than the truth."

A gleam flashed across the floor as the piece of metal above the door swayed. The bell shook as well, and Marta took her basket of knitting with her to the next room. Kai stood to open the door, and I picked up a few bobbins beside the loom, pretending to inspect the quality of the thread while keeping an eye on the door.

Kai waved me over. "They need your seal, Master."

I gathered the supplies from the table before meeting them at the door. Two men waited. The first, gangly and pockmarked with hands stained black from the reins of his horse peered around Kai, inspecting the walls of my workshop. The other, bearded and short, waited with parchment extended.

"Now hold on there," the bearded one said. "We need the master to sign, not another slave." He pointed to my face where the brand of four interlocking circles ran from my temple to cheek.

I unrolled my sleeve showing the 'HL,' the brand for Homme Libre or Free Man white against the soft flesh of my wrist. The man's eyes widened at the mark, and I took his moment of distraction to seize the parchment and set my seal. Then I stepped back into the house, allowing Kai to dictate the rest of the instructions.

With Kai's help, a large wooden crate was hauled in from the lane where a wagon was parked. The bearded one's face turned purplish-red as his eyes bulged. His gangly mate fared only a fraction better while Kai carried the other side of the crate with a straight, determined face. They set it on the floor beside the table, and the bearded one pulled off his hat and fanned his face with it as he leaned, one hand upon the box.

"A good evening to you," said the gangly one, jabbing his elbow into this partner's ribs. The bearded one righted and walked to the door with his arms dipped low behind him. With the quick tip of a hat, they were gone into the night.

"They did not comment on the weight," I said, and Kai frowned. "They always comment about the weight."

Kai said, "Perhaps their suffering was obvious enough, they did not think it needed to be said."

"Do you smell that?"

"There is something foul, yes."

"Quick, open the crate."

With the fire poker from the hearth, Kai pried off the lid, and I ripped out the fabric lying within, tossing them on the table. Blinking up at us in the dim light, a woman crouched in the bottom of the box. Her dark hair was matted, and a bit of sick sat dried on her chin. The brand of a star marked her temple.

Upon seeing the sick, I sighed with relief. I had feared the smell to be that of death.

Marta entered from the other room, and the woman's face softened to see someone of her sex. "Oh dear," said Marta as she quickened her pace, "are you unwell?"

"I'm so sorry." The woman stood, and the roundness of her belly showed, accentuated by the shadows of candlelight. "I couldn't help myself. It came on so quick."

Turning from the box, I ground my teeth. Damn whoever it was who had sent her in this condition! Not only was it a risk to her, but us as well. And the smell had been so pungent, I doubted the merchants had not noticed.

I stepped to the shuttered window beside the door and opened it a crack. The horse and wagon had departed and the streets appeared abandoned, but that could change in an instant.

Marta had poured a basin of water while my back was turned, and she dabbed at the woman's soiled clothing. The dress had been patched and re-patched, and I doubt gray had been the original color.

"Open the hole," I ordered Kai. "We need to get her hidden right away."

"But Zayim," Marta said, "she needs food, water, and a bath."

"The merchants were not acting right. She needs to be hidden immediately."

Kai took the leg of my loom and lifted it from the floor. Using the opposite leg as a pivot point, he turned it out until it lay perpendicular to the wall. Then he knelt and lifted the secret latch between the boards.

The metal above the door swayed once more as the bell jostled. I spread my arms wide as if to say "You see?"

Taking the girl's hand, Marta led her to the hole, and the girl ducked inside. The trapdoor closed, concealing her. Kai lifted the leg once more, and the metal flap swung with vigor. The bell toppled from its hold, striking me on the top of my head.

Rubbing my skull, I pointed to the storefront door, ordering Marta to leave by that exit. Kai swung the loom into position, and I waited with my hand upon the latch for him to distance himself from the spot. I picked up the bell from the floor before opening the door wide.

The man at the door stood with his hand upon the bell cord. His long cape drifted just above the floor, and the broach upon his shoulder marked him as a captain of the magistrate. Two guards stood behind him, their faces hidden by helmets. A pike stood aloft in the hand of one guard while a sword swung at the belt of the other.

"What the devil is this about?" I demanded. "Visitors at this hour, and ones with such determination to wake the house, they break my bell." I held it up for him to see.

"My apologies," said the man in the cape. "I am Captain Vernard. We received a report from some merchants that a suspicious delivery was made here and have come to investigate."

"And that gives you the right to damage my bell?"

The Captain looked over his shoulder to the men behind him.

"If you are going to speak, you must face me. I am deaf and cannot read your lips through the back of your head."

The Captain scratched his temple as he took me in from my brown, curly hair to my deerskin boots. "You are Zayim the weaver, are you not? Your reputation precedes you."

"As I have never heard of you, Vernard, I cannot say yours does."

The Captain laughed, but his face did not appear sincere about his humor.

"A package arrived, yes," I said, "but the merchants should be investigated, not me. What was delivered has been damaged. Come, see for yourself." I motioned for them to step inside, and the Captain obliged.

"You say you are deaf, weaver," said Vernard. "But how did you know about the bell or our presence at the door?"

"The metal above the door moves when the bell rings, letting me know someone is pulling the cord." The Captain turned to see it, and I waited until he turned back around before continuing. "The bell alerts my man, Kai, to the door when I am not in the room. Since you broke it, you are lucky anyone answered at all. I just happened to pass by and—"

Vernard held up his hand, and I stopped my ranting. "I apologize for the bell," he said. "I'll see that it is fixed before I leave. This is Kai?" He nodded to the big man.

"My slave, yes."

The Captain's brow furrowed as he stepped closer, inspecting Kai, whose eyes remained on the ground. "You elected not to brand him."

I laughed. "Do you see a man like me being able to brand a man like Kai?"

The corners of his mouth curled upwards. "Perhaps not."

"But the package—just look at these wares." I showed him the soiled and ruined fabric lying on the table, and as he peered into the crate, the Captain wrinkled his nose.

"What is that, do you think?" I asked. "If it is rat piss, it is from no rat I've encountered before. If you ask me, those swindlers did something to my order, and now they're trying to turn it around somehow by reporting a 'suspicious package' to you!"

The Captain rubbed his chin. "That's possible I suppose. But whenever a report like this is made, it is still protocol to search the home. May we?"

"I...uh...of course. But protocol, you say? It is not one I've heard of."

"Oh, indeed. Quite routine." He waved in his men, and they went about the workshop opening cupboards and checking under tables.

The one with the pike entered the storefront, and I prayed Marta had made it out. "I would like to go with them," I said. "There are some articles of high value that—"

"They will harm nothing," said Vernard. "You have my word on that."

The remaining guard approached my loom, and I reached for him. Vernard, however, pulled me back by my elbow. "Please allow me or Kai to help. If you shift the loom wrong, the warp will fall off and I will lose a year's worth of work."

"A year? Truly?"

"Yes, tapestries are a delicate and tedious artform."

Vernard turned to speak to the guard, and the man nodded, his helmet shaking as he did. While he looked behind the loom, he did not move it.

"You know, weaver," said Vernard, turning back to me, "you do very well for a man in your condition. There has hardly been a word I've spoken that you've missed, and you make yourself quite plain."

"I've run a shop for nearly twenty years, sir. I've gotten a lot of practice."

Vernard looked past me to the door leading to the storefront, and my eyes widened to see Marta standing before him, her arm clasped by the other guard. She had loosened the bindings of her frock, and her sleeves hung off her shoulders exposing the depth of her breasts. Her cheeks were flushed, and her curls hung undone beyond her shoulders. Both my mouth and Kai's popped open to see her, but I sealed mine quickly and swallowed hard.

"I found her hiding in a wardrobe upstairs," said the guard.

I cleared my throat and averted my eyes from hers, but a grin spread across the Captain's face. "Weaver, I am impressed! Lady, are you not the daughter of the tailor down the lane?"

She bit her lip and peered at the floor. "I'd rather not say."

"Indeed," said Vernard, and I blushed. Oh, the rumors that would spread of this night!

"You checked the floors of the other room?" Vernard asked the guard.

"Yes, sir. All clear."

"Then we will check the floors in here and be done. And you will forgive us this intrusion, will you not, weaver?"

I cleared my throat. "I…uh…yes. I will think nothing else of it." But I felt my eyes wandering to the loom, so I walked in the direction opposite of the call.

Using the fireplace poker from the table, the Captain went about tapping upon the floor. I watched him closely, wondering what this was about. I had expected him to inspect the floors visually. Could the hearing find a hidden room by sound?

"Captain," I said, hoping my voice would cover any tonal distinctions, "how should I go about reporting the crime of the ruined merchandise?"

"Come by my office in the morning," he said without stopping. He rounded the table, going along the sides of the cabinets and past the hearth, closer and closer to the loom. "We shall file a report."

"Last time I came to your office, I was turned away."

He paused and stood upright, and I held my breath in order not to release a sigh of relief. "When was this?"

"When I was attacked some years ago. Your officers made it clear I should expect no protection from the office of the magistrate due to my former status as a slave. It is why I had to purchase Kai."

He continued tapping, and I winced. "I do not recall that. I will, however, personally file a report on this."

"I appreciate that, as I would like to know whether it is the merchants at fault or their supplier. It's important I think—"

The Captain reached the loom and cocked his head to the side.

"I have been with the supplier for some time and…"

He tapped in the same place again.

"…and would like to continue using them if possible."

Vernard slammed the poker against the floor, and Marta covered her face with her hand. She pulled it back enough for me to see her lips and mouthed one word: "Run."

I turned for the door, and the guard reached for me. Kai shoved his shoulder into the man's chest, and I darted past him into the next room. I raced through the storefront past the shelves of woven fabric and thread and into the abandoned streets with no idea where to run. Booths and covered merchant's stalls passed by me in a blur.

I ducked into an alley and kept running in the general direction of the docks. As I glanced over my shoulder to see if I was being pursued, I crashed into a pile of crates. My shin complained, forcing me to limp several paces, but I continued onward, running blindly through the dark streets.

A man stepped out of his door as I rushed past, candle in hand. He opened his mouth to me, but I did not linger to make out the words. Upon reaching the sea, I ran down the length of the shoreline passing dock after dock. Some fishermen just arrived from their nighttime duties raised their hands and stood as I went past. My goal was to reach the boat of a smuggler I knew in hopes that he would hide me for the night. As I looked over my shoulder again, I saw a horse galloping down the shoreline to me.

I quickened my pace looking left and right for an escape. The horse gained on me, and I made out Vernard as the rider, his silver broach reflecting off torchlights as he passed. I could not swim and I had few friends within the city. I doubled my pace, racing for the smuggler's boat.

The horse grew closer, and my lungs burst for air. The smuggler's boat came into view, but I knew not where the smuggler was, nor could he hide me with Vernard so close upon me. To reach him now would do nothing but show my alliance to him.

Heart pounding, chest heaving, I stopped and bent at the waist to catch my breath. There was no point in continuing. I was caught good and well by my own deeds.

Vernard slowed his horse to a trot and reined in the beast beside me as I looked up. "Weaver, giving up so soon?"

Although I continued to pant, I straightened to speak to the man. I recalled the anxiety of tonight and many nights before it, the long days praying the runaway slaves beneath my floor would make no sound, especially when the hearing were around to know of it.

For years I had feared this, but now, for no reason I could fathom, the fear had dissipated.

And so I swallowed away the dryness of my mouth and said, "It has been a long run, and I am tired. In more ways than one."

He dropped from his horse, landing with grace before glancing over his shoulder. He acted as if expecting a trap of some sort to descend upon him, but I had thought little of this moment until now.

"Very well then," he said, and from inside his cape, he produced a coil of rope. I thought he would tie my hands behind my back, but he made no move to do so. Clearly, my small stature and soft middle were no threat to a lean man like the Captain.

"Tell me," I said as I extended my hands. "What did you hear that gave me away?"

He looped the rope around my hands, cinching it down snugly but not overly tight. "When I slammed the poker down the final time, the woman screamed."

"Ah. That would do it."

"Indeed. And now perhaps you can enlighten me. Why did you do this, weaver? A free-born would have faced a fine, but you?"

I looked out over the sea, to where the streaking light of the moon reflected on the waters. "Because a house in a port city is valuable," I said. "And no free-borns were willing."

Vernard's mouth formed a line as he considered me. Then he gestured for me to follow him to the castle. We passed the gallows on the way, and I knew I would gain a closer look at them soon.

CHAPTER TWO

The jailor shoved me into my cell, and the wave of wind from the door's slamming blew back the hair from my neck. My fingers tingled as if still numb, but the ropes had been removed from my wrists several minutes earlier. I stood in the entryway of my cell breathing in the dank smell of the underground quarters and absorbing the coolness of the stones on my bare feet. Gray light entered through a ventilation slit upon the wall opposite the door, the only break in the granite boxing me in.

The numbness from my hands spread and settled over me as I stood there, staring at the slit as the colors turned from gray to brilliance. Something bumped my leg, and I turned to see a bowl of porridge leaning against my bare foot.

They took my shoes. Protocol, they had said, but I knew the truth. Those shoes were worth three days' wages. It seemed Vernard's kindness did not extend beyond himself.

I gathered the bowl and sat on the stone shelf that formed my bed. To my surprise, the porridge was still warm and did not taste foul. I was relieved for a moment, then wondered if I was losing my mind. I dropped the spoon into the mush.

After pacing a bit, I tried pulling myself up to see out the window, but I could barely get off the floor. The air shifted as the door opened and the jailor appeared. His straggly hair stood at odd angles as he considered me with a curled lip.

"They say you're deaf but can read lips. Is this true?"

"As long as you face me and speak clearly, I can manage," I said.

"Your sentence has been declared. In fourteen days, you will hang."

"What? I have yet to have a trial!"

The man laughed, exposing his brown, rotting teeth. "You are slave-born! You do not get a trial, only a sentence." He slammed the door.

My shoulders sank forward as my legs turned to lead. Dizziness overtook me, and I laid down on my ledge as the granite swayed and weaved. I had seen this coming. I knew the risks of smuggling slaves, so why was I worried now? Had I been in denial about my fate?

Or hopeful?

Was this dizziness due to relief? A final solution to all that pained me? Or was I afraid, here at the end of all things?

I pressed my hands against my face as if doing so would clear my thoughts. Had I wanted to die, I would have hung the noose myself. Or in my cowardice, my fear to commit the mortal sin, had I forced the magistrate to do it for me? My friends would consider me brave, offering my life for the freedom of others. They overestimated the value of my life.

And so, I lay upon my bed, cursing the world and everything in it. But more than that, I cursed my destiny and the scant part I had been allowed to determine.

* * *

As the first rays of light crept through the window of my cell, I sat up on the ledge and rubbed the patchy growth upon my chin. The marks on my wall counted seven days. Seven days of being alone. The hearing could gain comfort from the footsteps within the hall and the sound of people passing by my tiny window. I, however, had the stones for company and the dust motes for entertainment. Not even rats visited my cell.

I crossed my legs and stared at the opposite wall. The granite worked as a blank page of parchment allowing my memories to flow across. Already, I had sat for hours like this as my life played out before me. The first time I touched a loom and learned to weave, the time I sprinkled salt over parchment and then dyed it with berries to create the night sky, the face of my newborn son.

The daughter of my master, Alonya, and her sweet smile as I pronounced her name correctly. Then her blood drying on my hands.

The hatch at the base of my door opened, and a bowl of porridge slid inside. Only the thrice-daily deliveries marked the passing of time. I ate the bowl without tasting it as the memories continued to play before me.

Then a feather floated down from the slit, fracturing the scene, causing it to fall into pieces on the floor. I set the bowl to the side and picked it up. It was not a feather after all, but a piece of parchment.

> "My Dear Zayim,
> We are seeking a way to secure your release, but the magistrate has refused our ransom. We, however, will not cease trying. Do not give up hope, and do not for a moment forget my love for you. I will see you soon.
> Marta"

I ran my hand through my curls then crumpled the paper and tossed it into a corner. She was sweet, but my fate had been sealed on the first day I had offered my help to those seeking freedom. I had told her that from the start.

I returned my attention to the wall, trying to bring forth a good memory, but my mind selected the pictures on its own.

"How do you think of such things?" Marta gestured to my loom and my half-finished cloth. Flowers repeated in patterns surrounded by ringlets of gold on a green background, a picture inspired by the home of my first master. "Father would pay handsomely to make clothes from that."

I slid the coin purse across the counter to her. "Add a little commission, and I'll have it done by next week."

"You would steal from your master? Zayim! I thought you were above such things."

"Nothing for myself, but Sloan craves those fat orange melons. If I could bring even a piece home, she would be delighted."

Marta took the chair meant for my master's son and flipped her green velvet frock over her ankles. The boy was off courting a girl on the other side of town leaving me to run the shop in his absence. "When is that baby coming anyway? It seems she's been with child long enough."

"She's due any day, and I'll be glad for it to be over too. She's quite intolerable in this state."

"Zayim!" She smacked my knee as I grinned. But it was true! The larger Sloan grew, the more troublesome she became. And I too had grown impatient waiting to see the young child and to cradle him in my arms. Master had allowed me to weave a blanket for the baby, and I looked at it each night before bed.

"Marta," I said, "I know before when you have talked about my liberation, I have turned you down."

Marta cocked her head and leaned back in the seat.

Studying my hands, I continued, "A deaf man like me is lucky to have a warm bed and a plate of food. But the child, if it can hear...I would like it to have a chance at a destiny greater than my own."

"Of course, Zayim."

"We will wait until the child is weaned. He will not be branded until he is five after all, then I would like to get Sloan and the child out of the country."

"And what of yourself? Your master will not approve if you help them escape then expect to stay."

"I don't know what I would do in another country around people who do not know me or how to speak to me."

Marta took my hand. "Of all the people who could make it, Zayim, it would be you."

I smiled at her, and warmth flooded over me from her touch. "Thank you, Marta. You are a good friend."

When we packed up for the day, I found a whole melon waiting, hidden within the fabrics. Marta winked at me from her stall.

How many chances had I had to flee? If I had just run, perhaps Marta would have married, had a life and children. Instead, she waited around for me, hoping for the love I was not capable of giving her.

The memory shifted to the morning of my son's birth, but I stood to pace once more. No. That was not one I would endure. And for the rest of the day, I paced, refusing to dwell longer on what could have been.

***

I screamed into the void of my cell with all the air my lungs contained as I leaned against the wooden door. My head pounded and my throat pleaded, but still, I yelled. There were no words, just air rushing out of my mouth. Finally, I felt the vibrations of someone pounding against the door. My jailor, probably, wishing to shut me up.

"I can do this all day!" I shouted in reply. "I am not the one who has to hear it!" And I let out another wail.

The door shifted behind me, and I stood and backed away. The jailor appeared, his face red. "What is the meaning of this, deaf man? You have stirred up the whole prison."

"I am to die tomorrow, sir. I would like to see a priest."

"A priest? A priest! Damn your soul to hell, you do not deserve a priest!"

"Either a priest or I shall continue in my disturbance. The choice is yours."

He pulled a club from his belt. "I shall have you beaten!"

"And I shall scream louder! This time with a cause!"

His lip curled up revealing the rotten teeth once more. He mumbled something unclear before closing my door behind him. An hour later, a priest arrived. A young thing, he sported the strange bowl haircut and the brown, hairy garb required by those of his order.

"Father, would you care to sit?" I gestured to my ledge.

"I would prefer to stand," he said, glancing about the room. "You wish to receive last rites?"

"Yes, sir. If you will grant them."

"You are from Burganne, but I do not recall you attending Mass."

I played with the seam of my tunic. "Yes, Father. I apologize for that. I cannot hear and so my attendance felt a bit—lacking."

"You should have come anyway," he said, and I bit my lip. "Regardless, if you will confess your sins, I will absolve you of them."

I found the ledge behind me and sat. I wished he too would sit. My cell was not dirty in the slightest. "When I was a slave, I fathered a child with a woman who was not my wife."

"Did you ever marry her?"

"We were not permitted. And after the boy was sold to foreigners, she refused to speak to me, so no. That was never done. I did, however, free her and the boy once I gained my own freedom, and I send money to them weekly."

"You should have married her."

"To this day, she refuses to speak to me."

"That should not matter."

I pressed my fingers into the stone, holding back a retort. "I suppose I should have. Can I receive absolution?"

"What else do you have to confess?"

"I cursed my master behind his back daily for five years after my son was sold."

"Have you sought forgiveness from your master?"

"He did not know of it."

"You should have sought it out anyway."

I rubbed my hands over my eyes. "Forgive me, Father, but I am to die tomorrow. Can we speak of absolution rather than what is no longer within my power to achieve?"

"Let us come to the matter for which you are facing execution, your smuggling of slaves to other countries. Would you seek absolution for that as well?"

I shook my head. "I have no sorrow over the crimes that led me to this place. While they are sins of the state, I do not believe them to be sins to God."

"God has placed the king in authority over you. Any sins against the state are sins against God."

"I…just don't know that this is true. The king is a man like other men, and his rulings are not infallible."

"You aided in the theft of property from other men, godly men. You're dying because you are a thief."

"No man should be in control of another's destiny."

The priest barked a laugh. "I suppose that would make sense from a condemned man. You wish to believe your punishment unjust, the product of another man controlling your destiny. But the crimes which you have committed are yours to bear, and until you can accept your waywardness, I cannot and will not absolve you from your sins. Guard!"

"Now, wait a minute." I stood. "You would damn me to hell for disagreeing with you?"

The door opened, and the priest stepped backward to it. "You damn yourself to hell, weaver. I had nothing to do with it."

"Wait! Don't go!" I cried, but the door slammed closed, and I was alone once more.

With a cry, I tore at my hair. I had always feared it, but now I saw it was true. God hated me. He, my master first and last, desired to abandon me during my time of most need.

I fell to my knees and pulled at my tunic. Air burst from my lungs as I pressed my forehead to the stones and wept. I knew no prayers, I had no words, but I let out a stream of grumbles and pleas. "Father do not forsake me. Do not forsake me. Do not forsake me…"

This wretched life! My wretched soul! Would I now be turned away from paradise too?

I lay upon the stones, my face pressed against their cool surface watching the dust motes dance within the light. Twirling, tumbling…

After seven days of solitude and now the rejection of my God, my mind started slipping like molasses through my hands, and I made no effort to stop it.

Then a shadow flitted above my head as another parchment floated on the breeze as it drifted to the ground. I lunged for it, breathing in the words written upon the page. The handwriting was slanted as if it had been written in a hurry, but unmistakably Marta's.

> "My Dear Zayim,
> I saw the priest leaving and inquired of his visit with you. He is the vilest, most distasteful man I have yet to meet. And although he proclaims a rank of holiness, he too is but a man like other men. And he is wrong. God alone can judge you, Zayim. And God's judgment is always right. You are a good man, and what we do is righteous and true. He will see that, and I will see you if not in the flesh than with Him in spirit. We have not ceased to try, but—"

A few words were scribbled out.

> "In the past, you have forbidden me to lie to you, and I will not lie now. We have no plan and no solution. But in all things, we do hope. I love you, Zayim Free Man.
> May God go with you as he always has.
> Marta."

I leaned my back against the wall and rested my head upon the stones. I had no further tears to shed, no further confessions to state. What had been done to me was wrong and the actions of tomorrow would be too. I considered praying for a miracle but found that I had achieved peace.

Or insanity.

But at this point, what did it matter?

***

My dreams disagreed with the peace of my waking hours. As I slept, I dreamt of Alonya, the daughter of my first master. We played among the poppies beyond her father's field, and I weaved a crown of flowers for her. Poppies—my first word spoken due to her insistent coaching. Her chestnut hair bounced against her shoulders as she ran from me. She stole a glance over her shoulder, and her face changed to that of horror.

A man with four interlocking circles branded on his flesh, a brand that matched my own, stood over her with a knife. The poppies turned to blood, dripping on the fertile lands, and I raised my hand to see the blood there, drying in the sun.

Suddenly, I stood upon the scaffold, hands tied behind my back as a bag was pulled over my head. The drop came without warning, and there I fell, dangling by my neck as my body shook.

And shook.

Rough hands shook me, and I peered up at the jailor through slits. Yellow light flooded my cell around the man with crooked teeth. Did my body believe I could escape this day by ignoring the sun's presence?

The jailor jerked me off the ledge and did not release my garments until I stood steady. "It's time," he said.

I yawned and rubbed the sleep from my eyes. So be it. Better to be dead in reality than dangling in the purgatory of my dreams.

He motioned me toward the door, and I shuffled to it on my bare feet. I wished for breakfast, but the porridge cooling by the door would go uneaten.

We had not descended deep into the prison to reach my cell. Perhaps it had been purposed for criminals such as myself—those with short stays. My jailor placed manacles about my wrists, tightening them down with a screw. Funny, he had not done so in my cell where there was no place to run. Was I truly so little a threat?

Yes, the answer came, and I shrugged it away. I had never struck another man in my life, although, as a slave, I had indeed been struck.

My body ached from the stone slab and I rolled my neck about my shoulders. I was sure my appearance matched how I felt. The patchy stubble upon my chin had grown, making it feel scragglier than ever. Would they be decent enough to provide a razor and a comb before the drop?

The guard led me up the stone steps, and the smell of must cleared some. A plane of light lay across the corridor from a chest-high window. I had forgotten what fresh air smelt like and I breathed deeply, tasting it.

The jailor led me through the winding halls of the tower. How nice it was to feel his presence beside me. I missed people more than I thought I would, and even though my destination ended with a broken neck, I drew comfort from him.

We stopped before an oak door with wrought iron hinges. The jailor's mouth moved, but I could not discern his words. I was about to ask him to repeat what he had said when he opened the door and pushed me inside.

The room was circular with vaulted ceilings, and a cherry desk sat in the center of the room. A portly man took up the space behind it. Light shone around him from the window as if he were somehow holier than any other artifact in the tower.

I shuffled forward a bit, uncertain of the circumstances that had brought me here. A tapestry on my right caught my attention—a woven map of the man's country home. The body of water was called Willow's Ford, and the surrounding forest was called Willow's Wood. On the edge of the wood was a cottage marked by a single purple iris.

When I turned my attention back to the man, his face wrinkled in a scowl. Clearly, he had tried to say something and I had not caught it. He gestured to the chair, and I read his lips clearly, "Sit."

As I sat, I gathered the heavy chains into my lap. I felt small and silly sitting there surrounded by his fine desk, well-fed body, and the expensive woven art upon the wall. But I held up my head as if I belonged there.

"Zayim the deaf weaver." The man shifted a paper across his desk. "A freed slave-born awaiting death for harboring fugitive slaves. What a life you've lived. Full of contradictions."

I had nothing to say to this. At least, nothing that would not antagonize him. And I had no energy for such things without having had breakfast first.

He nodded to the tapestry. "You noticed your work on the wall. Do you know who I am?"

"You are the Duke of Willow's Ford, sir," I said.

"You have a good memory."

I glanced at the tapestry once more. You have a dull name.

"I am also the magistrate overseeing your case. Which means I have the power to save your life."

I leaned forward in my seat. "Prove it."

A thin smile crept up one side of his mouth, and he set the papers back down on the desk. "I'd love to watch you hang, and all the other slave-borns who think they deserve a place in our society. You are closer to an animal than a person."

The dichotomy of thought that must take place in such a person. First, they purchase your handcrafted work and place it prominently on their wall, then they determine your destiny in this world to be equal to that of a horse. I had no time for such people.

"You are coming to a point, I assume, or am I to be tortured before my death as well?"

He glared at me but did not continue his tirade. "I have a proposition for you. In exchange for your help, I will grant you your life."

I did not believe him. If he had refused a ransom from Marta, why would he be offering this to me now? But I decided to play his little game. "There are some things I will not do, even in exchange for my own life."

"Then it's good this is up the liberationist's alley." He slid a paper across his desk made of thick fibers. Painted on it was the face of a young man in his early twenties with brown hair and eyes.

"My son was captured in a battle outside Durban. Word has reached me that he has been sold to traders in Aquilla. I want you to find him using your liberationist contacts."

I slid the portrait back. "Impossible."

"Your people specialize in smuggling slaves. You tracked down your own son after ten years and purchased him back, and you would have me believe you can't find my son?"

"I never lost track of my son. In regards to smuggling, people come to us, not the other way around. Your son could have been bought and traded again to any other place in the world. He could have caught ill on the boat and been buried at sea without your ever knowing."

The duke slammed his fist on the table. "He is not lost!"

I jumped at the outburst and the chains rattled out of my lap. His brow twitched as I regathered them. For the first time, I entertained the thought that he may be serious. I cleared my voice and said, "He is lost. Accept it. And accept that it is your willingness to endorse a system that treats humans like cattle has contributed to his demise."

The duke rose from his chair, nearly toppling it. "I should have you—"

"What? Hanged?"

He sneered. "Drawn and quartered."

I looked to the floor and took a deep breath to quell the flood rising in my chest. When I returned my gaze to him, his sneer had turned to a smirk, and he retook his seat. "There is time yet to bring pain before your neck snaps."

I tapped against the chain as I looked at the tapestry once more. The chances of finding the lad were dismal indeed, but what if...

"As I am sure everything I once possessed has been seized by the state, I will need resources," I said.

"You will get them."

"And I will take my slave, Kai, with me."

The magistrate played with the papers upon his desk. "It has not escaped me, the hypocrisy of owning a slave while claiming to be a liberationist."

"Will he be available or not?" I asked through clenched teeth.

"Why not?" He shrugged. "I will instruct those holding him to bring him here."

"You seem certain I will not take these resources to another country and run. What other leverage do you intend on using?"

The magistrate leaned back into his seat. "If you run, I will enslave your son once more, weaver. He and his mother."

"Ah," I said. "So either I find your son and help him escape, or both our sons end up as slaves."

"Will you take this job or not?"

I peered around him to see out the window beyond his chair. Waiting in the morning sun were the gallows. A rope fitted just for me hung upon it. But if I swung today, I feared the magistrate would punish my son now for spite.

"I suppose it is a better alternative to my other plans. Why not?"

CHAPTER THREE

My jailor shoved me through the doors of Chateau Burganne, nearly sending me down the stone steps headlong.

"You know, I can follow spoken instructions," I said turning back to him.

He grinned cheekily and closed the door in my face. Rubbing my raw wrists, I glared at it in hopes my look would carry through the door.

The massive stones of the castle, now smoothed by the elements and stained black in some areas, stood over the city like a sentry. The design, like most of the oldest structures in Burganne, was Roman with four stalwart towers at the corners and a central tower serving as the main entrance. I had been let out through a side door, a less-traveled spot on the first floor of the west tower that opened into the main courtyard.

I shielded my eyes as I dismounted the stone steps and quickened my pace upon the cobbles before my feet roasted. Upon finding a shadow of a statue to stand in, I gripped the foot of the stone man, and I inspected my filthy soles. Then I looked up to see St. Peter frowning down upon me.

"My apologies, friend," I said, removing the hand. "It seems we will keep our appointment another day."

So busy was I in speaking with the saint, I did not notice the ox of a man waving at me from across the courtyard beside the gate until he was nearly upon me. Moisture stains collected around his neck and beneath the arms of his sage-green tunic. The material had been torn in three places, and the leggings were not much better. There would be no saving them. I would have to make him another set of clothes.

"Why the devil are you still here, Kai?" I asked. "You should have fled the city days ago."

"I did not wish to leave until I knew your fate," he said, then looked over my shoulder to the castle. Descending the steps came Captain Vernard who had arrested me, the broach of the magistrate ever on his shoulders.

"Weaver!" he called.

"Captain, surprised to see me beyond the walls?"

"Without a rope around your neck? Indeed, weaver. But the day is still young."

I raised the corner of my mouth, unsure whether he was serious or joking. Or both.

"By rule of the magistrate," he said, "I am to join you on your mission."

"The magistrate does not trust me, I see."

"You are not known to be trustworthy."

I flicked my brows up, acknowledging this fact, before turning to Kai to ask, "Do you have a new master now?"

"They assigned me to city labor. It was to be made permanent after today."

Vernard rounded to stand before me. He chewed on the corner of his lip as if I had insulted him by turning my back. Facing someone fully, however, was my only means of clear communication, so he would have to leave his offenses behind.

"They did not brand you," I noted of Kai.

"They elected to wait," Vernard said. "At least until your feet stopped twitching."

Kai's nostrils flared and he bit his lip, but he had enough sense to hold his tongue. I, however, was surprised by this change in tone from the man who arrested me a fortnight ago. He had been austere, yet polite, and as far as I was aware, nothing I had done had caused his opinion of me to falter.

"You will be a merry addition to our traveling party," I said.

"I continue to think it strange, weaver, that you did not elect to brand your slave before," Vernard said. "It is offered at the auction house for a small charge, and you are not a poor man."

"I purchased Kai for self-defense. And I did not think starting our relationship with hot metal searing into his face would be wise. An unhappy bodyguard, in my estimation, would be a poor bodyguard, or do you disagree?"

Vernard sneered, and he glanced to the doors of the castle. "Indeed."

I scratched the patchy stubble on my chin and glanced at Kai. If we were in the company of this man for long, we would have to be more careful with our secrets. Kai really should have run.

"Yes, well, I believe our first action should be to return home, plan our trip, and gather supplies. Any objections to this, Captain?" The man shook his head, and we left the courtyard. The guards upon the gates eyed Kai and me as we passed, but nodded greetings to Vernard.

Makeshift shops covered in canvas lined the streets of Burganne as vendors called out their wares. I did not live far from the castle, and most we passed were my neighbors. They halted and turned to us, but I ignored their strange looks. I did not know which drew their attention more: my release on the day of my execution, or my missing shoes.

My shop sat between a potter's house and a baker's kitchen. The smells of the latter caused my stomach to rumble, and I hoped that some of my food stores had been left untouched.

The door of my home hung on broken hinges, and my shingle lay fractured on the cobbles outside. Scattered upon the floor of the shop were tangles of thread, yarn, and torn fabric. Not one shelf was left upright. I expected no less and stepped over my broken belongings on my way to the back room.

The warp on my loom had been cut and one of the legs was broken in half. The half-finished tapestry lay in a heap, and the space beneath the trapdoor stood open and empty. Upon this, I had to pause. A year's worth of work and bleeding fingers made for a sorrowful sight indeed.

I did wonder momentarily about the fate of the woman. Unless her master were a debaucherous pig, which, considering the state in which she came, was not impossible, she would have revealed his identity and would have been sent back unharmed by the magistrate. Although her master may lay a hand on her. If, however, she remained silent and no master could be found, she would have entered the custody of the state to work as they demanded. Not the best life, but a life nonetheless.

I searched through my cabinets in vain. Not even a crumb remained. And if they had found all the food, surely they had found my silver as well. I did find, however, a clean tunic, breeches, and a pair of boots in my room upstairs. They were a bit old but would do the job.

As I re-entered the shop, I was surprised by the tears in Kai's eyes. "Zayim," he said, taking in the damaged property. "I never came back here. If I had known…"

I should not have been taken aback by the sentiment. The shop had been his venture. I, content to work the loom until my fingers ached, did not waste time with customers. He had proposed the shop as a way to increase my income. The extra money was completely unneeded as I made plenty from my tapestries, but I feared he was growing bored in his service to me and allowed it. I did not wish to see him unhappy.

Unhappy people left.

I did not wish to dwell on the tears of a man twice my size, so I turned to the Captain. "The Magistrate said he'd finance our mission. I'm assuming that includes food?"

Vernard, who leaned against the doorway of the shop, nodded.

"Then be useful and go buy bread."

He narrowed his eyes at me, clearly unwilling to take orders from a branded man. He opened his mouth to speak, but a woman brushed against his arm as she entered the shop.

"Zayim!" Marta exclaimed and crossed the room. In a flash, her arms were around me, then she stepped back to take me in. "I cannot believe you are here. I was so worried, I could not breathe. How did you manage to get out?"

"We have company," I said, and she turned to see Vernard by the door and clutched her chest.

"Marta, am I right?" Vernard asked. "How have you been since we last spoke?"

"Just fine, thank you," she said tightly.

"Your friend here, whom you inquired about so diligently, has been assigned a task. If he completes it, he will not be hanged."

Marta looked between me and Kai. "Wh-what kind of task?"

"This man was sold at auction in Aquilla." Vernard showed the portrait of the magistrate's son. "You told me you had no contact with the liberationists, yet you approached the magistrate with a sum of money a tailor's daughter could have no hope to collect on her own. Will you continue in your story, or will you help us find this man?"

"Marta knows nothing," I said. "She is a friend from down the street, nothing more."

"But," Marta said, "I do have family and friends in Aquilla. My mother is from there after all. I will inquire of them and let you know if they have seen the man."

Vernard narrowed his eyes. "Indeed."

"May I see the portrait?" I asked, and he handed it to me. I searched the floor of overturned items until I located a pile of unruined parchment. With Kai's help, I righted the table, sat, and propped up the portrait against a fractured jug. As I sketched the portrait with charcoal, Vernard peered over my shoulder.

"Will this do?" I asked upon finishing.

Vernard's eyes widened. "It took that artist nearly two days to capture Dorsey's likeness, and you've mastered it in minutes."

I took another page, pressed it against the drawing, and ran a piece of wood across the surface. Upon separating the two pages, I now had three portraits of the magistrate's son. It missed a couple of details that I filled in with the charcoal but looked quite well in the end.

"Go over the lines with the charcoal again," I told Marta and Kai, "and we will make as many of these as possible before nightfall. You can send it in your inquiries, Marta. Vernard, do be useful and get that bread, will you? Or I swear I will faint soon and be of no use to you at all." I said this without looking up to see his reaction, but when I glanced at the door a few moments later, he was gone.

Marta wrapped her arms around me once more, and I breathed deeply, taking in the lavender smell of her curls. Today, her usual green frock was replaced by a gray one that tapered at her waist. It was attractive enough, accentuating her curves, but had a dismal air to it.

It was a dress of mourning, and suddenly I grew ashamed of my attitude of the day thus far. While alone in my cell, I had certainly felt sorry about myself as I reviewed my life but had not thought once of how my death would affect anyone else. I had not tried to send a letter of farewell to her or even my own son. I doubted I would have been successful, but I should have at least tried.

Kai dragged a chair near and sat at the table. "What's going on, Zayim? Are we really going to help find the magistrate's son, or are we going to run the minute our feet hit foreign soil?"

I glanced to the door knowing the spy would return soon with the bread from next door. "If we don't do as they want, my son's freedom will be revoked."

Marta gasped. "I'm sorry, Zayim. I should have gotten Sloan and the boy out as soon as you were arrested."

"I should have gotten them out long before that."

"There was no way to foresee this," Kai said. "We thought they would kill you, not extort you."

Marta took the chair beside Kai. "I will smuggle them out of the country as soon as possible."

"Something about this does not feel right," Kai said. "For two weeks we tried to petition your release, and just before your execution, the magistrate's son goes missing, and now they're offering you freedom in exchange for finding him?"

"We are at war." Marta shrugged. "Such things do happen."

"You are wondering if this Dorsey exists," I said.

"What do we know of him?" Kai asked. "That portrait is real, sure, but this Dorsey could have been killed in battle months ago. He could be someone else's son for all we know. This whole thing could be a ruse to get you to give up your contacts. That is if you didn't give them up already."

I tilted my head to Kai. Did he really think I would talk?

"You were gone for two weeks, Zayim," Kai said, "and you barely have a scratch on you."

"Did I talk, Marta?" I asked, turning to her.

Marta curled her finger and pressed it against her chin. "No, Kai, he did not talk. If Zayim had talked, we'd have more trouble than Captain Vernard by this point."

The door opened, and Kai and Marta turned from me, both suspiciously rubbing the backs of their heads. Some members of a secret society they were. I stepped forward and took one of the two bread loaves from Vernard. Splitting it into pieces, I distributed them to my friends before devouring my portion.

"We need to discuss travel arrangements," I said as I retook my chair. "And supplies."

Kai pressed the charcoal to the paper and said something. Marta started to reply but turned her back. Had they already forgotten? I slumped in my seat and muttered. "I can't hear you."

Both turned to me and apologized. I should be good at letting such things go, but it was a skill I had yet to master. Nonetheless, I waved my hand for Kai to continue, and Vernard joined us at the table.

"I said, I can go fetch supplies," Kai said. "With Vernard's money of course."

"We should go as merchants," Marta said.

"With what wares?" I gestured around my ransacked shop.

"I snuck in and salvaged as much as I could when the guards were out," she said.

Vernard pointed a slender finger at her. "Those are property of the crown!"

"Be still," I said. "They'll be used for the crown." But I looked at Marta in question. Why the hell had she said that bit out loud? She shrugged in reply.

"There is no need for us to travel as merchants," Vernard said. "A peace has been bargained with Aquilla, and I have gained permission to enter the country for this purpose."

"And you think the men at the auction house will care?" I asked. "Part of their business is discretion, and some soldier showing up trying to track down one of their customers will be turned away in an instant. Any records they may have had on your Dorsey will be destroyed the minute they see you coming."

"According to the Treaty of Durban, the houses—"

I looked at Marta's untouched piece of bread, ignoring whatever it was he was saying. She nodded for me to take it, and I actually tasted this second piece, enjoying the airy texture and buttery coating.

"Why do you need me again?" I asked with my mouth full. "Because every other person you've sent on official inquiry has come up empty-handed. But if we go in as merchants looking for a cousin or missing brother, the chances of having a productive conversation with these people will go up."

"It will feel more like a business transaction than a government inquiry," Marta said.

"I thought you were the daughter of a tailor," Vernard said.

"Which is why she knows so much about business," I said. "Marta, would your father be able to supply us with more appropriate dress? Kai's tunic is hopelessly in shambles and I won't have time to mend it."

Kai looked down at his shirt as if noticing the holes for the first time.

"Certainly," said Marta. "Will I be posing as a merchant's wife? Or another slave?"

"You will be staying here."

"But I—"

"I haven't seen any other neighbors come by and wish me 'welcome home.' I'm going to need you here to…" I glanced at Vernard. "To be available for contact in Burganne."

Marta drummed her fingers on the table but did not argue further. I needed her to get Sloan and the boy out, not sail across the sea with me. Not to mention that she was in enough trouble as it was.

Marta and Kai, now set with their tasks, went to them immediately while Vernard and I were left alone in the shop. I held out a bit of charcoal to him, but he chuckled and leaned back in his seat. "I am no artist."

"You're tracing lines, not painting a sunset." I set the charcoal piece and a sheet of parchment before him. "If we're going to do this, Captain, then you're going to have to get used to doing things you would not normally do. Like speaking with people you would normally arrest."

He picked up the charcoal and inspected it. "Like your 'slave?'"

I reddened. "Like me."

* * *

Captain Vernard had a page bring over a cot and some luggage for the trip and set up his bed beside the back door in my workshop. The front door had been nailed shut, and I suspected he chose that location to prevent my sudden leaving. But while my son, Etienne, was still in the country, I would be going nowhere.

We worked late into the night, tracing the portrait, planning our route, and writing letters to Marta's 'relatives,' each of which were conveniently named Jean. The information provided was basic: height, build, hair color, eye color, and circumstances of capture. The poor boy had no memorable features in which to aid the search. He would be one among hundreds in a system where no one cared.

As the evening grew long, heads drooped and the covering of yawns became frequent. More than once, Marta caught me looking at her, replying to my gaze with a smile. Each time I ducked my head and continued with the work, but I owed it to her to say something. Without her words, I would have been reduced to a heap, unfit even for the rope.

As midnight neared, Kai pushed back from the table and stood. "I'm going to turn in. It's been a long day." Vernard looked up at him with a crinkled brow, and Marta folded her lips inward. He followed up the statement in haste, "With, uh, with your permission, of course, Master Zayim."

"You may go," I said, internally rolling my eyes as he left. If this continued, we would never be able to return to Burganne without Kai's head getting fitted for a noose.

"Marta," I said, "I would like a word in private if that is possible."

We rose from the table and entered the shop. Two chairs sat behind the bench from where Kai ran the business, both overturned. Upon righting them, we sat looking out over the ransacked shop.

My hand lay on the armrest inches from her fingers, and more than once I had to draw them back from touching her. I could imagine the feel of her fingers, soft and warm interlaced with mine. I placed my hands in my lap and folded them.

"I wanted to thank you, Marta," I said. "For your letters. They meant more to me than you can know."

Her pink cheeks gathered and a dimple showed. "Oh, you got them! Good. I was afraid I had sent them to a murderer by mistake!"

"I got them, yes."

"That damn priest. I could have punched him right in the nose for what he did. I sent a letter to the Abbess in Candorlan immediately thereafter."

My jaw slackened. "You wrote to the Abbess? What was she going to do about it?"

"Well, if nothing else, I hoped she would find someone else to absolve you if the priest would not."

"Does that work? Absolving someone in another town after they've died?"

She pressed a hand to her forehead. "I don't know, Zayim, but I had to do something. I couldn't—" Tears breached her eyes, and I felt guilty for pressing the issue. I should have just accepted the gesture and moved on.

"I've never felt so helpless in my life," she continued. "To know you were there, awaiting death while I stood unable to stop it."

I wrapped my arms around her, bringing her against my chest. Her shoulders bounced, and I closed my eyes, smelling the lavender of her hair. "How poor of a friend I have been to you," I said, and she pulled back from me.

"What do you mean?"

"You should not have attached yourself to me. I will only bring you grief."

She pressed her soft hand upon my cheek and caressed it with her thumb. "You are my greatest friend. And although my heart would shatter from your death, I would never abandon you to spare myself from such a thing."

I placed my hand over hers, taking in the warmth of it. "Why do you treat me with such kindness?"

"Why do you refuse to believe you deserve it?"

But the answer to this I would not give. So, I sat there, clinging to the hand I knew I could not keep, knowing soon I would have to let go.

CHAPTER FOUR

The next morning, Kai, Vernard, and I boarded a ship bound for Aquilla. When she saw us off, Marta planted a kiss on my freshly shaved cheek, and I smiled as the tenderness of that kiss lingered. Kai caught me touching the place as we boarded and said, "That woman would marry you if you asked her."

"I know. Which is why I never will."

Kai frowned at this, but there were some things I would not discuss, even with him. I only hoped Marta would stop waiting on me and make a life of her own. She almost had that chance, had I not come back from the dead.

"When you said we would travel as merchants," Vernard said to me, "I assumed you would be the merchant and your slave, well, the actual slave."

I took in Vernard's gray tunic, tan breeches, and the ridiculous hood I had convinced him all merchants wore. His beloved broach poked out from where it was hidden beneath his jerkin. Kai, who wore a similar outfit, grinned at the man, clearly amused by this switch in roles.

"What makes more sense to the common man?" I asked. "The deaf, branded man being the slave, or the particularly large one? The fewer questions asked, the better."

"And if they ask to see his papers?" asked Vernard.

"How often do you ask an unbranded man for his papers? More likely, it will be me who is asked, not him."

"I'm starting to wonder about seeing his papers myself."

"Well, it's a shame I do not have them on me. If you insist, I'll rummage through the crate—"

Vernard held up his hand. "Never mind." But he continued to eye Kai with suspicion, unable to see past the piece of paper determining his status in the world. This was a man of black and white. Right and wrong. Incapable of seeing a man just as a man, without any status or strings attached.

I had spent most of my life around such people. Many of those who purchased my works from my master would not step foot inside my shop once my own name swung above the door. That is until the king's chamberlain entered my shop and purchased an order. Had he seen my brand, he might have left the store, but Kai attended to him that day while I wove in the back. After that, all my neighbors had to own something created by me.

Our ship cabin was small with two beds stacked one on the other and a place for storage below them. Vernard took the bottom, and Kai tried to insist I take the top. On a ship, however, entry by the crew could occur without warning at night, so I slept in blankets on the floor. I talked a good game about it, reminding Kai I was once a slave too, but my back reminded me I was not as young as I once was, and I would later nurse an ache for days after we landed.

That day, after dragging our crate full of woven cloth and tapestries below, the captain of the vessel assigned me to work with the cabin boy. The job entailed running messages, delivering meals, and performing other errands on board throughout the journey when I was not needed by my 'masters.' The fourteen-year-old cabin boy found it most entertaining to command a man of my age and had me running to and fro across the ship for his amusement. After carrying goods from the forecastle to the steerage deck, then from the rear castle to cargo more times than I could count, I feigned orders from Kai and slipped into our quarters.

Vernard sat upon the lower bunk going over some of the magistrate's papers, and Kai sat in a chair repairing a tear in his shoe. I had yet to see Vernard speak to Kai but did not press the matter. Instead, I climbed onto Kai's bunk and placed my arm over my eyes. While Kai was awake, he could prevent any crew from entering.

Kai tapped me on the shoulder. "Okay, Zayim?"

"I'm hiding from the little tyrant," I said.

Vernard, still shuffling papers, stood and leaned against the bunk. "For a former slave, you certainly aren't good at being one now!"

I leaned up on my elbow. "I was a fantastic slave and made my master very rich."

"This is true. No one can dispute that. The question is why he ever let you go."

I shrugged. "He decided it would be more profitable to release me than to keep me."

"It's a shame you were not still a slave when you were caught. Your master would have been fined, but you would have been released instead of facing the rope. Unless—" And a grin spread across his face. "Unless there have been slaves hiding beneath the floors of Zayim the weaver for longer than we suspected and that is why your master got rid of you."

I continued to shrug as if his discovery did not matter, but as I covered my eyes with the crook of my arm a pound of worry settled on my gut. Our greatest defense, I realized, was the arm's length at which I kept the general public. In this instance, isolation could be considered a perk of being deaf. Most people were lazy and did not take the time to understand me. Although—my comings and goings did receive close observation on more than one occasion. The day I brought Kai home was one of those times.

I had left Kai's iron bindings to rust outside the auction house, but his clothes and condition marked him as a slave without the brand. In the marketplace, children romped and tumbled, excited to discharge their energy after the rain of that morning, but they stood slack-jawed as we passed, their games forgotten at least for a moment. Each time I glanced over my shoulder, I too, was surprised to see him lumbering behind me, in part, because he had chosen to follow instead of run. I think he was curious about the odd little man who had just purchased him.

Kai ducked as he entered my shop and turned in a circle, taking in my works on display. I led him into the back room and dipped out two servings of stew hanging from the pot over the fireplace. I placed one for myself and the other across the table for him. "What is your name?"

The name he gave, I did not catch. And after I failed to repeat it on the third try, he shortened it to Kai. And either I got this right, or he grew bored of trying to teach me.

"Who is our master?" he asked.

If it had been in fashion, I would have worn a tunic with shorter sleeves to decrease the frequency of my explanations. I slid down the fabric about my wrist, showing my brand of the free man, and said, "I am under my master no longer."

Kai frowned at the mark, then looked upon me with greater suspicion. I motioned once more to the seat, and he eased himself into the chair as if afraid it would not hold him up. He stirred the stew around for a moment then set the spoon back on the table.

I removed his slave papers from my inner pocket and spread them out on the splintered wooden table. "Do you read and write, Kai?"

He shook his head. "But I know what that is."

Flipping the page over, I located the transfer of ownership lines and scribbled my name. "If you sign your mark here, you will be a free man." I slid the paper across the way, dipped the pen once more, and set it on the table beside him.

Kai rubbed his chin as he studied the papers then took a bite of stew. "A man does not buy a slave just to set them free."

"You're right," I said. "I have a job offer for you. But I will not hold power over you in the same manner that was done to me. Each man should have a say in their fate."

"What is the job?"

"Born-slaves now free are not popular among my people. I need protection. In exchange, I will provide you with food and shelter as well as give you payment. I will also teach you to read and write if you want."

Kai crossed his arms and leaned back in his seat. "What weaver needs protection?"

I raised my shirt showing the bruises along my ribs, and Kai tipped his head to the side. Earlier that week I had been attacked by two boys a street over. I had reported the beating to the magistrate, but they had turned me away.

"I'm not hard to sneak up on," I told Kai, and he laughed.

Kai slid the papers toward himself. "In my country, there is always something more. Something hidden. What are you hiding, weaver?" He leaned across the table. "What will you do if I take my papers and leave?"

"There is nothing I can do. The papers are legally binding. Since you are not branded as a slave, you could leave this house and go back to your people without the brand of a free man. I certainly have no power to prevent you from getting out the door."

He laughed again, and I felt the vibrations of it through the table.

"Now as to what I am hiding," I said, "I agree you should know the whole story before being expected to protect my secrets. But you also need the freedom to say no and to leave. If you do not want to stay, I do not want you here."

Kai's dark eyes bore into mine as if he could see into my very being. He was assessing me, determining what sort of business I had managed to get wrapped up in. Then he took the pen and made his mark on the page. "What secrets do weavers keep?"

"For starters, you have no idea what truly goes into our dyes," I said, and he shook the floor with his laughter. I rose from the table and dipped out two more bowls of stew. After moving the loom, I rolled back the rug from beneath it, found the latch hidden within the cracks of the floorboards, and raised the trapdoor. The faces of two terrified women with brands looked up at us.

Kai froze with the spoon suspended as he looked back at them with wide eyes. One was old and wrinkled while the other young and smooth of face. Their clothes were tattered and their skin clung to them.

"It is alright. Kai is a friend." I knelt beside them and handed over the bowls. "It won't be much longer now. A guide will be here for you tonight."

"Thank you," the older woman said, and I lowered the trapdoor back over them.

The big man swallowed hard as those eyes continued to bore into me. "Their accents—Those women are from Soren," he said. "That is just north of my home. They could be my relatives."

I shrugged between bites of stew. "I don't know where they are from, nor do I play those games. All I know is they are slaves that need to be free."

"We have slaves in my country," said Kai. "I have never been a liberationist."

"But you have no love for my country either."

"Our countries are at war. Well, they were at war."

"Then I ask that when you leave you tell no one of what you saw."

"I did not say I would leave," said Kai. "I just—" And he stared into the corner once more.

I cleared the table, and upon turning back to him, it was clear he was ready to speak.

"I will stay for now," he said.

That had been eleven years ago. I had planned to announce his freedom, but Kai believed it would add to my neighbors' scorn of me. We agreed to keep his freedom a secret, at least for a time. In the end, it was good we had done so; otherwise, we would have had matching nooses. As a former slave, Kai's assistance in freeing slaves would be seen as an attempt to start a slave rebellion. If, however, he had been acting under the orders of his master, the crime committed would belong to me alone.

Kai tapped my shoulder, and I removed the arm from my eyes again. "They gave the call for dinner," he said, and I let out a sigh.

Dinner meant meals to be delivered all across the ship, but I slid down from the bunk nonetheless, thankful that the boat ride would only take a few days.

* * *

The rail of the vessel warmed my hand as I looked out over the vast sea. The rise and fall of the ship breathed with the waves. The wind rushed through my hair, billowing out my clothes and the sails, and I breathed deep, savoring the salt in the air. For a moment, the young tyrant had forgotten about me as the ship made preparations for docking, and I absorbed my free time by taking in this vista.

When Kai's thick hand clamped down upon my shoulder, I jumped.

"Are you alright, lord?"

I inhaled deeply, stifling my nerves. "I'm alright. But I'm still not your lord right now."

"Ah, I see," said Kai. "Which means you'll take no interest in this letter addressed to me—"

I snatched the folded parchment from him and inspected the writing: Marta's writing. Beyond Kai, the sailors raised boxes from the cargo hold and carried them ashore. We had landed without my realizing it.

The note stated that one of Marta's contacts had found a possible lead and would meet us outside the auction house in Lasen tomorrow. I showed this note to Kai and then tossed it into the sea.

CHAPTER FIVE

I did not know what was in Vernard's bag, but it weighed twice that of mine and Kai's. As I carried it, I stumbled down the gangplank nearly flinging it and myself into the drink.

"Need some help?" Kai, who walked before me, turned to ask. I grunted in reply and kept going.

Vernard looked over his shoulder and grinned. "Still sure about that role assignment, weaver?"

"Are you unfamiliar with the concept of packing light, Vernard?" I asked. "It feels as if there is a second man in here."

He stepped off the gangplank. "Or it's just a half-one carrying it." He laughed at his own joke, but heat rushed over my chest and face.

"Oh, leave him be," Kai said, noticing my discomfort. "He might not be as broad as you or I, but he's twice as smart and you know it."

Vernard turned to him sharply. "You are still a slave as far as I am concerned and have no right to address me in such a way. Do not allow your temporary status to cloud your vision of where you truly belong."

I set the bags upon the wooden dock and pressed against my lower spine. "In chains beside your beloved Dorsey?"

Vernard smacked me across the face with the back of the hand, and I stumbled back, shielding my face from further blows. Kai dragged me behind himself as he stood chest-to-chest with Vernard. He spoke near the man's cheek as if concealing the sound, and Vernard's nostrils flared. Fire sprung to his eyes, and I expected him to lash out, this time at Kai, but he sneered and walked away.

Rolling my jaw, I rubbed my cheek where warmth began to spread. "Apparently, Dorsey is a sore spot," I muttered. "What did you say to him?"

"I reminded him that he has entered a country with few alliances," said Kai. "And that all I have to do is shout 'spy' and he'll be swinging from the nearest tree. He will not be striking you again."

"Have I ever told you that you were the best purchase I ever made? Next to my son, of course."

Kai's face lifted as he beamed from ear to ear. "A few times, Zayim. But I still like to hear it. Now, are you done trying to be a good slave, or shall I help you with these bags?"

***

It did not take long to find the auction house as the smell of feces and stale urine rose distinctly above that of stinking fish. Human waste has its own particular stench, and, just as it had done in Burganne, a memory just beyond my grasp came to mind. Had I been sold at an auction house when I was a tot?

There was no one alive who knew that answer. My original papers had been lost, and my new ones had been drawn up when my last master inherited me. I could recall neither mother nor father, only this stench.

We did not stop at the house that day but journeyed instead to an inn. Captain Vernard had gone in search of horses and a wagon to purchase, so Kai and I rented a room while he was out. The inn smelled of pipe ash and booze, and a slick surface of grease lined the tables of the barroom. A round woman with an apron stretched across her middle glanced over her shoulder as she shoved a log into the fire.

"That's fine," said Kai, answering a question I did not catch. "She'll be with us in a moment," he told me.

The woman dusted soot from her hands and rounded the bar. "Need a room?"

Kai leaned his arm against the bar so he could face both me and the woman. I appreciated this about Kai. Even if it were not necessary for me to be part of the conversation, he always made sure I could see his lips.

"Yes," Kai said. "Two. My companion will be along shortly."

"Not that I wouldn't like to take your money," she said, "but there are two beds per room."

"As you can see, there are two of us."

The woman eyed me, paying close attention to my brand. "We do not rent our rooms to slaves. He will sleep in the stable around back."

Kai looked at me, but I could not signal my decision one way or the other without appearing authoritative. "Alright," Kai said. "But he is deaf. If there is trouble, come get me."

She quirked her brow. "Are you expecting trouble?"

Kai shrugged. "From him, no. He can make himself quite understood if he wishes. But others are less patient."

The woman, seemingly satisfied by the answer, gave us the key to our room, and I hauled our bags upstairs. The room was comfortable enough with two beds, a table and chair, and a trunk, although I did wonder whether Vernard would approve of sharing his quarters with Kai for this leg of the journey as well. If he had an issue with it, however, he would have to make his own arrangements.

Kai sank into the chair and peered out the window that looked down upon the busy street. I joined him for a time, and we gazed upon the people of Lasen going about their business, just as they did in Burganne. And just as at home, the sense of restlessness grew within me. But I had no loom to work or orders to fulfill.

That in itself was strange. I wondered if I would ever weave again. Looms were expensive, and it took me nearly a year to reimburse my last master for the previous one after he freed me. I doubted I would return to my little shop and began contemplating how to have the loom shipped to wherever I ended up. A logistical nightmare that would be. Perhaps Marta could help.

My restlessness mounted, and I tapped my thumb against the table. Kai looked from me to it, apparently bothered by the sound. Abruptly, I stood. "I'm going to walk the streets for a bit to get a feel of the place."

"Alright," Kai said, standing as well. "Where do you want to start?"

"I was thinking I would go alone. The overclasses rarely look twice at a slave."

Kai laughed. "Don't I know it? But be careful. We're already searching for one needle in a haystack. No need to make it two."

As predicted, no one paid me any mind as I walked the streets of Lasen. No matter how long I maintained my freedom, it seemed I would always function better in society as a slave. I knew the rules of that status, how to look at people, how to walk with my head slightly lower than the others. But as I walked the streets, a sense of disappointment grew within me.

There was nothing wrong with Lasen, per se, but the similarities to my own home were magnified. Same wattle and daub houses lining cobblestone streets, same weather-beaten Roman structures where officials held their business, same merchants selling surprisingly similar wares. I had never traveled this far north and had hoped to see something new, at least before I died.

I stopped still on the cobbles and a man nearly rammed the back of me. I was still thinking like I was going to die. Sure, my son, Etienne, was in trouble, but my neck was no longer fitted for the noose. I ran a trembling hand over my face, then shook the hand to rid it of vibrations. A coldness flooded me starting from my head and falling to my feet. This was all wrong. In my cell, I had felt numb about my death, and now I was scared?

Or was I scared of living?

I gripped the stall of a booth as heaviness settled on my chest and I struggled to breathe. Perhaps I should have brought Kai after all. Maybe the lack of his lumbering shadow was what caused this now.

Townspeople passed me in a blur, a few of their faces looked at me with furrowed brows, but none stopped. Then something struck me in the back of the head.

A woman working the stall upon which I leaned held her arms out wide and then swept a hand across her wares. She spoke, but my mind could not perceive what she was saying. Someone else approached from the street, pointing between me and the booth.

"Wait," I said. "Wait—I do not understand—"

A man from behind grabbed my arm and shoved me against the door of a shop. His breath flooded my ear, warm and moist.

"I'm deaf!" I cried as I tried to crane my head around. "I cannot hear. If—if you wish me to speak—"

He twisted my arm, and I cried out as he shoved his shoulder against my back, pressing my face against the metal brackets of the door. He shoved his hand into my pocket.

"I am deaf!" I shouted. "Please, whatever you want—"

A hand seized the man's arm and pulled him back from me, and I turned to see Vernard, hand on the hilt of his sword. Clutching my injured arm, I inhaled relief.

"What is this?" Vernard demanded.

"The woman saw him steal from her booth!" the man said. "I asked him who his master is, but he refused to tell me!"

Vernard shrugged. "He's deaf."

"He's playing a game! I heard him speak."

"He's not dumb, just deaf. And he's my slave."

"Your slave's a thief, he is!" The woman pointed a fat finger in my face. Vernard turned to me. I shook my head.

"I will vouch for him," Vernard said. "But if it will make you feel better, you can search him as well. Zayim, arms up." He gestured this last bit for emphasis, and I raised my arms from my sides.

The man patted me down, setting the contents of my pockets on the booth: a few silver coins, papers proving my freedom—although I doubt this lot could read them—and a small mending kit. The woman sold pears and could hardly claim that came from her shop.

"Well, why was he hanging around my shop then?" the woman asked. "I don't like him hanging around my booth like that."

Vernard slid two of the coins across the booth and took a couple of fruits. "Will that settle our differences?"

Her lip turned up in a sneer, but she nodded nonetheless. I took my papers from the stall and pocketed them deep.

"Good. I apologize for any inconvenience." Taking my arm, he led me from the street. Heads continued to turn as we passed until we were further down the lane. Once we were far enough away from the commotion, Vernard stopped and asked, "Does that happen often?"

"Most people of Burganne know me," I said. "Some are asslings, but they all know I cannot hear and that I am no thief."

"This is true," Vernard said. "All of my men know you at least by reputation. You should stay near Kai or me in the future, at least in the market. Where were you trying to go?"

"I was going to go by the docks and observe the slaves working the auction house to figure out who is who," I said. "While you and Kai speak with the auctioneer, I will speak to them. There may be information the slaves have that their masters will not tell you."

"Very well, I will go with you," he said. "We will pick up some fish while we are there."

While we shopped among the fishermen, I surveyed the building in question. The foundation was made from stone, but the upper stories were formed from the usual wattle and daub covered in plaster. Black iron bars welded in grid formation were fixed to the back of the three-story structure. Some of the cages were covered on top by canvas or wooden slats, but most were left open to the elements. Thin, filthy fingers grasped the bars as eyes peered out at me.

The last time I had gotten this close to an auction house was the day I had purchased Kai. At least on that day, I had been able to save one man. I had looked through the bars wondering who I would meet that day and what sort of life he had lived. Today, however, I could not meet those eyes. There was nothing I could do for them.

"See those three men?" I indicated a trio speaking to each other outside the cages to Vernard. "They work the house itself."

"Are you sure? Their brands don't match."

"The house gets to pick out any slaves they wish that comes through their doors. Fresh off the boat would probably not meet their needs. But if you watch, they speak exclusively to each other, never saying a word to the ones inside the cages. And since we have been here, they have not left the area for the shops."

Two of the three slaves I estimated to be in their twenties while the third was closer to my own age – somewhere near forty. The older man gave orders to the younger. He I would approach tomorrow.

One of the younger men dumped food into the cages through a panel on the side. Those inside scrambled for the food, shoving and stepping on anyone who got in their way. I bit my lip as I took in the desperation, but Vernard crinkled his lip. "They're like animals."

"They are people, just like anyone else," I snarled.

Vernard's brows shot up. "I…okay?"

"You just called them animals. I say they are people."

"I did not say that out loud."

"Well, apparently your lips move when you think. The people in there are starving. They've been stolen from their homes to be sold to the highest bidder. You could take a prince and put him in that cell and he'd be reduced to that state in days." I slapped a coin onto the table of the man selling fish—and watching us with a baffled look—and took up the purchase.

Vernard laid a hand upon my arm, turning me to himself. I withdrew from him and flinched, half-expecting another blow. Vernard, however, released my arm, holding up his hands in peace. "I am worried about Dorsey, that is all. He has been missing for a long time and I—" He looked back to the cages. Worry lined his face, aging him in an instant as dark collected beneath his eyes. Had he been sleeping?

"You told the magistrate the task was impossible," said Vernard. "Do you truly think this?"

"You are a military man who has seen war. Do you recall the fate of those you have captured?"

"In truth, I cannot recall one of their faces."

"Expect the kindness demonstrated by your own men to be the treatment Dorsey is receiving now." The rubbing against the brow intensified, and I feared the hairs would fall out. I grasped the man's shoulder, bringing him back to me. "But we will follow this road wherever it leads. My resources are not unlimited, but they are efficient. Which creates better odds for Dorsey than anyone else around him."

Vernard nodded, still unassured by my words. I created no further sense of optimism. The state of things was dismal, and I prayed Marta could get my son to freedom before we failed.

CHAPTER SIX

The stables attached to the back of the inn were comfortable enough, although the smell could have been better. I doubt, however, that there are stables in existence where the same could not be said. Using straw from the horse stalls, I rubbed down the brown mare Vernard had purchased that afternoon. Her neighbor, a white colt, tugged at my sleeve as I did, and I petted his soft nose. He nodded his head in approval and winked with his massive brown eye, and I smiled as I ran my fingers through his thick, gray mane.

Vernard had purchased a pair of fine horses—too fine really for a pair of traveling merchants and their slave, but I did not say anything to him about it. He had, after all, gotten me out of a pinch that afternoon. And I had a love for horses, although I never needed to own one myself. As I continued to rub down the mare, the colt mussed my hair, causing my curls to flatten and stick to my scalp.

"You're a jealous thing, aren't you?" I said as I went to him next. His body tremored beneath my hand in reply as his tail swished.

I was nearly through brushing him down when I caught sight of someone entering the barn. He was tall and straight as a bean pole with a brand on his temple like interwoven vines—an oddly fitting pattern. The colt's chest rumbled as he pranced about his stall.

The bean-pole leaned against the stall door. "Who the hell are you?"

"Just a traveler," I said. "My masters are staying in the inn."

"You talk funny. Where are you from?"

"Not far. I'm deaf so it sounds like I have an accent."

"Deaf? But you're talking to me right now."

I sighed inwardly and wished I could make wages from explaining my situation so many times. I opened my mouth to answer only for him to turn and look toward the door where another man entered.

"New guest," said the bean-pole. "Says he's deaf."

The second man sported a matching brand but had olive skin and raven black hair. "If he's deaf, how can he talk?"

"Practice," I said. "And I can read lips which is how I know what you're saying." I grabbed my satchel and stepped into the aisle. "Is there a place I can make a bed for the night?"

"Sure," Bean-pole said and nodded for me to follow. He led me up a ladder into the loft where a series of makeshift beds were made from hay. He looked at the beds for a minute, then turned back to me. "Sorry, I guess I didn't say that while facing you. You can sleep there."

"Thank you."

Bean-pole looked behind me as a sly grin crossed his face. I turned around to find the raven-haired man banging together two blocks of wood behind my back.

"You look silly doing that," I said, and he stopped with a frown.

Bean-pole bent at the waist and laughed. "Sorry, my friend! You know we had to check is all!"

I supposed that might be true. Many other hearing persons had done similar actions, although I did not for the life of me know why one might fake being deaf.

"How long have you been with the inn?" I asked.

"I've been here my whole life," Bean-pole said, "but Maccario came, what was it, five months ago?"

"Six months," Maccario said and brushed his fingers over his brand. It was raised and a shade of pink while Bean-pole's was pale and nearly flat upon his skin. "Where are you from, deaf man?"

"Burganne. And my name is Zayim. My masters are expanding their trade routes, but we're here in Lasen for a specific reason."

"Oh?" Bean-pole sat in the hay and placed his hands behind his head. "And what reason is that? I'm Lucius by the way."

"A son of a noble was sold at the auction house here in Lasen." I sat on the wooden slats and leaned against a post. "The family wishes to have the boy back, so we've been hired to track him down."

Maccario sneered. "What'd he do to get sold?"

I shrugged. "Not sure. From what little the family told my masters, it's probably something like gambling debts. Honestly, had the slavers been smart, they would have held the boy for ransom rather than selling him. The family has deep pockets."

Lucius shook his head. "The Lasen Auction House does not reveal their clients' identities. Most of the houses in Aquilla don't."

"When the slaves arrive, they are given a number," Maccario said. "And that number is what goes down on the ledger. No names, no descriptions, so even if the auction house wanted to tell you, they couldn't."

"That is less than inspiring," I said. "As someone in, you know, our situation, I kinda wanted to help the guy."

"You wanted to help a loser with gambling debts?" Maccario scoffed. "You know how I became a slave? Someone came up behind me and hit me over the head. Next thing I know, I'm in irons sailing to some god-forsaken country I've never heard of. I had a wife, a beautiful daughter. Now I'm mucking up horse shit for a two-bit swindler like the innkeeper. Nobody has taken pity on me."

"Keep your voice down," Lucius said.

"I guess our only solution is word of mouth then," I said. "Descriptions from people who might have seen him at the auction house. What do you know about the three slaves running it? Mainly the older one."

"That'd be Rike," Lucius said. "He'll be of no help. Guy has his nose so far up his master's ass, it's turned brown. And the guys working with him have only been there for a few months—after he got the old guys flogged and sold."

"Those guys were stealing shoes and other valuables from the other slaves and selling it to merchants," Maccario said. "They took the bracelet my daughter had made me after I managed to hide it from everyone else."

"Yes, that was unfortunate, but you don't go telling on your fellow slaves!"

"Can Rike be bribed?" I asked. "What does he like?"

"Don't even try that," Lucius said. "I'm telling you, he's not worth messing with. He'll turn you over to the law before giving you anything. And the others are too afraid of him to say anything either."

***

The next morning Kai and Vernard collected me from the taproom where I had been enlisted to clean every damn tankard in the place, and we journeyed to the auction house once more. Instead of hanging around the back, we stepped onto the front porch and were greeted by an attendant at the door.

"Wishing to sell?" asked the attendant, nodding to me.

"Uh, no," Kai said. "But we would like to speak with the auctioneer."

"Really? Aged scar and a strong back, bring in a good price."

"I'm deaf," I said.

He staggered a moment in his pitch. "Well, my boss is fair. He'll see you're compensated as you should be."

"The deaf man brays like a donkey, does he not?" Another attendant with graying hair protruding from the sides of his cap joined the first. "I will take care of them, Poe. You may go." Then he gestured for us to accompany him to the side of the building.

"So, what is it that brings you here?" the attendant asked as he tried and failed to hide a cheeky grin. "That is if you're not selling the donkey."

I scratched the back of my head. The man's grin faded, and Vernard showed him the portrait. "We are looking for a man."

"Ah," the attendant said. "Are you family?"

"We've been hired by the family to find him," Kai said.

"Well, come with me, and I'll be sure the auctioneer sees you soon."

We were escorted through a side door and told to wait. The attendant ushered Kai and Vernard into two of the three straight-backed chairs set at a small circular table. The room had a musty smell, but dark stains dotted the polished floor here and there. I guessed them to be blood stains, left there by slaves unwilling to be sold so easily.

Displayed prominently on the wall was a tapestry woven into a map of the town. This time, a single lilac marked a house on the edge of the city.

"Isn't that one of your works?" Vernard asked. The attendant, who was leaving the room, paused to look back at me before shutting the door.

I nodded and leaned against the wall beside the table. Kai, however, tugged at his collar, and I knew he was thinking the same as I was. The room we had entered was probably set aside for deals to be conducted between the auctioneers and slave sellers. This meant every slave who came through this auction house had the opportunity to study the tapestry. It had not been hung there by accident.

The door on the other side of the room opened, and the auctioneer entered. His tunic was long and maroon, and in the belt around his waist was a wooden rod with a handle. The shaft of the rod was discolored.

"Half a pound of silver," the auctioneer said. "And that's mighty generous since he's deaf."

Kai crunched his hand into a fist. "He's not for sale. We're here on other business."

Vernard stood and withdrew the portrait from his pocket. "We are looking for this man. He would have been sold through here. Do you remember him?"

Kai stood as well and hurried to speak as the auctioneer eyed Vernard suspiciously. "We intend on purchasing him back, of course."

"Who is he?" the auctioneer asked.

"He's—" Vernard started.

"He is nobody really," Kai said. "Just the son of a merchant caught in the wrong place at the wrong time. But the family wants him back, so we've been hired to find him."

Vernard glared at Kai but kept his mouth shut.

The auctioneer handed back the portrait. "I do not know this man, but I wish you luck in finding him."

I nodded and turned for the door, forgetting my place for a moment. When I turned back around, Vernard had his hand around the back of the man's neck as he pressed the portrait closer to his face.

Kai wrenched Vernard's arm away and shoved him into the table. He held up both hands in a placating motion as a snarl filled the auctioneer's face. Vernard pressed up from the table with venom, but Kai grabbed his tunic and hauled him out the door. I took hold of the door, nodded to the auctioneer, and closed it behind us.

Once outside, Kai and Vernard continued their argument, shouting back and forth at each other. I stepped between them, grabbing a handful of both of their shirts. "Enough!" I shouted.

Vernard ripped my hands from his shirt and started shouting at me. I, however, did not heed his lips and stared at the cobblestone instead. When I finally looked up at him again, his teeth were barred, but he appeared in greater control of himself.

"What?" I asked.

"The man did not even look at the portrait!" Vernard said. "How could he have recognized Dorsey if he would not even glance at it?"

"The man runs a business," I said. "And a good business does not allow their clients to be hassled by previous owners of their merchandise, or in this case, their families."

"You swore you would find Dorsey!"

"I said I would try. And I shall. While you go back to the inn, I will stay behind and speak with the other slaves."

"But—"

I turned to Kai. "Buy Vernard a good ale, stick him next to the cheery fire of the taproom, and keep him there until I come back."

"Are you sure that's a good idea after yesterday?"

"It will be better than having this hothead around."

Vernard swore at me, but I turned away from him. Finally, he went with Kai, and I looked to Rike who had watched the whole display a stone's throw away. But there was no need to speak to him any longer, so I stepped past the man and made my way to the small house on the edge of the city.

CHAPTER SEVEN

I knocked on the door of the house, and a child near six answered. At first, I assumed I had come to the wrong address, but I had studied the map closely during the weave, and dried lilacs hung over the lintel.

"Child, is your papa home?"

But then the graying attendant from the auction house stepped in from the garden and waved me inside. I entered and barred the door behind me. Upon turning around, I became enveloped by the arms of the man.

"It's good to see you, Zayim," he said, releasing me from his embrace.

"Jules, you look well," I said. "I wondered if Marta's contact would be you after all."

"Come inside, have lunch with us." He motioned me forward. "And I apologize for my remark about the donkey earlier. It was done in jest. I never meant to insult."

"It was the presence of the spy that kept me silent. No offense."

Jules's brows disappeared beneath his hair. "A spy?"

"He's with the magistrate in Burganne. I guess Marta did not say?"

"I should have guessed something like this," said Jules. "Her letter was quite cryptic, and she called me Jean. I will have to be more careful in the future."

"Indeed."

Jules's home was small with the kitchen, dining, and sleeping quarters all on the first level. An additional loft housed the children, of which he had five. Jules led me to the table in the next room, and his wife poured me a glass of ale.

"You say you are unsure if this Dorsey exists or not," Jules said. "Was that what Kai and the spy were fighting over before you left?"

"Vernard speaks of Dorsey as if he is real. I am still unsure but am beginning to believe the boy exists. If not, Vernard is an excellent liar – better than I am at least."

Jules slid a folded paper across the table. "I made a list of three buyers for you that purchased men matching Dorsey's description. My boss does not keep records of such things, but I do for just this reason. Unfortunately, I did not catch a name."

"This is more than what we had. Thank you. And my compliments on the placement of my tapestry. That may be the best I've seen yet."

Jules grinned. "You would not believe how many have come to my door because of it."

I bit my lip. "Be careful, Jules. You have children to think of."

"I am a free-born, Zayim. I will face a fine, nothing more."

"From your king, yes. But your neighbors will view you as a traitor if you are caught. I would be more worried about them than the authorities."

Jules nodded and looked at three of his little ones playing on the floor with carved wooden dolls. "I will keep this in mind. Thank you."

"So, you're the weaver who made the tapestry at Papa's work?" Jules's eldest son Faustin, asked as he joined us at the table. The boy was near fifteen, slender, with a mischievous gleam on his boyish face that caused me to like him instantly. "Papa talks about you all the time. You are famous here in Lasen!"

"This is true," said Jules, leaning back in his seat. "I send Marta many orders, but she said they will take a long time to fill."

"A good tapestry takes a year at minimum," I said. "I've taken to working smaller ones for the liberationists, but most of my clients pay commission for bigger sizes. I have enough work on order than I have life left at this point. All I'm lacking now is a loom, thread, a shop, and free time."

"What you do is invaluable, Zayim. I'd say hundreds of people have been freed because of those tapestries already."

"I'd say thousands!" said Faustin.

"And hundreds more are brought to replace them." I took a sip of wine. "Until the whole system is shattered, I am not sure what we do means much."

"We change individual lives," Jules said. "That matters."

"I know you speak truth but sometimes the weight...."

Jules nodded and refilled my cup. "I know. And I also know about the weight that recently landed on your shoulders."

I laughed. "You mean on my neck."

He grabbed my arm. "I am so glad, my friend, that it did not come to that. You know we raised money and tried to offer the magistrate a substantial ransom. When he refused, we talked of rescue, but penetrating the castle of Burganne was outside our reach."

"Marta told me. Thank you, Jules. It means more than you know." I raised up the charcoal picture of young Dorsey from the table. "For better or worse, this man, in a way, saved my life. Whether or not I'll be able to return the favor hangs in the balance."

"You will find him," said Faustin. "If anyone can do it, it's you."

I smiled at the youth and the red curls and freckles that lined his face. "You have quite the confidence in me, young Faustin."

"I've heard the stories," he said. "Of you and Marta sneaking slaves out under the noses of guards and shipmasters! Someday, Papa will allow me to help in his work."

"Perhaps someday, Faustin. When you're a bit older." Jules squeezed the shoulders of the lad. "Now, Zayim, you may stay as long as you like, but I am expected back after my lunch."

"I should get back too." I stood and shook his hand and Faustin's hand as well. At the door, however, I paused. "There is a man at the inn we stayed at named Maccario. He was recently purchased and has a wife and children. I believe he would possess the motivation to get home if he knew how."

"I will make some inquiries."

"Oh, and by the way, Jules, if you think I bray like a donkey, you should keep in mind that you smell like a whore's latrine."

Jules smiled from ear to ear at my belated retort, but a child tugged upon his tunic. "Papa, what's a whore?"

I laughed as I stepped back onto the road and cried over my shoulder, "Good luck!"

CHAPTER EIGHT

"They gave you three names, just like that, huh?" Vernard sat turned in his seat on the wagon as Kai drove the horse from Lasen. I sat upon the crate filled with my work and held on with my fingernails as we bumped along the road.

"It's all in whom you ask," I said.

"So, you're telling me a veteran slave recalled not just three slaves matching Dorsey's appearance, but their numbers, the names of the buyers, and the towns in which they live?"

I shrugged in reply. He could suspect all he wanted, but without knowing any names, there was no case to build against my friends for the magistrate. I could tell this infuriated the man, but I was not about to open my mouth further just to satisfy his curiosity.

We journeyed to the closest town on the list, a hamlet known as Flores. Right before we arrived, I moved to sit on the back of the wagon where a slave would ride. It was peaceful here, and I found myself enjoying the solitude. After spending so many days alone in my cell, the constant presence of my companions had become a bit jarring. I was just getting settled in my own thoughts, however, when we pulled into the hamlet.

Wooden fences lined the entry of the town where curious faces watched us from the fields beyond. The place consisted of twelve main buildings, and I was surprised such a place could even afford a slave. As we passed, a white-haired man with a long staff stepped from a house marked by the carpenter's symbol above the door.

"What business have ye?" the man cried out. "Best not be selling spirits! We'll have none of that here!"

Had I read his lips wrong? But then a younger man came from behind and pulled the old man in. He bowed as they withdrew. The young man's face was branded, and as we passed, I saw the elder man's face was too.

I raised up from the back of the cart to see an old Roman structure at the top of a hill. The structure consisted of four sides and a rotunda, typical of most monasteries. Men in monk's habits exited the building to watch us ascend the hill.

I unfolded the list of names once more. The first listed was P. Chapin. With a name such as Chapin, I had assumed him to be a cobbler, not a priest.

This was not a welcome turn of events. If Dorsey were here, then he was now owned by the Church itself, not just a man. In my experience, what went to the church rarely returned, people or goods. Perhaps they flowed out to other monasteries or nunneries but to the general public? Not in my knowledge.

Tightness gathered about my throat, but I could not understand why. It came upon me suddenly, like it had at the marketplace. Like a noose closing in.

"I do not speak," I said, and both Kai and Vernard turned to me.

"You what?" Kai asked.

"I do not speak," I repeated. "I am deaf and dumb, do you hear me?"

"I…uh…okay," Kai said. "So be it, I suppose."

Vernard opened his mouth to reply, but I turned back to face the rear. Other slaves emerged from the houses as well as a few unmarked craftsmen. I kept my head lowered but watched them carefully.

When the wagon stopped, I hopped off the back and rounded to the front. Continuing to keep my head lowered, I watched the lips of my companions and the Abbot that met them. He was an older man with a scant amount of hair clinging to the back of his head. His gray scapula was brought in by a belt, but his belly hung over the brown rope. A thick gold chain with a crucifix hung around his neck.

Beside him stood a younger monk with a wooden cross held up by a leather cord. While the Abbot smiled warmly at my companions, the other man scowled, narrowing his eyes, especially at me.

"I have no servant by that name," the Abbot told Kai.

"We have a record, Father," said Vernard "that shows someone from your monastery purchasing a slave matching the boy's description." He snapped his fingers at me, and I handed him the list.

The younger monk eyed Vernard as he took the parchment. "A man of average height with brown hair and brown eyes. Yes, that could fit half the population of Aquilla." He handed back the page.

"Even if we did purchase the man," said the Abbot, "you must know that he is now property of the Church."

"We do not seek to dishonor the Church," Vernard said with a bow. "And will pay whatever is required for the man's return."

"Very well. I will not pull the men from the fields, but you may observe them this evening when they return for supper. Brother Pierre will show you a room where you can lodge for the night, although your slave will sleep in the slave quarters."

I began to wonder if Brother Pierre was actually nearsighted and not narrowing his eyes in suspicion. If he squinted any more at us, his eyes would have been shut. But the corner of his mouth twitched as did his nose in perfect imitation of a mouse — or a rat.

The Abbot excused himself and we were left with the rodent. "I do not like the way your slave looks at me," he said. "He does not know his place, I would wager."

Typical. Here I was trying to appear submissive and being accused of being arrogant.

"He's looking at your mouth," said Kai, "not your eyes. The man is deaf and is reading your lips."

"Still – I do not like the look of him."

"Zayim," Vernard said, "go tend to the horses."

It was the first order from the man I could fully endorse. When the horses were groomed and eating in the stables, I brought in our luggage, minus the giant crate still sitting in the back of the wagon. Marta had done well to secure so many of my fabrics that I wondered if the magistrate had managed to get any at all.

The cool stones of the monastery kept the space protected from the summer heat, and the graceful arched ceiling along the corridors were adorned with statues of angels and saints. I kept my head down, averted from the saints, and for the first time understood my decision to be mute. After being damned to hell by the last priest I encountered, I had no desire to speak with another. If they agreed with the priest of Burganne, I was certain my fate would be redoubled.

Marta said I should bear no guilt, but what if she were wrong? Nearly everyone I knew believed slavery to be an acceptable role for man. Was I in the wrong? Did these saints and angels now stand in judgment of me?

With a shuddering breath, I raised my gaze to the nearest one. It was Moses standing before me, clutching two tablets of stone. Beside him, his brother Aaron and further down Joseph. Three former slaves. Three men who knew of our chains and the burns beneath the shackles. And they did not look upon me with scorn.

Nor, perhaps, would God our Father.

Vernard and Kai were already in our room sitting on their opposing beds with their knees side-by-side when I entered and set our belongings on the floor. The space was tighter than the ship, and I suppressed a laugh. "There is room in the slave quarters, I'd wager."

"I'm tempted to venture there." Kai stood and moved to exit but had to wait for Vernard to pull his legs into the bed before he could pass. "You'd think a place like this could afford better rooms."

"The priests live a life of denial," said Vernard. "Instead of fine things, their belongings are simple, their living spaces small. That way they can keep their mind on the work of the Lord rather than on physical goods."

"Yes, well, I'm going to spend some time in the dining hall," said Kai. "Judging from the belly of the Abbot, I doubt there is much denial taking place in that realm." He closed the door and we walked down the hall a bit before speaking.

"Do you think the monks would be able to get a letter to my sister?" he asked me.

"Probably," I said. "If anyone can get a letter to an abbess, I'd say it would be an abbot. And this time you can use your own name to send it."

"She will be glad of that. She's never been in much favor of our ruse."

"And for good reason. It's a terribly dangerous ruse."

"Indeed." Kai winced as he said this and placed a hand upon his back. I cocked my head in question of this, and he redden slightly. "It's nothing, Zayim. Last night's bed was rough is all."

But I rose on my toes and tugged on the collar of his shirt, peering at his back. Raised red lines crossed his back like a spider's web. "Holy Mother! Kai, why didn't you say anything?"

"It's fine, Zayim. They're scabbed over and healed for the most part."

"Who did this to you? Your new master?"

Kai bit his lip as if deliberating upon answering or not. Then he nodded to our chambers.

"Vernard?" I demanded.

"Well, not him personally, but on his order."

"Son of a bitch!"

"Listen, Zayim, it was just," said Kai. "I struck some of his men when you ran. I would have struck him too if he hadn't had his sword."

I pressed my hands to my face. "Damn Vernard and the sodding magistrate! Damn them straight to hell."

Kai pulled my hands from my eyes. "You're in a church, Zayim."

"I do not care. That should not have happened."

"And this is why I didn't tell you. You are making this more than it should be. It was unpleasant, yes, but a flogging is better than hanging from the gallows."

I swatted at the moisture gathering in my eyes. "I am sorry, my friend."

He placed his giant hand on me and smiled. "You are sorry because you are a good man. And a good master. But do not let this form a rift between you and Vernard. As long as they have your son, we need him on our side."

***

After depositing my bag on an empty bunk in the slave quarters, I managed to find a job tending the garden at the center of the monastery. Anything to keep my mind off the terrible scars striping Kai's back. More than one man had succumbed to disease from the whip, and it was one of the most common and most feared punishments. It was an abhorrent practice and one I would never have permitted to occur even if Kai had been my legitimate slave.

How many floggings had the Captain ordered, I wondered? I doubt he had ever held the whip himself.

For the first hour within the garden, I dwelt upon these thoughts and the cruelty of man. Why could we not live as the monks did, in harmony in a garden such as this? Why did we have to murder and steal from each other?

Over time, the tempest in my chest settled as I worked the soil, adding compost and pruning wayward vines. Never before had I seen such a beautiful arrangement of plants. Purples, reds, blues, and yellows collided and rippled with the gentle breeze, each on display in their tiers. Vines heavy with grapes climbed a dome trellis at the center of the garden. Light tinted green streamed through the vines onto the fractured flagstones below. I could have spent my life beneath such a ceiling. In any case, I now had inspiration for my next weave.

As I knelt plucking two blighted leaves, the first I had seen during my time in the monks' garden, a young woman took the bench beside me. She closed her eyes and leaned back, allowing her raven hair to cascade from her shoulders as sunlight shone upon her face and chest. Her linen dress was white, although a spiral brand at her temple marked her as a slave.

Her garb marked her as a consecrated virgin. As a slave this meant the decision was likely not her own, but her promise to keep at her own peril. Likely, the priests wished to keep her near to appreciate, but maintain their sense of piety.

When she opened her eyes, she caught me admiring her. Warmth of embarrassment flooded my cheeks, but she smiled and asked, "Do you have a name?"

As pretty as she was, I would not break my ruse. I tapped my ear and signed my word for "Zayim," although I knew she would not understand.

"You are the deaf man traveling with the merchants," she said. "I am sorry if I—"

I waved my hand, showing no offense taken, and she smiled her pretty smile once more. "The garden is lovely, isn't it?" she asked. "I know you don't speak, but do you mind if I talk to you?"

I shook my head, knocked the dirt from my hands, and sat on the flagstones beside her. I had all day. I pointed at her and mouthed, "Name?"

"Ranae," she said.

I signed the letters of her name, and the smile grew. I really should have moved on instead of engaging with the girl, but I felt mesmerized by her beauty. She was like the flowers or the stone walls that captivated my attention, inspiring me to create works of art around them.

Ranae turned her head to the other side of the courtyard where a woman motioned for her. Her shoulders fell as she looked at me. "It was nice to meet you."

I nodded, and as quickly as a butterfly lands upon the finger and flitters away, she was gone.

But there was nothing I could do about it, so I returned to my work once more. I had not worked in a garden since I was a boy, and the feel of the warm dirt between my fingers and the smell of the earth brought me back to my first home, a farm in south Visconia known for small, red, oval plums. I had not seen plums of such shape and taste since I left there and wondered what became of the place.

As I imagined the taste of the plums, so sweet and juicy in my mouth, the face of Alonya, my master's daughter, filled my mind once more: her pink cheeks and flowing chestnut hair as she shared the secret dessert with me beneath the yew tree. It was she who taught me to form my words and worked as translator whenever I stumbled. My constant companion and the only friend of my youth.

I loved her. And I loved her father, my master.

But my fellow slave, Eglis, had a quarrel with our master. The foolish slave had grown affectionate of a slave girl belonging to a family nearby. He begged my master to purchase the girl as his wife, but Master refused and the girl was sold to traders from afar.

Eglis slaughtered my master in his sleep, he and the children, even the youngest daughter who was barely a tot. As I held the body of Alonya in my arms, he offered his hand to me, promising me freedom if I came with him.

I refused.

Being still a youth, I did not know what to do in the empty house surrounded by bodies. If I had sought help from the town, I doubt they would have understood me as the clarity of my speech came later while working in the weaving shop. I cleaned and wrapped the bodies in fresh sheets as I had seen the women do with Alonya's grandfather when he had passed. It was not until the next day that someone came by and found the state of things. I was discovered sitting beside Alonya's bed, clutching her cold fingers.

I was thirteen.

By our laws, any slave who murders his master sentences the other slaves to death. But the brother of my master took pity on me and brought me into his home. Eglis, fool that he was, returned three years later in another bloody attempt to free his love. The watchmen of the town subdued him, and he was taken to Burganne for trial. He was the first and the last execution I attended.

A hand rested on my shoulder and I spun around to face Vernard as my chest heaved. "A bit jumpy, aren't you, weaver?"

I pressed a hand to my temple and shook my head clear.

"The slaves are being assembled. Let's go see if Dorsey is among them."

I dusted the dirt from my hands and followed after the Captain. Upon exiting the courtyard, Ranae smiled at me, and I nodded in return. Vernard's brows rose as his eyes lingered on the girl as we passed. "Made a friend?"

I tapped my closed mouth, and the corner of his own raised. Whatever it was that amused him, I did not know. Nor did I care after what he had done to Kai. I wished to yell at him, but it would have done no good. The man would not feel shame for his actions. He was a servant of the magistrate, no more.

"Why are you in such a foul mood?" asked Vernard.

I glanced about to ensure we were alone before asking, "Why are you in such a good mood?"

Vernard grinned. "One of the monks told me their most recent purchase was captured in the Battle of Durban. I showed him the portrait, and he said he recognized the man. I think we have found him."

But as soon as the slaves assembled, I knew we had not. Undoubtedly, Dorsey would have been waving like a madman upon seeing Vernard, yet none of these men knew why they were being assembled, nor did any step forward. Vernard was invited to inspect their faces, but this only confirmed my thoughts.

Upon returning to our rooms, Vernard collapsed onto his bunk and ran his hands through his hair. The Abbot came by, inviting us to dinner. The Captain stared at the flagstones in dejected silence, and I grew tempted to rejoice in his suffering. At least he was getting a taste of the realities of slavery and what it was to be lost.

Two long oak tables ran the length of the dining hall with benches on either side. The wood had been polished to a shine, and the plaster of the walls gleamed white. Two wrought-iron chandeliers lit the room, and a low fire burned in the hearth.

Since I could not hear the requests of those we were serving, I was instructed to keep the fire stoked. An easy job, I leaned against the stones of the hearth and observed the monks in their conversation. I picked up very little, just fragments of conversations, but the room inspired me nonetheless. I had hoped to see something new upon my journey north, and the monastery had been it. There was something about the motion of eating and talking, the movement of gray-brown sleeves across the table, and the often too-serious gazes the monks gave each other that caught my attention. Rarely had I attempted to incorporate people into my weaves, but this interesting scene might be an exception. Drinks flowed and laughter became common.

As the night grew late, my eyes grew heavy. Most of the monks left the hall for bed, but Vernard stayed at the table, engaged in animated conversation with the Abbot. I glimpsed a couple of phrases and knew the topic to be church doctrine. Was there really that much interest in the holy books that caused men to stay up so late? Since I did not read Latin, I did not know. All I knew were the stories Kai's sister, the Abbess, had shared.

When Vernard finally rose from the table and said his farewells to the Abbot, I doused the fire and glared at him as he strolled past me to the door. I quickly caught up with him, intent on giving him a piece of my mind about staying up so late. But as we entered the courtyard to the garden, Vernard held up his hand.

"What is it?" I asked.

He tapped a finger to his lips and stepped deeper into the garden. Branches shook and moved in the moonlight. It was too much motion to be a mouse or squirrel, or even a dog for that matter. My eyes grew wide as Vernard drew a short sword from beneath his cloak and sprinted around the corner.

Someone rose out of the shadows and took off across the garden, and Vernard gave chase. I stepped around the corner to follow, but on the flagstones lay a form. White garments reflected by the moon gave way to legs uncovered. The white dress, please, no, let it not be—

But it was Ranae.

CHAPTER NINE

I fell to my knees beside Ranae, trying to take her hands in my own, but she pulled away. "It's alright," I said, and she peered up from behind her trembling hands. "I will not hurt you."

For a moment, she stared at me, astonished by my ability to speak, then wrapped her arms around my neck and clung to me as her shoulders heaved. I petted her dark hair and rocked as if she were a child.

Light from torches came from the other side of the garden, and fire rumbled in my belly when I saw a man being dragged through by others. Until I recognized the man to be Vernard. He resisted them, shouting words I could not make out. The grave face of the Abbot was among them. Kai, too, stepped into the courtyard, having heard the commotion.

"What is this?" the Abbot demanded of Vernard, and Ranae buried her face further into my chest. "I invite you into my home and—"

"I did nothing!" Vernard tugged against the men restraining him. "Sir, I had just left your side! How could I have? I found the man, Pierre upon the woman."

Brother Pierre stepped out from the crowd and into the torchlight. "Lies! I found him in the garden with the woman. It was he who—"

"Enough!" I shouted, and Ranae jolted in fear. I covered her head protectively as the eyes of those gathered turned on me. "I was with Vernard. He tells the truth."

"You can hear?" the Abbot declared. "You can hear, and you accuse others of lies?"

"I can read your lips, sir, and I can speak."

Pierre's lips moved incomprehensibly until he found a reply. "Of course, he defends his master! But you would take the word of a slave over mine? I saw them making eyes at each other over the meal! The rendezvous must have been planned for when you went to bed."

I reached into my jerkin and pulled out my papers, showing them to the Abbot. A torch was brought near. "You are a free man?"

"In that, I did deceive," I said. "It is easier sometimes to be what is expected."

The Abbot's face crinkled further, clearly not understanding my reasoning. I did not blame him. A man such as the Abbot delighted in status, but Ranae looked up at me as well, a question on her lips.

The Abbot bent before Ranae, his old features full of gentleness. "Tell us. Who has done this?"

She looked to me, her sudden protector, and I petted her arm and nodded. "Pierre," she said before her chin collapsed to her breast.

"Your Grace." Pierre knelt on the ground before him. "It is…it is clear I have been found out. But the devil of a woman tempted me so! I could not help but find myself drawn by her presence."

"She was consecrated!" cried the Abbot. "You have destroyed her!"

"Have mercy upon me, your Grace!" He fell to his face. "I shall – I shall pay for her and she shall be mine."

The Abbot sneered at the monk. "Indeed you shall, or it will be taken from your back!"

"What?" I cried. "You would allow the man who harmed her to own her?"

"She is a slave!" said the Abbot. "And an unholy one at that. She has been ruined!" The man turned to leave us. Others began to follow him out of the courtyard, but Ranae clutched my jerkin tight. Gently, I pried her fingers from my clothes and stood.

"Abbot," I said, and he turned back to me. "I will pay for the girl."

"You?" His aged brow contorted in disbelief. "And what do you have of worth?"

Vernard tapped me on the shoulder. "Zayim," he said with mumbled lips, probably in an attempt to whisper, "my money from the magistrate is not inexhaustible."

"Kai, get the crate from the barn."

A woman led Ranae away while we entered the dining hall to discuss the price. When Kai opened the crate before the Abbot, his and the eyes of the surrounding monks grew wide. The Abbot raised the article on top and ran his thumb over the textiles.

"I recognize this work," he said. "These are done by the weaver, Zayim. His work hangs in the halls of my king—" The Abbot turned to me, sudden recognition in his eyes. "It is said that the man of such talent is deaf and a former slave. But you?"

From near the bottom of the crate, I brought out an article and set it on the table. "For the woman."

As the Abbot ran his hand across the weave, his demeanor concerning me changed to one of awe. "This is as soft and light as air itself. Is it silk?"

I nodded.

"The only man I know who possesses silk is His Holiness in Rome…" The Abbot raised the cloth, and it gleamed in the light of the chandeliers.

"Do we have a deal, Father?"

The Abbot ran his hands upon the cloth, caught in rapture by the material. The softness, the gleam of such a fine thing. The man knew what was of value in material, but not in flesh and blood.

"What is your answer, sir?" I asked.

What he said, I did not discern as his head remained downward, so I looked to Vernard instead.

Vernard scratched the back of his ear. "That was a yes."

"Then we will ride with her in the morning."

***

Since my image as a slave had been broken, Kai insisted I take the bed that night as he slept on the floor between our beds. My weary back was most grateful. Although I slept through the night, my dreams were plagued by rotting poppy flowers dripping red in the meadow.

The next morning, we said our thanks and farewell to the Abbot in the courtyard of the monastery, and Ranae was brought to us. They had exchanged her white linen dress for a hairy garb similar to the monk's. Her eyes were red and swollen, and she clutched her arms tight against her chest. The slaves about the courtyard paused in their work to watch the poor girl be handed over to this band of strangers.

"Go to him, girl," ordered the Abbot.

A tear rolled down her cheek as she took staggering steps toward me. She did not raise her head but continued to embrace herself. Good reasons or not, the monastery was likely the only home Ranae had ever known. And I was tearing her from it.

"Who is that?" I nodded to the woman I had seen with Ranae yesterday, peeking out behind a pillar. A matching spiral marked her temple and tears cascaded down her cheeks.

"My…my aunt. My mother's sister."

"If the Abbot permits, you may say your farewells to her."

"I—" She clamped a hand to her mouth and then steadied herself with a breath. "I have already said them, sir."

I nodded. "Very well. Then we shall go."

Kai had already hitched the wagons, and we took our customary places. Before Ranae climbed onto her place on the back, I scanned her head to toe, taking in her measurements. Her eyes grew wide as I took the place beside her, my legs dangling above the ground. She scooted to the corner, as far away as possible from me.

Once we were away from the hamlet, I brought out some of my fabrics and sewed them as we traveled. Ranae wrapped her arms around her legs and stared into the countryside as we rocked along the road. In her hand, she clutched a necklace, probably her only personal possession.

Around midday, the crate bumped me in the back, and as I looked over the wood, Kai tossed a water pouch to me and a sack of food. I laid the morsels out for Ranae as well, but she only took a crust of bread. I took a draught of water and set it within her reach. "You do not need to fear me."

Ranae looked over her crust of bread at me, her beautiful green eyes inspecting my features. She picked up the pouch, running her thumb around the rim.

"I know you have questions, Ranae. You may ask them if you wish."

"Why did you purchase me?" A tear tumbled down her cheek. "I have little value to a group of merchants except—" She clamped a hand over her mouth.

I bit my lip. She was right to be afraid. From her view of things, at best, she had been purchased as a wife. At worst, a whore. "Ranae, the last man in the world you have to fear is me, do you understand? You will come to no harm within my care."

She studied me once more before flicking away a tear and staring into the woods. Her breathing became labored and she rocked back and forth ever so slightly.

I sighed and picked apart my crust of bread until there was nothing left of it. "Ranae, if you could go anywhere in the world, where would you go?"

She spread her arms wide then brought them down with her shoulders slumped. "I don't know. I know very little about the world, sir."

"Some place nice, though, am I right?

"Well, of course." She picked at a loose thread on her garb. "Some place without winter, if it exists."

"That is a good answer. And what would you do in this place?"

She pinched her eyes shut and rubbed the space between her brows. "I don't know, sir. It is not my place to say."

"You are afraid, and that is fine. The world has many places and many roles to fill." I stood and rummaged through the crate once more. After finding a pen and sealing wax, I pulled out two sets of parchment from deep in my pocket. My own pages, I put back, but hers I set upon the floor of the wagon. Her eyes grew wide as she scanned the document, taking in the Abbot's seal.

"What if it were your place to say?" I asked.

Her petite mouth parted as she looked from the document to me, then back again. After dipping the pen into ink, I signed my name, placed my seal, and slid the parchment over to her.

"I purchased you, Ranae, because I believed you could do better in determining your place in this world than Brother Pierre."

Her slender fingers brushed upon the parchment as if it were the Abbot's silk. A higher value to her was this page anyway, higher than any who had held it before could estimate. "You cannot be serious, sir—" Then she tilted her head and peered over the top of the crate toward Kai.

"What did he say?" I asked.

"He said you are very serious," she said. "And Vernard said 'I knew it.'"

I smiled, imagining the exchange. "What I want for you is to have a life of peace. And for that, you need to be free. So, make your mark." I nodded to the page.

As she raised the pen, it shook in her hand and another tear slid down her cheek. "I…I don't know what to say—"

I shrugged. "Then say nothing. It is your right, after all."

Her look of disbelief shattered into respite and she took a shuddering breath. The mark she made was a spiral, matching the one on her temple. Then she folded the parchment up and slid it into the pocket at her waist. Tears fell from her cheeks unfettered, and she breathed two words: "Thank you."

I nodded and gathered the sewing back into my lap, but Ranae launched from her side of the cart and wrapped her arms around me in an embrace. I laughed as I petted her hair. "It is alright, girl!

It was nothing, truly." But when she released me, I swatted away my own tears.

CHAPTER TEN

The return to Lasen had been planned from the start, as the monastery had been to the south, and our next location to the north. Upon reaching the city, I hollered for Kai to stop just within the walls.

I dismounted the wagon and motioned for Ranae to follow me. "We have some business to attend to."

"I take it your smuggling friends live near here," said Vernard.

"I have been here but once, Vernard. How many friends could I have made? Kai, secure passage to Candorlan for the lady while I'm gone."

"Right, Zayim." Kai flicked the reins and the cart lumbered along the streets.

Jules lived several blocks from here, but I had stopped just in case Vernard decided to try and locate him once this was all over.

Ranae watched the crowded streets with wide eyes. A horse trotted past, and she clung to my arm. "I have never been to such a city."

I patted her hand and led her down a side street. "I remember the first time I came to my home in Burganne. It scared me something terrible: people coming up behind me without my knowing, children tumbling out of doors, wagons rushing past. It takes some getting used to, but you are going to a place similar to where you came from – a nunnery in Candorlan."

"A nunnery?" Turning to me, she clutched the collar of her dress. "Oh…I—"

"Not to stay. That is, unless you want to. The Abbess is a friend of mine. She'll help you find lodging and employment. Here we are."

When I knocked on Jules's door, he opened it and pulled me into an embrace once more. "I did not expect to see you so soon! Who is your friend?"

As I stepped into the home, I tripped over a young child, and Ranae grabbed my arm to keep me from crushing the boy. I dropped the clothes bundled beneath my arm and they covered him like a phantom. "Sorry." I collected the fabric and patted him on his head as he glared at me. "This is Ranae."

Jules took her hand and bowed. Her eyes grew wide at the greeting, still used to being treated like a slave. "It is a pleasure to meet you."

"I have purchased and freed Ranae, but she needs safe passage to Candorlan. Do you have—?"

"Of course." Jules exited to the kitchen and returned with a small box. "My wife and the kids put these together." He slid the lid open. "You have some money, a list of names, and a small map to follow once you step off the boat. The box should fit nicely into your pocket."

I scratched my nose. "I…uh…was hoping for something a little more – personal. There was an attack recently, and I would feel better if she had an escort."

"Zayim, I cannot leave my job without giving warning to my employer—"

"I was thinking of your son."

Both Ranae and Jules looked to the kitchen as a bench toppled over with Faustin riding it to the floor. With a sheepish grin, he righted himself and the bench. "I could go! Father, I could—" He stopped still in his tracks, opening and closing his mouth like a fool as his face grew red. The corners of Ranae's mouth turned upwards.

"I could escort the lady," said Faustin upon finding his breath. "We could travel as merchants as Zayim has done."

"Or she could go as a friend of the weaver, Zayim," I said. "And you could be her escort. Once she reaches the end of her journey, she will not be among enemies."

"Oh," Faustin said, a bit crestfallen. "That shall work as well, I suppose."

I unfolded the fine blue linen garment I had sewed along the journey and handed it to Ranae. "Go ahead and get changed, my lady."

"I did not imagine…" she said taking it. "Are you sure?"

"What sort of name would I make for myself if I allowed a 'friend of the weaver' to walk around in that garb. Go and get changed!"

With a great smile, she took the dress and went upstairs for privacy.

"Faustin," Jules said, "if you are to do this, you will need to behave, my son. The lady is to be shown utmost respect. Your duty is to protect her at all costs, do you understand?"

He nodded vigorously. "I do, father."

Jules tousled his hair. "Good boy."

Ranae returned from upstairs, and Faustin smacked at his curly locks in an attempt to right them from his father's hand.

"Before we go, there is one bit of business left to attend to." I removed an iron brand from my pocket, the mark of a freeman.

"You are aware the brand has no meaning in my country," Jules said.

"Yes, but it means something nearly everywhere else."

"Brand?" Ranae asked, brushing her hand against the spiral on her temple. "Brand where?"

I showed her the mark on my wrist, and she relaxed some.

Once the brand was red hot in the fire, Jules pressed it to the inside of her wrist, and her face pinched in pain. I quickly submerged her hand in a bucket of water, and we applied a wrap coated in ointment.

"You are free, my lady," I said.

"Yes, but forgive me if I do not feel it until we are in Candorlan."

After saying our farewells, we journeyed to the docks. Faustin carried a staff and a pack of provisions his mother had prepared. Nobody seemed to notice Ranae or me as we traveled, but a few people nodded at Faustin. Upon reaching the docks, I was surprised to see Kai and Vernard, and my surprise only grew with what Vernard held in his hand.

"I was granted access by a Marquis within your country and have extended his power to you through my seal," said Vernard. "This letter will give you unfettered access to the port of Nostria and on to Candorlan. Travel well, my lady."

Once more, the young maid stood dumbfounded before us, and I feared another tear was about to surface. "I…I do not know what to say. I did not believe such people existed." She planted a kiss upon Vernard's cheek, and he turned a shade of crimson.

The boat was due to depart the following morning, but the crew allowed her to stay the night on the boat. Their chambers on the boat were satisfactory, although I would have preferred them to have separate quarters. Faustin grew red once more upon seeing the space and declared, "I will keep watch, my lady, outside your door." And he stacked two crates together and leaned upon them.

"Thank you, Faustin," said Ranae from the doorway, "But I'll keep the door open for now so that neither of us gets lonely."

I suppressed a grin as I turned for the gangway, and Kai tapped me on the shoulder upon reaching the docks. "I do not think the lady will tolerate him being outside for long."

"Yes, I believe the stack of crates will be abandoned before nightfall."

"Who knew you were such a matchmaker, Zayim?"

"I'm only surprised, Zayim, that you let her go so easily," said Vernard, joining in our conversation. "I was sure the lady Marta was about to gain competition."

"Young Ranae could do much better than an old bachelor like myself," I said. "Besides, I am married to my work. Kai knows this to be true."

Kai laughed. "In truth, Zayim, I would prefer you to get a wife. Then perhaps she could cook and clean for you and make sure you change your shirt."

"Really? You must remind him to change his shirt?" Vernard said.

"I must remind him to eat," said Kai.

"I am not some helpless babe!" I said.

"It is worse, of course, whenever the muse takes him," Kai continued. "The man will not sleep for days as he works upon his canvas!"

"And Marta tolerates this?" Vernard asked, then chuckled. "She is a better woman than I imagined. You should have married her long ago, weaver."

Kai held up his hand to Vernard. "You may wish to tread lightly there on the subject of Marta as it concerns marriage. It can be a testy one."

"There is no subject for which to dwell upon," I said. "Marta and I are, and will continue to be, just friends."

"That is not what I saw a fortnight ago," said Vernard. "I believe you lost claim to that title long before now."

"Oh, upon the night when she was caught in my house with a runaway slave and needed an excuse for her presence?" I said. "Marta is a good and upright woman, and I will not hear of her reputation being sullied."

"I have not sullied it!" said Vernard. "If her provocative display was indeed a ruse, then it was she who did the sullying!"

"I will not tolerate such talk about her!" I shouted, wagging a finger in Vernard's face. "You will not speak of her in this manner again!"

Vernard's eyes grew huge as he stared slack-jawed at my finger. I, too, became surprised by its presence and the heat upon my face.

Kai placed a hand on my shoulder, pulling me back. "And that's probably where it needs to end. Come. It looks strange, a slave and a master arguing like this."

I turned from them and stormed down the docks without a glance back.

CHAPTER ELEVEN

Upon returning to the inn, I collapsed onto the hay pile in the barn, exhausted from our journey. I was still a bit shocked that I had lashed out at Vernard. Kai knew me better than I did myself. He had predicted the encounter, but I did not recall raising my voice at him over anything concerning Marta. Still, Vernard should not have implied what he did.

"Hey, deaf man!" Lucius smiled as he ascended the ladder. "Didn't expect to see you back! Find what you were looking for?"

"No, unfortunately," I muttered. "Which means more days on the road."

I was not the rogue, intrepid hero of the liberation movement as Faustin supposed. In fact, I had not left my hometown in nearly two years, and then only on actual business. I was just a weaver with a hole in his floor. "Where's Maccario?"

Lucius leaned forward as he glanced about the hay loft. His enunciation deteriorated, and I guessed him to be whispering.

"If you move your lips without a sound, I can understand you better," I said.

"Oh, sorry. I said Maccario disappeared yesterday. Just up and walked away from the inn. Vanished without a trace."

I feigned surprise. "Do you think he managed to find passage back home?"

"That's what I would guess. He was always talking about his wife."

"Did he tell you he was going to leave?"

Lucius looked about the loft once more then nodded.

I tried to make my voice airier and therefore "softer." "Why did you not go with him?"

He shrugged. "I've been a slave all my life. Where could I run?"

I nodded, understanding his position completely. It was rare for us to escort born slaves to freedom. Most would prefer to stay with what was familiar, even if familiar was horrible.

"Besides," Lucius continued, "my master has promised me a wife at the end of the year – if he hasn't changed his mind after Maccario. But—" He pulled a bit of cloth out from beneath the hay and passed it to me. The hand-sewn map stitched on the fabric did not lead to Jules's house. Since the map was in no way hidden, I guessed it led to a less incriminating rendezvous with one of his contacts.

"If you would like to run," Lucius said, "this will get you there."

I folded up the fabric and passed it back. "You should consider freedom, Lucius. Especially if you are looking to start a family. A man should be his highest master."

"Take the cloth," he said. "A philosopher like you would be better served by it."

I studied the man, considering his worth and ability to keep his mouth shut. I had a job to do and could not face another noose, especially in a foreign country. But then again, he had frowned upon Rike's talebearing and had covered for Maccario. I rolled up my sleeve and held out my mark.

Lucius grabbed my wrist, eyes wide. He looked up at me as if seeing a new man. "You are – you are free? But why are you here in the barn?"

"What better way to meet friends like Maccario?"

He continued to stare at me, as if not being able to comprehend what he had seen. Then he leaned back his head and laughed. "Is there anything about you deaf man that is as it appears?"

I smiled in return. "Very little."

***

Vernard roused us the next morning before dawn, eager to continue the hunt for young Dorsey. I could feel the anxiety in his manner, the way he packed his bags and hurried us along. The longer our journey took, the further Dorsey could slip from our grasp.

The next village was a two-day ride from Lasen into the hilly region of Aquilla. Each of us took turns driving. When Kai took the reins from me once more, I took my place on the back, intent on taking a nap, but Vernard rounded the wagon to sit by me.

"I had been meaning to speak with you since morning," said Vernard, "but it is hard to converse with you while you drive."

"Would you have preferred me running the wagon into a ditch?" I asked, and he smiled.

Vernard picked apart a leaf that had fallen into the bed of the wagon down to the stem. "You are a craftsman of much fame, yet it puzzled the magistrate to find so few possessions to your name. Of course, this—" he pounded on the crate "—explains part of the missing goods. The affair with the girl, I believe, may explain the rest."

I leaned back against the side of the wagon and crossed my arms over my chest. In truth, I was not nearly as charitable as the Captain suggested. I had bought four slaves in my lifetime: my son, his mother, Kai, and now the girl. The rest of my money I had used to purchase a vineyard then had immediately deeded the property to my son, naming Kai the manager of the estate until the boy came of age. The vineyard was a successful endeavor and had provided nicely for Sloan and Etienne thus far. If I wished for the boy to have any inheritance at all, however, I knew I would have to keep my mouth shut, so I shrugged in reply.

"You are a man of conviction, I will give you that," said Vernard. "Misguided convictions, perhaps, but convictions nonetheless."

"What do you mean?"

"The entire liberationist agenda," he said. "Do you really believe the world would be better if all slaves were made free?"

"I do."

Vernard looked out to the road as it passed, started to speak, then remembered to turn his head. "My father owns a number of slaves on his estate, so when I say I have been around them most of my life, it is not hyperbole. They are filthy people: unwashed, unkempt, and a highly unintelligent group as well. If you were to release such people into the masses, they would not be able to recognize their own hunger to prepare a meal for themselves."

For a moment, I was held in silence by the severe distaste for what I believed to be my fellow man. Then I cleared my throat, "And what of your Dorsey?"

"Well," Vernard faltered, "granted most of the slaves on our estate are born slaves. I do recognize that there are exceptions to what I have described. You are one, of course. But can you imagine the sheer impact the release of such a large population would have on our economy? Freeing a couple here and there by the rare master who finds their slave worthy of freedom, I can tolerate, but blind sweeping mandates freeing so many at once?"

"You are a man of war, sir. When is it that your men fight the hardest?"

"I…uh…when the glory of their kingdom is at stake."

"Is it?" I asked. "Or is it when their families are at risk?"

"I suppose that would impact how a man would fight, yes. In fact, I prepare the men for battle in this way. Upon defense, I ask them to think of their children at home and how their stand today will impact their future safety."

"You remind them of what they have to lose."

"Of course." The last of the twig dissolved and he knocked the crumbs from his lap.

"And what does a slave have to lose when even their children do not belong to them?"

"A slave works for the profit of their master."

"Would you expect a mercenary to fight as hard as your countrymen when they know they will receive neither pay nor prestige from the victory? But a master expects that of a slave. This failure of the economy that you worry so much about, I believe, is the other way around. If a man has something to gain, or lose, he will give it his all. As is, you have a group of people breaking their backs under the whip of their masters for no hope greater than their next meal. But if you free these people, you unleash their possibilities as well. Who knows where we will land? Perhaps in a kingdom rivaling Rome itself."

The corner of Vernard's mouth rose as he selected another leaf to mutilate. "You have an infectious optimism about you, Weaver Zayim. No wonder people follow you."

"Perhaps. But the reasons for liberation are stronger than any economic rationale. It is not right to own another being as one would a beast. To allow them no say or protection of their own body or work is wrong."

"You are a free man now, Zayim. Do you believe the state has no right to dictate laws over its citizens?"

"The state does not rip children from the arms of their mothers to be sold to foreigners."

Vernard rubbed his chin. "Yes, I did believe that had something to do with it. You are bitter over what your master did to you."

"For a decade, my child and I were separated. I missed the whole of his childhood. When I arrived to redeem him, he did not know me and was reluctant to go. Since I, in good conscience, could not leave him behind, I was forced to tear him from a family he loved to reunite him with a mother he did not know. Now, just as the boy begins to see the value of his freedom, the magistrate threatens to revoke it as a way to extort his father. Am I bitter, Captain? Of course. Would you not be?"

The Captain adjusted his collar as if it had begun to tighten around him. "I am not above compassion, weaver. I have two daughters of my own. To endure the loss of either of them would be to lose part of my soul itself. But a master is not just a man, but a business owner as well. I would not be amiss, I believe, to assume the boy was sold due to the deafness of his father?"

It felt as if my chest caved inward, falling into the depths of my stomach. "No," I breathed. "You would not be amiss."

"A master must be able to consider his own business and what brings profits to it. He must be permitted to do as he sees fit—"

"Just as Brother Pierre would have done as he saw fit to young Ranae? As a father of daughters, surely you cannot approve of that."

"I find it abhorrent," said Vernard. "But according to the laws of our lands—"

"Have you considered, Captain, that the laws of our land might be wrong?"

"A king rules with the blessing of God—"

"And what of Moses?" I asked. "Was he wrong to demand freedom of Pharaoh? Because I believe God gave a resounding answer to that nation."

Vernard leaned back his head and laughed. "And you consider yourself to be Moses, do you? Do you intend to part the sea as well?"

"Hardly. I am but a thread in a tapestry. But the Lord will have his way, or the nations shall suffer. That, you can believe."

His eyes glinted as he smiled at me, humored, or perhaps impressed by my response. "That, weaver, is something we can agree on."

And with that, Vernard dismounted from the wagon and jogged alongside before pulling himself into his seat on the front. Back into the seat of a free man. But he had stepped down for a moment into the seat of a slave, and I did not take that for granted.

CHAPTER TWELVE

The further we traveled from the city, the fewer travelers we passed. I did not know whether to be thankful for such a decrease in traffic, or nervous. Fewer people meant faster travel, but a dwindling population also seeded the land for bandits.

When dark began to settle, we stopped for camp in a small clearing just off the road. The sky was clear, so Kai and Vernard elected to leave the tents rolled for the night, and I was sent for firewood.

They did not ask me about the tents, and I feared my position as a 'slave' was beginning to be taken too much to heart. But, not wishing to be viewed as weak for desiring the illusion of protection by fabric walls, I wandered into the woods and collected the requested kindling.

As I searched the underbrush for dried twigs, I barely noticed the steep escarpment before I tumbled down it. I looked out over the view, immediately enraptured.

Such beauty could not be put adequately into words. The hills we had climbed were not mountains, but a river had cut through the terrain creating a bluff on one side. The water below shined orange with the setting sun as clouds of purple, blue, and gold reflected on the surface. The wind rippled across the bluffs, and the trees shook and bowed before the sight. My clothes ruffled as the wind swept across me too, and I became lost in the moment of shifting lights and colors.

Then I remembered myself and the imminent darkness and continued gathering my sticks. By the time I returned, Vernard had lit a fire from the surrounding underbrush but welcomed my load to give it strength. Kai hopped down from the wagon, and I noted with curiosity the crate sitting on the ground. A canvas sheet had been strung from one side of the wagon to the other with a tall stick creating a peak at either end.

"I thought we weren't pitching tents," I said.

"Vernard and I aren't, but I know you don't like to sleep outside." Kai shrugged and joined Vernard at the fire to prepare a stew.

For a moment, I did not know what to say. It was not the rocks and pebbles that stuck into my back when sleeping upon the ground, or the dew that settled on me that caused my dislike for sleeping outside. It was the all-encompassing darkness among the shifting shadows of the woods. Unlike Kai and Vernard, who could sleep sure with the knowledge that most threats would be heard in enough time to act, I had no such surety. My previous thoughts of loss in status were replaced by embarrassment.

"Thank you, Kai," I said, although the words did not feel adequate. He looked back at me and nodded with a smile before continuing to cube potatoes and drop them in a pot of water.

If the ground was hard, the wooden planks of the wagon were harder. Kai and Vernard kept watch, which put me further behind in my debt as it concerned security, but I was comforted by them nonetheless. Although I was stiff upon waking, it was an easier night than it would have been upon the ground.

At sunrise, we packed up and continued on the road. After midday, we reached a village and were directed to a farm just beyond the borders. We passed a few peasant homes along the road, but our destination commanded a hillside overlooking acres and acres of land. The house was stone, three stories high with a pitched roof. A stone wall with a wrought iron gate enclosed the area.

The gates were open for the day, but we did not pass by them unnoticed. Several branded faces peered up at us from a garden near the front of the property. A boy ran for the house, undoubtedly to fetch his master. In the meantime, a foreman exited a shack near the gate and greeted us, and Kai reined in the horses to speak with the man briefly before we continued up the drive.

The master, an octogenarian with hearing about as proficient as my own, met us at the door. He leaned heavily upon his staff, cupping his hand to his ear as Vernard introduced himself.

"Peddlers you say?" the master said. "Peddling what?"

"We are searching for a man," Vernard said, extending the now worn portrait.

"A clan? We are part of no clan."

"A MAN!"

Truly, the man would do well to study lips.

A younger man with a neatly trimmed beard emerged from the house and descended the stairs. He extended his hand to Kai and Vernard. "My apologies," he said, nodding to his father. "What is it that brings you here?"

Vernard went about with his usual spiel, and the younger man bellowed a rough translation in the ancient man's ear. It was clear, however, that this translation was a mere courtesy. The younger man, Henri, was the son of the patriarch and ran the day-to-day of the villa now that his father had grown so far in years. Whether or not the octogenarian was aware of the demotion was unclear.

"You realize, of course," said Henri, "that if this man is among my slaves, he is mine by right. Family ties or not, the decision regarding my property is just that: my decision."

"We in no way wish to show disrespect to you or your father," said Kai. "We have come with money and intend on paying whatever is deemed reasonable."

The corners of Henri's mouth raised for a second before he returned his face to concern. If Dorsey were here, it was clear we would be paying quite the sum to reach what was "reasonable."

After providing the patriarch an abridged version of what was discussed, Henri assigned a slave boy to our horses and led us to the fields behind the house. A well-worn path ran between the fields, but I struggled to keep up with the discussion as I dodged marshy places and other soakers. I managed to get the gist of the conversation, however.

"I believe I know which man you are seeking," said Henri. "He is one of four I purchased that day. Quite the mouther, he is."

"What is that sound?" asked Vernard.

"The new ones are always the mouthers. It takes a while to learn one's place, it seems. This morning, he complained about his food rations. Had this been a one-time incident, perhaps I would have overlooked it."

A crowd gathered around a cleared place beyond the first field where a solitary post stood. Back a ways stood a foreman, arm raised as a cord trailed behind him. With swipe of the arm, the cord came down onto the back of a man secured to the post. The body of the man jerked upon impact as a line of blood emerged on his flesh.

CHAPTER THIRTEEN

Vernard swore and took off for the post. Kai tried to grab him, but the Captain shrugged him off as Henri shouted after him. The foreman raised the whip once more but turned around at the commotion.

Vernard slid to a stop before the post, causing mud to fly, and raised the flogged man's face to his own. Then, jamming his hands into his hair, he took a step back and turned on foot, wandering off toward the field. The crowd parted, allowing him passage.

"Not him," I said.

Kai shook his head as he placed his hands on his hips.

"I'll go see to him." I jogged after Vernard as he stopped before the wheat field, looking out over the golden heads swaying in the afternoon breeze. I joined him but stood silent. Streaks of moisture lined his face.

"Dorsey is a very proud man," Vernard said. "It would not be unlike him to…" He pinched his eyes shut and pressed the bridge of his nose with his thumb and forefinger.

"Your brother is from a proud family. There is nothing wrong with that. It may keep his head up longer."

"Or get him killed," Vernard replied then he turned to me fully. "I never told you he was my brother. How did you—?"

"I drew his face over and over again, and each time I look at your face, I see it once more."

The Captain shook his head as he stared at his mud-covered boots. Then he raised his eyes to heaven as if preventing the fall of more tears.

"Dorsey's chances in this have always been grim," I said. "But there has also been one thing going for him that is not true of the others. His brother is searching for him."

Vernard took a shuddering breath. "Yes, that and a small, deaf weaver."

I did not know whether he was teasing me or being insulting. I erred on the side of the former, however, and forced a smile. "Then he's better off than a king."

Vernard chuckled, but then his eyes wandered to the beaten man being removed from the whipping post. "May God help us all."

***

We did not stay at the villa much longer after our task was done. Not wishing to keep only to myself, I sat upon the crate as we drove back out the wrought iron gates and onto the road once more. Neither Kai nor Vernard spoke, although Vernard continually glanced in Kai's direction as if about to speak then deciding otherwise.

I had forced Kai to allow me to see the marks on his back. Most were healed, although some were still scabbed. The flogging had taken place according to the law of Burganne, but the order had still come from Vernard. Doubtless, the man had attended many of these floggings on slaves or on wayward free men, but I suspected the thought of his brother being a possible victim of such treatment had never crossed his mind until today.

The subject was never broached, at least not while I was present, and upon the setting of the sun, we stopped to make camp in a clearing near a brook. I gathered kindling as usual, and soon a cheery fire danced within a ring of stones.

Kai, who was an excellent cook, made another hearty stew, which I partook of readily. Vernard, however, ate slowly. He stared at the glowing embers as his mouth moved mechanically over the food.

I rose from my log seat and went to the crate. Near the bottom, I found a bottle of wine that Marta had managed to secure from my home and brought it over to the fire. Vernard's gaze rose upon seeing the bottle. I poured some into a wooden vessel and handed it to him.

"What is the occasion, weaver?"

"Thirst and your forlorn gaze. It is making us all depressed." I passed a cup to Kai and then poured one for myself.

"Sorry. I am just worried is all." His goblet hung low in his hand.

"Of course you are," I said. "Which is why I did not hand you water."

With an attempt at a smile, Vernard raised the cup and took a drink. "Thank you, weaver. You treat me with more kindness than I deserve."

I stretched out upon the ground, using my log chair as a backrest. "This is true. But I hold little in account for grievances when things are done for family. I have very little in that regard, so I understand the value better than most."

"Yes, what of your family and your origins?" Vernard asked. "Your name is unusual. Where did you come from?"

"In truth, I do not know. My first master and his family were slaughtered by a fool with a grudge. If anyone would have known, it was them."

"But you had papers, surely—"

I shook my head. "None that were found. Either they never existed or were lost. I don't know where I came from, just that I am. My son is, and will always be, my only family."

"You are that committed to your work?"

I smiled thinly and nodded. "Your father could not have picked greater collateral."

Vernard took in another draught of wine.

"Tell me about your brother," I said. "And how a well-connected family like yours could not secure his ransom."

"During the battle of Durban, two dukes, a marquis, and a prince were taken captive as well as my brother. During the negotiations with Aquilla, the second son of a duke was not brought to the table. My family sought to ransom Dorsey independently, but there was a mix-up. Our page went to the wrong location to find Dorsey, and by the time he arrived in the correct one, Dorsey had already been sold."

I added a log to the fire and stirred around the embers. "I am sorry."

Vernard sighed. "The king was sympathetic in the matter. He allowed me leave from the army after Dorsey's capture to be present with my family. I had actually only returned to Burganne the day we met. Once the king heard of our misfortune, he sent men to inquire about the matter on our behalf. When they discovered nothing, he personally negotiated my passage into Aquilla to find my brother. It was he, too, that agreed to your clemency in exchange for your assistance."

"Ha! The king knows who I am?"

"From what I understand, he's quite the admirer of your work."

"Hmm. I shall not let that go to my head."

"He will completely let it go to his head," said Kai from across the fire.

"Your family must be pretty well-liked by the king to have received such favor," I said.

"The king and my father were childhood friends," Vernard said. "My grandmother was the previous queen's lady-in-waiting."

"You are truly a noble through and through."

He cocked his head to the side. "Does this cause you to hate me?"

I paused for a moment, considering this. "It helps me understand you. I cannot say that a high nobleman such as yourself has ever come through my floor, but more than one lower one has. Your status does not bother me, but it does not impress me much either, Captain. We have a saying among the liberationists that a man is a man like any other man. The same basic wants, desires, passions, and flaws flow through each. Power comes from the response of such titles by the masses, but it is, in my opinion, all illusions."

He sipped on his wine as I spoke, but his eyes watched me intently as he listened closely to what I said. Finally, he said, "You have little respect for authority, don't you?"

I grinned. "As someone who has started from the base of society, climbed to the recognition of the king, then fell once more, I would say it is not so much disrespect but more of a different perspective."

"We shall call it that, at least."

"But tell us about this Dorsey, Vernard. I would feel better about this journey if I knew a bit more about the man."

Vernard stirred the fire with a stick as a faint smile reflected the memories of his brother. "My mother favored Dorsey as many mothers do their youngest. He had a knack for getting into trouble, but always charmed his way out of it. Sometimes I hated him for that, but other times he charmed me as well…"

He leaned upon the log and his eyes grew ever more distant. "There was a man, the son of a friend of my father's. He was courting a girl and was insanely jealous of her. He would throw down a challenge against any man who would look at her sideways. Dorsey was caught snogging with the girl by the man! And I don't know how the devil managed to pull it off, but he convinced the man to get a drink with him. By the end of the night, the two had become the best of friends. They're still friends to this day!" Vernard laughed, and then his demeanor changed to sadness once more. "If something should have happened to him – God, my poor mother."

We did not stay up much longer after that. Tomorrow would bring another journey and another desperate attempt at finding a lost man. There was one place left on our list, however. As I lay upon the wooden planks of the cart that night, I scrambled for another idea on how to find Dorsey but came up empty.

As the gray dawn turned to yellow, I opened my eyes to see light streaming through the fabric of my makeshift tent. When I crept out from beneath the tarp, my back protested its poor treatment of late, and I stretched to release the crick in my neck. Kai nodded to me from where he sat leaning against the tree for his watch, and I waved in return. Vernard continued to sleep, wrapped in his blankets.

Good. Judging from the gray beneath his eyes, he needed the extra rest.

After performing the necessaries on the other side of the cart, I returned to the fire and stirred up the coals. "Are we out of wood?" I asked.

"It was a chilly night," Kai said. "I could—"

"No, it's fine. I can." I stood and arched my back once more before twisting a couple of times. "Go lay down in the cart or something. I'm up, and it is daylight now."

"I'd rather rest on the road. The next town is another two-day ride. I'll start packing up here."

I had to walk a little further into the trees than last night to find sticks, and my back ached all the more from having to bend so often. Part of me wished I had sent Kai after all, but as I was the only one who had received a full night's sleep in the past two days, it was the least I could do.

Something darted across my path, and I dropped the armload of sticks I had gathered. The creature swooshed his giant fluffy tail at me before ascending a tree and hopping along the branches. "Damn squirrel," I muttered, collecting the sticks once more. Oh, my poor back! The first purchase I was going to make once this quest was over would be a good bed.

I came across the brook on my way back and, after checking that no one was about, washed quickly before returning to camp. Privacy was a rare thing when traveling in such a small group, and I did not take it for granted.

I was busy considering how to create a good breakfast from dried fish and oats when I stepped back into the campsite. Vernard was no longer lying upon the ground in his blankets. Instead, he stood by the wagon with his hands up as a brute of a man held the Captain's sword to his chest. Beside the fire lay Kai, the back of his head bleeding.

CHAPTER FOURTEEN

I dropped the bundle and rushed to Kai, but another man bearing a club barred my path. "You have killed him!" I cried.

"He's not dead," said the man, "only unconscious."

I looked at Vernard. His lips were sealed tight, although he glared at the man who now possessed his sword.

"Was this the big rescue you promised?" laughed the man with the club. "A puny slave?" His own large belly jiggled with laughter.

"Yes, well, give me back my sword and we shall see a fair fight," said Vernard.

"Do we look as if we care about fairness?" said the clubman. "Tie his hands up, Sylvain, and I'll get these others done. Stay where you are, slave, or I'll beat your head in!"

"Do as he says, Zayim," said Vernard. "No point in getting killed over a robbery."

"That's very good instructions!" said Sylvain. "Listen to your master, boy."

I swallowed hard as I looked from Vernard to Kai. The big man's chest moved up and down, which was a relief, but I still did not like the look of the blood trickling down his neck.

Damn my useless ears! Had I heard the ruckus, surely, I could have done something instead of stumbling like a fool into the situation.

What I could have done differently, I did not know. I had no skill in this area. And if I tried to intervene now, I would, as Vernard suggested, only get killed.

"Alright, now you." The clubman stepped over Kai with the rest of his rope. With a venomous gaze, I extended my hands as he cinched the bindings tight. Then, using the remaining length, he pulled me to the wagon and secured my hands to the back. "Now, let's see what you have in this crate!" The clubman opened the top, and Sylvain craned his head over to see.

Vernard flipped the blade away from his chest and elbowed Sylvain in the face. As he lunged for his sword, however, the club smashed against his face, and he fell into a heap. The man raised the club once more, ready to pummel his head into the ground.

"Wait!" I cried. "For God's sake, don't kill him! Tie him next to me or something, but I implore you, don't kill him."

The bandit lowered his club while Vernard gasped, spitting blood from his mouth as it spewed from his nose. The clubman turned to his companion, and I did not see what was said. Sylvain, however, grabbed the Captain by the arm and dragged him along the ground until they reached the nearest tree. A rope was slung around the base, and Vernard's hands were secured to it.

"That's a rare thing." The clubman strolled to me, his weapon dragging the ground. "Such loyalty from a slave to his masters. I'll have to mention that to the auctioneer. Perhaps I'll get a better price."

"Auctioneer?" I said. "I am a free man. I cannot be sold. Check the mark upon my wrist."

The bandit's brow furrowed as he slid the binding and my sleeve upwards. "Ah, I see! And if you were not in Aquilla, that might mean something, little man. But here, it does not." He slid the bindings down and turned from me. I gnashed my teeth behind his back, but then the man turned to Vernard as if hearing something.

"He will not fetch you a good price," Vernard said as he hunched with his back against the tree. Blood oozed freely from his nose, staining his tunic. "He's deaf."

The man looked back at me, studying me from head to foot. "You are lying. He just spoke to me!"

"He can read your lips," said Vernard. "Come on, it is not hard to see. The way he speaks, as if speaking from his nose, the way he stumbled into camp with no clue of your presence. His master freed him because he was not worth the trouble of keeping. He will cost you more to feed and water than you'll make at auction."

"Bah," said the bandit with a sneer, and I relaxed some, thinking they had been dissuaded.

The two brigands searched through our belongings, pocketing whatever valuables we had. They dumped the contents of the crate upon the ground, taking my seal and silver, but leaving the woven cloths. Fools.

All this they loaded into the wagon. So, we would be left without horses too, it seemed. Then Sylvain climbed up into the driver's seat as the clubman took the place next to him.

"Wait!" I cried. "I thought you were leaving me here."

Sylvain turned to me and said, "We never said that." He flipped the reins, and the wagon lurched forward. The rope went taunt, and I was dragged forward, leaving my companions bleeding behind me.

* * *

I prayed all along the route that the brigands would turn right at the fork, taking me back to Lasen. Jules would find a way to smuggle me out.

We turned left instead.

I tried to visualize the map and what lay in that direction. Since Kai had been doing most of the driving, I had led the navigation up to him. Damn, was that a mistake! What lay to the left? Was it a town I had crafted a tapestry map for? I could pass by the house of a friend and never know it.

Then I tasted salt, distinct as the first day I rolled into Burganne with my former master. Only one thing could cause the air to taste so. We were nearing the sea, and probably a port city as well. But still, I did not know which one.

The port city came into view, like a line of strange stones rising from the horizon. The town was not as large as Lasen or Burganne, although it was walled. A pair of guards stood before the gates, pikes in hand. Just as we were to emerge from the tree line, Sylvain reined in the horses, and the clubman rounded the wagon to me.

"Where are they?" the clubman demanded.

"Where are what?"

He pulled on the rope, drawing me to himself, and shoved a hand into my pocket. He pulled out the aged and folded papers that proved my freedom.

And he tore them to pieces.

"That's punishable by hanging," I snarled.

"You think this my first capital offense, deaf man? Why don't you let me worry about that?" The clubman hopped upon the bed of the wagon, and it lurched forward once more. But I would not give up so lightly.

"Guard!" I cried as we reached the gates. "Guard! He has taken me illegally! I am a free man by right, but he tore my pages. Guard, please! You must help me!"

"Halt!" cried the guard, but the clubman leapt forward, striking me in my face. I hit the ground and blocked the next blow by crouching beneath the now stopped cart.

The guard approached, clamped my arm, and dragged me out. "What is this?"

"My companions and I were traveling the road when we were attacked. I am a free man, not a slave, yet this man took me and would see me sold at auction," I said. "Here, I can prove my freedom." I rolled up my sleeve and showed him the mark.

The clubman dropped from the cart. "He lies! He is a runaway, and I have been hired by his master to fetch him, sell him, and return the profits. He is deaf and his master has dealt with enough trouble from him!"

"He took my papers and destroyed them. I know the mark means nothing in Aquilla, but it is all I have to prove my story. If

you send a patrol up the road, you will find my companions and—
"

"Do you know why we do not acknowledge the brand in Aquilla?" demanded the clubman. "Because it is so easily forged! I found this upon him!" He extended his hand and showed the brand that I had used on Ranae.

The guard took the brand and inspected it before placing it side by side with my own mark.

"If you would send a patrol up the road," I said, swallowing hard, "you will find my companions. Two men now bleeding. They will verify my story."

"Enough of this," sneered the guard. "It is clear from your dress and this seal what you are, slave, and I will not tolerate any more of your raucous tales."

"But sir—"

The guard struck me in the gut with the base of his pike and air rent from my chest. I knelt to the ground, clutching my stomach. I did not hear what was said next, but the rope went taut once more, and I scrambled to my feet to prevent being dragged as the horses lurched forward. For the first time, my fate truly sank in, and I was afraid.

The clubman and his mate led us through the town while I trudged behind them, eyes searching, praying for a familiar face. I was not given a second glance by the townsfolk as they carried on with their business. I was just another slave bound for the auction house as far as they were concerned.

I knew which building was the auction house as soon as we turned the corner. It could have grown wings and flown to Burganne to replace the house there without anyone's notice. I wondered if this was a design dictated by a cabal of slavers or just coincidence. Even though we did not go to the back of the building, the smell of the stocks reached me in a wave as they parked the wagon alongside the building. I forced myself not to gag.

The clubman disappeared into the building for a moment leaving me with Sylvain. He grinned at me, showing half his teeth to be missing while the remaining rotted. A piece of cloth wrapped across his head and disappeared beneath a black, floppy hat. Just beneath the cloth, however, was a scar that could be the beginnings of a brand.

The lead brigand returned in short order, seized my rope, and walked toward the door without a glance back. I trudged behind him sluggishly, determined not to make the job easier.

The warmth of the room we entered caused perspiration to break on my brow. Or was that just my nerves? I had never been sold, let alone at auction. No tapestry hung upon this wall, only pictures of runaways, written regulations, and pay scales. This was a place of business only, with no compassion allowed.

The auctioneer gripped my chin, pulling my gaze to him. I met his grisly face, although my eyes latched upon his lips and the graying mustache above it. "You are deaf, they say, but also that you speak."

I took a deep breath to calm the shaking in my limbs and met the man's eye. "There has been some mistake," I said as I rolled back the rope from my wrist, showing my brand of the free man. "I am not eligible for sale."

"That again, deaf man?" laughed the brigand. "He made the brand himself as a ruse to escape his master."

"It was made by the office of the magistrate in Burganne upon my release from my master," I said. "I am the weaver Zayim of Burganne."

"Slave or free, I do not care who you were," said the auctioneer. "Many come through my doors who do not think they deserve slavery."

"So," said the brigand, "in terms of price. He is deaf, of course, but the brand is old. That should mean something, should it not?"

"I have not yet had a look at him," said the auctioneer. "I can give no price until he has been inspected as a whole. Deaf man, take off your clothes."

Coals churned within my chest, and I wanted to spit in the man's eye and tell him to go to hell. Perhaps I should have. But the old chains wrapped around my soul once more and I, who had defied the magistrate just weeks before, found no fight to argue with a master.

I grabbed the back of my collar and pulled my shirt over my back and chest, letting it dangle around my still bound wrists. The men checked for marks of discipline, of which I had few, and I prayed they let this be the end of it.

"Your pants too," the auctioneer commanded.

I closed my eyes and breathed deep, but the coals churned over once more, and I delayed.

The auctioneer seized my arm and struck me across the face. "I said remove your pants!"

There was no point in fighting, I told myself. Either I could remove the pants myself, or they would be taken from me. With trembling fingers, I untied the string at my waist and let them fall.

Both men looked at each other in wonder. Then they laughed. "You are a eunuch!" cried the auctioneer.

CHAPTER FIFTEEN

"The price just doubled!" declared the brigand.

I looked away to the wall, fighting the moisture collecting in my eyes. I read no further lips, but could not avoid the cocked back heads and heaving of chests as they laughed. The auctioneer prodded at me with his stick and I closed my eyes completely. When I reopened them, I found myself all but forgotten as a price was haggled.

"I can create another eunuch in five minutes!" declared the auctioneer. "The price stays what it is."

"But a eunuch that is already healed? No, you will pay me what I am due."

"The price stays the same, but I will allow you to take his boots. They are nice boots after all."

I looked down at my mud-coated boots, the last pair to my name. "Are they really?" I muttered but was ignored.

"Eunuch, take off your boots," said the auctioneer.

So that was to be my new title. I tried to raise my shoulders, to stand before these men, but I could not feign such confidence with what I lacked. I stepped out of my boots, now complete in my nakedness within the stuffy room. The heat continued to climb even without my apparel, and sweat soon dripped down my neck.

The auctioneer and the brigand, so deeply engaged in their discussion of funds, forgot me entirely. Permission to redress was never granted, but I pulled my shirt over my head and my pants up anyway. Neither seemed to notice. Finally, a price was reached, and an attendant fetched me for the cage.

Upon entering the outside enclosure, I received a few glances but was otherwise unheeded. Just another slave up for the till. The smell this close however, burnt my nostrils, and I considered climbing the bars to the metal roof in order to escape it. Chances were, I would be beaten back down if I tried.

The soggy ground tried to take hold of my feet, and I made my way to stand against an empty part of the gridded wall. With horror, I realized there were no facilities for a man or woman to relieve themselves properly, which was undoubtedly the cause of the muck. Damn that man for taking my shoes!

As I peered out along the seaside watching the sails billowing up from the wind, the moisture in my eyes returned, and I wiped my eyes clean of tears only to have them return once more. I felt doubly emasculated by them but could not help their flow. They came silently, one after the other, and I clamped my hand upon my mouth. Damn this life of mine! Damn the magistrate and his son for not ending it when they should have!

Did God hate me? Had my very existence on this earth in some way offended him? Or was I, like Job, being tested?

Job had produced more sons and daughters after the death of his others, however. I was a dry tree.

Perhaps the wife of Job was the only sane one present by saying "Curse God and die." Yet I could not damn my soul to hell and thus continue the torment. I did not desire paradise either, just an end. Mere dust and ashes.

Peace.

About an hour later, a panel on the side of the cage opened and food was dumped inside – if it could be called that. The smell of rotted vegetables mingled with the stench of shit as haggard faces and half-starved bodies lunged for their piece. Clawing at the back of the horde were the weakest among us: a child no more than five clinging to the skirts of her mother, an old man with a terrible limp, a man with no shirt – I could count his ribs from afar. I stayed back against the wall, allowing the mob to have their fill. I was not yet desperate enough to partake.

Although I knew it would not take long to become so. I had been smuggling out faces such as these for nearly half my life now. Their stories were varied, but the pleading was ever-present. I never incorporated such pain in my weaving although visions of it were seared into my mind.

And as I was reminded of their stories, the reality of desperation, I grew ashamed of my self-pity. Even if my friends could not find me, the world I left behind would not be bereft of me, nor I it. My child and his mother were already estranged from me and hopefully close to freedom. Already my shop had been destroyed and my savings confiscated. So many of those around me were having their lives torn apart, but my life had already undergone such losses.

Since acquiring my freedom, I had spent my life preparing for my death. Acquiring freedom for my son and then his inheritance, giving instructions to Kai upon my demise from the first day of his employment, taking risks no rational man should. Slavery was not too dissimilar from death. No, I would be fine.

Unhappy, but fine.

Like most days thus far.

Except I would not be free…

Half a day went by in the slog pit, and I began to fear I'd be required to sleep here. It was a thought based on vanity rather than logic. If I remained here, there was a good chance Vernard and Kai would find me and purchase me back. But I did despise the idea of sleeping in filth.

As evening neared, I prepared myself more and more for the inevitable descent of the sun. But then an attendant stepped into the cell and called, "Eunuch!"

I waited a moment to see if anyone else would respond to the call, but as the seconds passed by, it was clear I was alone in my condition. I considered remaining as I was, pretending not to have seen the call, but that would delay things only slightly and probably anger the attendant to boot.

As I slogged to the door, the now familiar sensation of being noticed came over me. Only the attention was not upon my deafness, my lack of shoes, or the giant lumbering behind me. Most eyes lingered at belt level, and I felt heat creeping over my ears. Even the attendant glanced there as I stepped through the door. Then, without a word, he grasped the rope around my wrists and led me through the halls.

A door in the hall led to the side of the stage, but before sending me out, he ordered, "Take off your pants."

"You cannot be serious," I said. "It is not necessary to be seen—"

The attendant jammed his rod into my stomach, and I sank to one knee upon the sawdust floor as I gasped for air. Grabbing my hair, he raised my face to his own. "Take off your pants."

With staggering motion, I rose to stand. My body trembled terribly as I met the man's face. "I will not."

The rod slammed into my ear, and the next blow against the back of my neck. As I started to fall, he grabbed the collar of my shirt, tugged on the strings of my pants, and ripped them down to my ankles. With a hand of iron, he dragged me onto the stage. A podium stood next to the auctioneer, and he forced me to mount it as blood dripped down my neck.

I peered into the audience and immediately wished to close my eyes as the laughter flowed across the crowd. But I needed to search for a familiar face. Kai, Vernard, Jules – any familiar face would do. They would help me, buy me back if needed. But when I found none, relief flooded my chest. Only strangers knew of my shame.

As the auctioneer gave his speech to the crowd, I glowered at him, but he smiled impishly at me. The bidding took off with a flurry of hands, the auctioneer pointing to the one he saw first.

When I had gone to purchase Kai, I had watched the auctioneer in Burganne for an hour before finding a pattern to his cadence. He spoke quickly, although most of his words were the same repeated.

When I had raised my hand to bid, the auction attendants had tried to throw me out, thinking me a slave.

My freeman's brand had driven them away, but not before I missed the pattern of the cadence and what the bid number now was. I bid anyway, blind in the price, but hopeful. I went away with an empty purse, but with a new friend. I prayed for such luck as Kai, but the tightness in my throat allowed for little hope.

Hands flew up in a frenzy, and I looked to the auctioneer once more. Perhaps my state did bring in a pretty price, but doubtless another detail had been left untold. An otherwise whole man could fetch a good price, for sure, but one with other flaws?

And in that moment, I knew I could have my revenge, albeit ever so small. I shouted out into the crowd, "Don't let him fool you! I also cannot hear."

The club of the auctioneer slammed against my head, and I stumbled off the platform. He struck me again before dragging me back. "You speak when told to speak!"

But the damage had already been done. I did not know the sound of my own voice, but I knew it was unlike the hearing. The number of hands rising decreased to two or three, and the auctioneer glared at me. I matched his impish smile from earlier, and the glare turned to a snarl. But soon I was sold to a gentleman in the back, and as I stepped off the stage, I felt blood trickling down my ear.

* * *

A tall and slender man with giant, bony hands waited for me in the courtyard outside the alley. His face was a ghastly pale, and black, stringy hair collected in a bit of twine at his shoulders. I felt like a child before him, but I held my shoulders higher now that I had my pants once more.

"At least we'll be able to save on branding," my new master noted as I was brought forth. "I know you speak, but can you respond to questions?"

"If you look at me and speak clearly, I can read your lips. But if it matters to you, I have a mark of a free man." I showed him the branding on my wrist beneath the ropes.

"It does not matter to me," he said without looking, and I held in a sigh. "You're not particularly strong looking. What work did you do?"

"I am a master weaver, sir."

"I have no use for a weaver, only a house slave who will not sire a pup with my wife or daughters. Come." He tugged on the rope, and I stumbled after him out of the courtyard. On the way out, we passed the brander, burning a design into the face of a woman as two other men held her down. Her face twisted in torment as she screamed. I looked to the cobblestones, relying on the tug of the rope to find my way out. I was lucky enough to not remember that part of my life.

Waiting beyond the gate was a cart where another man stood tied to the back. Two interlocking diamonds were branded on his temple, white and raised above the skin – an old, healed scar. A third man guarded the other slave with a staff. My new master fixed my rope beside the other slave and climbed into the driver's seat.

The slave I traveled with had dark, shaggy hair and deep brown eyes that sparkled as if concealing a joke. "Your name wouldn't be Dorsey, would it?" I asked.

"Lons," he said.

"Right. I'm Zayim."

The cart lurched forward and us with it, and I immediately stepped upon a rock. I looked to the man with the staff – I later learned his name to be Sebastian, the son of my master, Regis. "Could I get a bit of cloth for my feet?"

Sebastian shook his head, and I prayed 'home' would be near.

Occasionally, I would look over my shoulder in hopes of seeing Kai and Vernard, but the path behind was empty. It would not be hard to trace me to the auction house; Kai would see it done even if Vernard protested. Beyond the auction house loomed in question, and whether or not they would have money to secure my release was another for which I had no answer.

The journey was not short, and my feet were cut and raw by the time we stopped for nightfall. I asked for aid, but this too was denied. I was not even allowed to tend to them myself, as my hands were tied behind a tree immediately upon stopping. Part of me wondered if I would have feet at all by the time we made it to wherever it was we were going.

We were fed, but only a little, and only while bound by rope. By midmorning the following day, my footprints were bloodstained, and my breaths came in heaves after such a fast-paced march.

"Master," I called up in gasps. "I do not wish to complain, but much more damage to my feet and I will no longer be able to continue."

Regis turned his head to the side and said something imperceptible.

I shook my head and breathed, "I did not hear you, sir."

Regis nodded to Sebastian, and Sebastian yanked on my rope, propelling me forward. I struck my head on the cart as I fell and was dragged several paces before I could find my footing once more.

Sebastian smiled a cheeky grin as he re-positioned the staff upon his lap. "He says, for a deaf man, you sure do talk a lot, Eunuch." Then he stood and joined Regis on the buckboard. I held tight to the rope, allowing it to carry me along the way.

Lons, however, glanced at my crotch with a grin. "You act as if you are new to this, Eunuch."

"I've been without a master for some time," I said. "And my name is Zayim."

"Alright, Eunuch."

CHAPTER SIXTEEN

By midday, all of my efforts were focused on staying upright. My strides came in bursts, and I pulled against the rope for aid. Only vaguely did I notice when we turned from the main road and entered through wrought iron gates. Tall trees lined the path, and light streamed down through their branches, swirling, tumbling around my woozy head.

Finally, the wagon stopped before a stone structure, an old Roman outpost now functioning as the house for the estate. I dropped to my knees behind the cart, my breaths shallow and fast. Lons was led away from the cart by a man clutching a whip, but I was left upon the ground.

Sebastian jumped from the cart and lifted my chin with his staff. "I'm not sure about this one, Father. Kind of a weakling."

"I have sat behind a weaver's loom for twenty years," I gasped. "And I'm past the age of pretending to be what I'm not."

Sebastian grinned. "What happened to your shoes, anyway, Eunuch?"

I tilted my head in question. "I am not a whole man, sir, and you wish to know what happened to my shoes?"

He laughed, and the rod beneath my chin rattled my aching head. "You have a bit of wit in you," he said. "It will serve you well, as long as you know when to stop wagging your tongue."

Sebastian took my arm and pulled me back to my feet. I scrunched my face in pain as I stood on them once more. With his knife, he sawed through my bindings and motioned for me to lead the way to the house. I hobbled ahead of him, rubbing my chaffed wrists.

Sebastian led me to the back of the home and into the kitchen where a female slave was ordered to see to my feet. The woman was not gentle, and I soon wished he hadn't bothered, but I held my tongue. Complaining had done me no good thus far, and I doubted it would endear me further to my master or his son to try.

In fact, as I sat there with my feet in the hands of this butcher, I realized my mistake. It was common practice to treat any new slave who showed a 'pampered streak' with a level of apathy and cruelty. After the standard was set for future expectations, a slave would often show a sense of gratitude for receiving even basic kindness such as food and shelter. The mere fact that my feet were now being treated was an olive branch of sorts to see if I was ready to accept my role or not. When my feet were wrapped in burlap tied by a string, I continued in my silence.

The self-proclaimed chamberlain, a free man who ruled over the house slaves, set me to task polishing silver, a job I could do while sitting. For two days, I continued like this, performing small jobs while sitting, until my feet were well enough to fetch firewood, clean out chimneys, and haul water from the well. Regis provided me a pair of rabbit skin shoes which were barely worth a half-copper.

My master had a wife, two daughters, his son Sebastian, and a newborn lad who looked nothing like his father. The 'mother' of the child neared sixty, and each time the boy needed nursing, a daughter took him into another room. The reddish tint of the boy's hair greatly favored that of the man who slept across from me in the slaves' quarters. Although these findings were never summarized to me, it was rather clear how I had come to find employment among this family.

All the while, I considered escape but would first need to learn the general geography of the territory. I had checked for my tapestries but was unsurprised to find none. If I behaved, I might be granted an opportunity to get to town, so I completed all my work with excellence. If I could make it to town with some stolen silver, I could bribe someone into sending a message to Marta. She would know what to do beyond that.

My days were quiet in the chateau, as no one attempted to speak or interact with me. When I tried to speak to the other slaves, they raised their noses at me. The red-haired man even walked off when I asked him his name. Finally, I cornered Lons as he mucked the horse's stalls and asked him, "Why does everyone here hate me?"

He looked past me to the door of the barn, but we were alone. "I don't know what you mean."

"I think you do."

Lons jammed the shovel into a pile of manure. "Listen, I'm new here too, so I don't know what's going on with the others."

"Then why have you stopped speaking with me as well?" I leaned against the post, determined to stay until I got an answer.

Lons's lip curled as he studied me. "You make them uncomfortable is all."

"Because I'm working in the house? I didn't pick my assignment—"

"No—" Lons glanced at the door once more. "I don't know how things are where you're from, but the only men I've ever heard of who lost their balls did not prefer the company of women if you understand my meaning."

I breathed deeply. "That's not the case with me."

"I'm not one to pry. It's irrelevant now as far as I'm concerned, but—"

"My master did not wish to contaminate his slave stock with deafness. This was done after the birth of my only son."

Lons' mouth popped open as I spoke, and redness filled his face. "Oh. I…uh…that's unfortunate. I'm sorry."

"Thank you for your honesty," I muttered and exited the barn. The rest of the day was filled with intrusive memories of the day my son was born. My very presence in this place reminded me of the event, and I began to sweat each time a vision of the day crossed my mind. I had to get out of here, but I could not hope to run and survive yet. My only hope here was to be found by Kai and Vernard, but even this hope soured my stomach. If the others found me, the secret I had been keeping for the past fifteen years would be revealed. Marta, who had waited so long for me to love her, would know why I could not.

Fifteen years… had it really been that long?

The birth of my son came early in the morning after a night of anxious pacing. Old Berta kicked me out of the slave quarters along with the three other men as Sloan labored. The men told me I was lucky to be deaf that night as her cries kept them all awake. But I wished to hear her screams. At least then I would have confirmation of her continued breathing. All night, I crouched beside the door with my hands on my head waiting for some sign of change.

Then the men tapped fervently on my shoulders, each saying "I hear it! I hear the child!"

I grinned as I pulled open the door only to be shoved back out once more. But it was not long before Old Berta allowed me to enter. A wrinkly pink babe suckled on Sloan's chest as his mother beamed. His tiny hand rested above her breast, fully formed, perfect.

Everything was perfect.

Until the door opened once more.

Two men I had never seen grabbed me, pinning me against the wall as a third strolled to Sloan's bed. She held the child to her and screamed, but the man pulled her hair as he wrestled the babe free. Sloan tried to get up to chase after them, but Old Berta restrained her for fear of her safety.

The men dragged me from the room as I kicked and fought, trying to run after the child. They hauled me into the barn. I continued to fight them, still thinking about my child, determined not to let him be taken from me. I had no fear for myself at that moment – but I should have.

"I'm sorry," my master told me as he stood by and watched as the deed was done in minutes, and the bleeding stopped soon after. Then I was bandaged and carried to my bed.

For the next week, I spoke to no one. And Sloan refused to speak to me.

She blamed me for everything. Logically, there was no reason for this, but I did not fight a mother's grief. It was, after all, safer to blame me than our master. Or, at least, it was safer to retaliate against me.

On the seventh day, my master sent me back to the shop on the street as if nothing had happened. And as far as anyone ever spoke, nothing ever had. But I sat there before my loom that first day doing nothing, thinking of nothing.

Until a warm hand rested on my shoulder.

I startled and turned round to see Marta standing behind me, tears in her eyes. "Zayim, I am so sorry." She wrapped her arms around me, pressing me against her shoulder. And I wept.

She never knew the whole story, only that the babe was gone. And I feared the part that was left out was the reason she remained so close to me. I was a slave for five years more after that, and in the ten after I could have married her. But I wanted two things simultaneously: for her to raise a family and for her not to leave me. A husband would not tolerate his wife to have such a friendship as ours, so I never told her.

I never told anyone.

These were the thoughts on which I dwelled as I brought in water from the well for the midday meal. When I entered the kitchen after just having left it, I found it abandoned. I stooped low and eased the yoke from my shoulders from where I carried two buckets full of water.

I looked around the corner from the kitchen into the hall, but this too was empty. I scratched my head, pondering what could have happened. Then a face appeared from behind a curtain. The woman who had tended my feet said, "Hide!" then hid her face once more.

CHAPTER SEVENTEEN

Had the estate come under siege? Were there marauders at the door? I turned for the door and nearly reached it, when the lady of the estate grabbed my arm and yanked me back.

"Finally!" she said. "Fifteen slaves on this property and I can never find one!" Taking hold of my sleeve, she pulled me after her through the house, flapping her mouth as she went.

"Lady, I cannot hear you," I tried, but still she continued, dragging me up the stairs behind her.

She dragged me into the drawing room and gestured with her hand. "There! Fix it!"

Several boxes lay upon the floor before me, containing an assortment of articles: candlesticks, tablecloths, curtains. Which she gestured to, I did not know.

"I apologize, lady, but I am deaf and did not understand my instructions."

"Deaf? Oh bollocks. Why did you say nothing? Now I will have to say all that again, and where to start?" She pressed a hand to her towering hair, and I nearly feared she'd topple it. "This room! This whole room is wrong! The cushions are faded, the tapestries are worn, and worst of all, the curtain rods are too low. You must fix it all!"

I looked about the room, unable to discern anything wrong. But then I shrugged, indifferent and numb about my chores. "Where would you like me to start, lady?"

"You call me mistress! Not lady! I am the wife of your master after all, not some woman off the street!" She picked up a goblet of wine and nearly sloshed it from the cup as she spoke.

"I…uh…yes, mistress. I apologize."

"Start with that box." She pointed to the large one in the center of the mess. "I purchased a tapestry last time we were in Lasen."

I did not know these people, of course, but that was true of most of my clients. For the liberationists, I made many small tapestries to be sold to wealthy homes. They would try to steer the buyers into purchasing a map of a place close to their estates.

As I lifted the tapestry from the box, however, I was disappointed to find a scene of a concert done by one of my competitors. "You are an admirer of DuBois, mistress?"

"DuBois?" she asked, snatching it from me. "What are you talking about?"

"That's the artist, DuBois. You can tell his work by his use of color and the work around the borders—"

"Who the hell do you think you are, slave? Trying to look uppity, are we?"

"In no way, mistress. I swear, I was only making conversation."

"Making conversation? Are you trying to seduce me? Lure me into your grasp?"

Did we all look alike to her? Had she missed the details about whom her husband had purchased? "Uh, no. That was not my intent, but I'll just stop talking now."

"Yes! You should! Or I shall have you beaten for your insolence!" She shoved the tapestry at my chest then pointed to a blank space on the wall. "Hang it there!"

I found the rod within one of the boxes, and soon, the tapestry was mounted upon the wall. DuBois did have an eye for color, and his ability to capture faces was far beyond my own. I would have liked to study the weave further, but she pointed to a crate of furniture coverings next before turning away to jabber. Never had I worked with someone who forgot so frequently about my deafness. After filling her goblet with wine for the third time, I began to understand why.

We went on this way for quite some time, her ordering me to perform a task, then her prattling on as I completed it. I dragged over a chair and removed my shoes before standing upon it to raise the curtains. She grabbed my arm, spinning me to face her, and my foot slipped off the seat. In my descent, I grabbed the drapes, and they rent from the rod, falling to a heap around my shoulders.

"What did you do?" She smacked me across the face, sloshing wine upon my clothes. "I told you not to stand on that chair! Now look at this mess!" She struck me again. While the sloppy blows stung, they did not damage, so I merely put a hand up.

The door opened behind her, and Sebastian appeared. "Mother!" He pulled her back from me. They spoke to each other as she gestured wildly at me from over her shoulder. I slid the drapes from my shoulders and gathered myself from the floor. The rod had not pulled completely from the wall, but bowed a little.

Sebastian pointed to the door and said, "Go!" For a moment, I thought he spoke to me, but he looked at his mother. She continued to ramble, pointing and stomping her foot, but he ordered her out once more. "I will deal with it," he said.

With a sneer, she gathered her skirts around her and left the room, glaring at me over her shoulder as she did. Sebastian pressed a hand to his forehead and turned to me. "She said you tore the drapes on purpose."

"I did not."

"I believe you." He dragged the chair over and sat. "This is a fine mess though."

I collected the drapes from the ground and examined the tear. The fabric itself had received some damage, but the majority of the injury occurred at the seam line. I sat upon the floor and placed my sewing kit in my lap.

"What is that?" asked Sebastian. "Where did you get it?"

"The slavers stole my papers and shoes, but left my sewing kit." I opened the case, showing him multiple sizes of bone needles and an array of basic threads. He furrowed his brow, but made no move to seize it. Upon selecting a color close to the drapes, I threaded the needle and prepared the cloth.

"You can fix it?" asked Sebastian.

I paused, setting the cloth upon my lap. "I mentioned to your father that I am a master weaver. No offense, sir, but I believe I can handle a simple tear."

Sebastian scratched his sideburns. "He mentioned something about that. I thought you were joking."

I nodded to the tapestry mounted on the wall. "The weaver who constructed that is a man by the name DuBois. He lives in Paris. And he is a competitor of mine."

Sebastian slapped his knee and laughed. "Now I know that you are lying. My mother paid a fortune for that. A slave could not produce such a thing."

"Ask around," I said, gliding the thread in and out of the fabric. "The person who sold that to your mother will know of Zayim, the weaver of Burganne. He may even tell you that the weaver is a deaf man and former slave."

"And upon doing so, you hope to gain your freedom somehow?"

"I did not ask you to tell them where I am or how I came to be here. But if you inquire of me and discover I am not lying, you may find greater benefit from me than just polished silver and mended drapes." After a few minutes, I finished sewing and cut the string with my teeth.

Sebastian took the cloth from me, bringing it close to his face. "I can barely see anything. It is as if the tear never occurred!"

I closed up my kit, pocketed it, and stood. "If I insulted your mother, I apologize. It is true I run my mouth more than I should."

"Considering your lack of hearing, that is a tremendous feat indeed."

"Yes, well, my master had me run his shop. Friendliness was considered a virtue rather than a vice." I tapped against my leg as I considered a way to further assuage the event. "I recognize my situation has changed, but it may take time for me to adjust fully. In the meantime, please believe that I am trying. A slave at odds with his master rarely fares well."

"You are an unusual man, Zayim, but I like you. And I will make inquiries, but keep in mind that if you cannot make friends with my mother and father, you will not go far here. So adjust quickly, or at least keep your distance. And try not to anger anyone."

"I will do my best."

And I did.

Keeping my head down, I focused on my chores regardless of my boredom. Pleasing my master had, after all, worked the first time. But during my previous term of enslavement, I had been naïve about freedom. Now I missed it so much it hurt. To be able to choose a pear over an apple in the mornings, to walk along the fields in the dew without being questioned. To be able to say no.

The good news was that once word got out about my skill with the thread, my work changed more to that area. The bad news was that the other slaves grappled for my attention and help during the few minutes of free time in the evening. Those who had refused to speak a word to me before now approached my bed with their frayed hemp garments. Repairing them to perfection would have been pointless, but I patched them so as to maintain function. In more than one garment, I sewed a hidden pouch for stealing "berries." I doubted fruit were the only things of interest.

As soon as one garment was completed, another was brought. More than once I contemplated putting a halt to this, but decided to act charitably. I was, after all, not intending on staying as long as they were. If nothing else, my loneliness improved during this time of usefulness. Also, since the others were now speaking to me, I was also able to gain information about my location, ascertain the distance to the nearest town, and discover if there were any slave patrols. Unfortunately, the nearest town was ten miles away and a slave patrol watched the road day and night. There was also a mention of wolves in the area. And of course, there was my deafness to consider if I were to attempt an escape.

I am not very good at sneaking about. First reason being is that I can't hear if anyone else is around, and second, I don't know if I'm being loud. Each night, one of the freemen sat in a tree blind watching over the property for bandits and escaping slaves. If I ran and was caught, a spear through the back might be my reward.

About two weeks after the event with the drapes, Sebastian returned from town with a package, and I was called into the drawing room. Regis, his wife, and one of his daughters waited for me upon my arrival as they lounged upon their couches. The newborn lad lay in a wooden bassinet at his grandmother's feet, and her leg pumped up and down to rock it. On the table lay an open package with a beautiful yellow fabric that practically glimmered in the candlelight.

"Eunuch," Regis said, "my daughter, Jeanette, has received an invitation to visit family over the course of the winter. You will make her some new dresses."

Jeanette, a fair lady with ruby lips tilted up in a perpetual smile, raised her brows at me as she sat straight-backed in the upholstered chair. In truth, I got the sisters mixed up, but, judging from the conversation, I did not think she was the mother of the babe.

"I am a weaver by trade," I said. "I can sew a dress if the design is not too complicated but do have limits to my skills."

"A day dress will do just fine," said Regis standing. "Nothing too ornate, but also not a servant's garb."

"Of course, sir." I nodded, and he stepped out of the room. "If you would like, my lady, I can make some drawings and you can choose which one you like best."

"There is a quill and parchment in the box on the table," she said.

I took the pages and pen and sat at the table to work. I thought of Marta drafting her projects in the firelight of my workshop. She would be better suited for this work, but I would do my best.

I ran the fabric between my thumb and forefinger. It was a thicker material, requiring heavy thread. I had been given access to the house's supplies and had a type in mind. Glancing every so often to capture the woman's proportions as she sat speaking with her

mother, I laid out three options of simple, yet elegant, design. I proposed a basic embroidery around the collar and sleeves, and if she had a leather belt, it would bring the dress together fully.

"Lady, mistress." I stood and passed the paper to them, then folded my hands as I waited for a response.

My mistress looked from the page then back at me. "You can sew a dress like this?"

I shrugged. Had she seen the gowns Marta sewed, she would not have been impressed.

"The second one," Jeanette said, holding out the page. Then her mother made a face as she peered at the little one. His face turned red as he cried out, and she scooped him into her arms. She rocked the tike close, swaying as she did.

Jeanette pressed the paper against my hand. "Hello?"

"Uh, right," I said, taking it from her. "I'll need to take your measurements."

The mistress stood and carried the babe from the room, and I ripped my eyes from them. The only time I had held my son was when he was ten years old. He refused to leave his master's side, and I had to scoop him up to take him away. He kicked and clawed against me.

With shaking hands, I took up the number-marked ribbon from my sewing kit and asked for Jeanette to stand. For the first measurement, I had to take the numbers twice for my mind to focus, and I scribbled it down immediately so as not to forget.

"I can have the basic shape of the dress completed in a couple of days if I'm uninterrupted," I said, sitting back at the table. "But I may have to make some adjustments before it is finished."

"I would like to make some… adjustments… now that my mother is not here." She pulled her chair close and sat beside me. "A dress like this is flat and accentuates none of my finer features." She undid the top toggle of her frock, exposing the crease of her breasts.

My throat went dry, and I glanced over my shoulder to the closed door. "I can make the neckline a little lower if you'd like."

"And what about the shape of the gown." She ran her hands from her breast to her hips, then hiked her skirt up past her knee. "Breasts such as mine should be appreciated, shouldn't they?" She took my hand and pressed it into her chest.

I pulled my hand away and stood, gathering the parchment and tucking the fabric beneath my arm. "I can make the dress in any way you like, lady. And if it does not fit according to your desires, I can make modifications." I stepped toward the door, intent on opening it if nothing else. She tugged my arm from the handle and shoved my back against the wall.

"You know nothing of my desires. Yet."

"Lady, I do not know what you expect, but you will not get what you wish in this manner."

"We shall see." She smashed her lips against mine and sucked my lip into her mouth. Then she bit it, and I pulled back in pain as the taste of metal filled my mouth. I pushed her away from me and grasped the latch.

Her hand covered mine and she turned my eyes to her lips. "Let go of the latch, or I will scream."

If she screamed, it would not matter what I said or any defense I could give. Her father would kill me without investigation or second thought. I slid my hand from the door.

"Why do you fear me, Eunuch?" she asked, her breath hot upon my face. I had to lean my head back to read her lips. "That's why father purchased you, is it not? So my sister and I could have fun?"

"My lady, I believe you have been misinformed about my condition. Even if I wanted, I could not—"

Her hand slid into my pants, and I inhaled sharply.

DuBois' tapestry stood across the way, and I studied it, taking in the choice of colors, the grace around the faces of his subjects, blocking out what the lady was doing. Along the border he had intertwined flowers: irises, roses, lilacs, into a mess of entangled vines. His attention to detail was what had brought him to fame, and I, as a fellow professional, appreciated his work as well. I would like to meet him some day. Perhaps we would be friends.

The lady released me, her efforts fruitless as predicted. As she stood, her lips turned up further in an impish smile.

"Are you satisfied, my lady?" I breathed, forcing my face to remain neutral, although my cheeks burnt hot.

"Hardly," she said. "But I am done with you, yes."

I fixed my pants, grabbed the fabric and parchment I had dropped from the floor, and left the drawing room in haste, racing for the stairs.

CHAPTER EIGHTEEN

I passed through the house, perceiving objects in my path only in time to avoid stumbling into them. Reaching the slave quarters, I closed the door tight behind me and drew in ragged breaths. My hands trembled and I nearly dropped the things I held. Then I swallowed hard and moved down the aisle to my bed.

The slave quarters were narrow with ten beds lining the wall and a fireplace at the end. It had been built as an addition to the east end of the house, and as the space was unoccupied during the day, it was a perfect place to be undisturbed.

I laid the fabric out upon my bed and marked the cuts with a bit of chalk. A few of the lines wobbled as I drew, and I had to repeat my efforts. It did not take long to do this part, however, and soon I was piecing together the bodice. The fabric truly was fine quality, durable, not likely to stain. It felt good to have something familiar in my hands once more.

The feeling of terror ripped through my chest, but I shoved it away and pulled the sewing kit from my pocket. I refused to think of anything but the dress and my sewing as a steady stream of moisture slid down my cheeks. Hours went by, and my hands began to ache. My stomach rumbled from missing lunch, but still I continued, not wishing to leave the safety of my solitude. When a hand clasped my shoulder, I retreated backwards on the bed and fell to the stones below. Sebastian looked down on me, a question on his brow.

"Sorry," I said, gathering myself and the dress from the floor. With my face averted, I swiped the remains of moisture from my cheeks. "I thought I was alone."

"What happened to your lip?" he asked when I was seated once more upon the bed.

I touched the place and winced. "Ah, it's nothing. I caught it on a branch fetching water is all."

"I saw you earlier when I returned from town. You had no mark then."

"Forgive me, it must have been later this afternoon." I gathered the fabric into a pile and set my kit on top. "Is there something you need from me?"

He dusted off the straw mattress across from me and sat. "I inquired about you in town at the shop where Mother purchased the tapestry."

A thread of sweat broke upon my brow and I swiped it away.

"She knew of you," Sebastian said. "The deaf weaver of Burganne. Although she did not have your works, she said she wished she did." He nodded to the fabric. "It seems we will have a dress made by you soon, however."

I forced a thin smile. "A rare item. One of three in existence."

Sebastian smiled in return, but it was as faint as my own. "You did not fetch water this afternoon. I saw you enter the drawing room shortly after I left. And judging from your progress, you've been here ever since."

"You must not have seen it is all."

"What did she do?" he asked, and I played with the latch on my sewing kit, diverting my eyes from his. He tapped me on the arm, drawing me back to him. "What did she do, Zayim?"

"According to the laws of this nation, nothing that was not in her legal right to do."

"I will speak to her."

"I would rather you not, sir. I'm hoping her curiosity has been sated and she will leave me alone for now."

Sebastian shook his head. "You do not know my sister."

"This is true. But presuming you do, will anything you say affect her actions?"

Sebastian lowered his head. When he raised it, the look on his face said no. "Father is content as long as another child does not come, so your best solution is to never be alone with either of them. And pray Jeanette is married off by winter."

"Avoiding your sisters is not easy while living in the same house with them."

"I know, but try." Sebastian smacked my arm, stood, and exited the quarters leaving me more disquieted than before he entered. I needed to get out of this place and soon. I checked my measurements to ensure no mistakes were made and applied myself to produce the best dress possible.

***

Two days later I sunk the final stitch into the dress and cut it with my teeth. Then I sat there for the next hour, dreading the moment I would hand it off to Jeanette. In order to do a proper job, certain things such as the length along the arms and legs needed to be checked, then I would embroider the edges. To confirm the length, I would have to be in the same room as her.

But I could not hide the progress of the dress forever.

So, I stood and entered the kitchen. Upon finding the chamberlain, I inquired as to my lady's whereabouts. He insisted on inspecting the garment himself first, which was fair since his mantle fell upon me as well. As he unfolded the dress and held it by the shoulders, he looked between me and it. "Are you sure you are not a tailor?"

"My good friend is a tailor, and she has taught me a lot over the years. But no, I am a weaver."

He handed it back to me. "Good job. She's in the drawing room."

I startled at the remark, as praise from any master was not common. I dipped my head in a nod, folded the dress over my arm and headed up the stairs.

As my hand clasped the handle of the drawing room door, I paused as tightness gripped my chest once more. The same sensation had gripped me each time I entered my master's barn after 'it' happened. I tried to tell myself an assault from Jeanette would not happen again, but this was stupid. I did not know what would happen.

Then the door opened and Regis jumped back, clutching a hand to his chest at my sudden appearance.

"I'm sorry," I said. "I have brought lady Jeanette the dress as promised."

His brows rose, and he motioned for me to enter. Sebastian and his mother were also present in the room, and I relaxed further to see him there. He nodded to me, and I to him.

Jeanette ripped the dress from my arm and allowed it to unfold to the floor. Then she spun, the dress rippling around her. "Oh, Papa!" she cried and kissed her father on the cheek. "Thank you!"

I released a pent-up breath at the pleased expression rising on Regis's face. If he was pleased then I was one step closer to town.

"Lady, I would like to confirm some measurements and make adjustments as necessary."

"Go try it on," said her mother, and she scurried from the room.

Sebastian took a sip from his cup and nodded at me with approval. I returned the gesture and stepped against the wall to await her return.

The family continued on with their conversations as if I did not exist, but when Jeanette returned to the room, she received their full attention. I had not dipped the neckline as low as she proposed, nor had I made the bodice exceptionally tight. Either adjustment would likely anger her father, not endear me to him. That being said, the dress fit her perfectly, flattering her image without being ostentatious. Only the hem around the arms and ankles needed to be taken in – which I had left purposefully long.

Her sister, Angelina, and the baby had re-entered with Jeanette, and they spoke rapidly to each other. From the glimpses of conversation, I gathered they were discussing the trip.

I took a stool from the side of the room and brought it to Jeanette. She mounted it while continuing to speak with her sister, and I made the measurements for the hem around her arms. They were to be quarter-length at the top, but the sleeve would hang low and wide.

Upon finishing the second sleeve, however, I looked up to see Jeanette and Angelina being the only ones in the room. Sebastian was nowhere to be found, and even the baby had been removed.

I glanced at the door, and it stood open. This gave me only marginal comfort.

"Nervous, are we, Eunuch?" Jeanette asked me.

I sat on the floor and began work on the lower hem, ignoring whatever she was saying. Angelina cupped my face in her hand and raised it up. "You're not afraid of my little sister and me, are you, half-man?"

"If it's all the same to you, lady, I would like to finish this dress and start on the others. There is quite a bit to be done."

"So, how did you lose your balls, deaf man?" she asked.

"Probably from humping his master's wife," said Jeanette.

"More like his master's son," said Angelina, and they both laughed.

My ears and neck flushed, and I turned back to the dress, determined not to engage in this. I knew from experience there would be no point adding to their fun, but Jeanette swished her dress about, preventing me from gaining an accurate measure.

"My lady, I must ask, what is the point of that?"

"I love the way he talks," said Angelina to her sister. "So proper, yet so – garbled."

Jeanette bent and pressed her hand against my face, rubbing her thumb against my cheek. I struggled to remain still, to appear unaffected by her hands that had already violated me so severely. How long would I have to put up with this torment before they grew bored with me? Would they ever grow bored?

I sat back on my bottom and placed my hands in my lap, determined to wait them out. Instead of looking at their mouths, however, I looked at their noses as they commented about my state and disabilities. Whatever was being said, it must have been hilarious, because more than once they threw back their heads in laughter. But the smiles soon faded as I remained quiet upon the floor before them.

"That was quite original, my ladies. I had not heard any of those before. May we continue?"

When neither replied, I leaned forward to take up the hem of the dress once more. Jeanette stomped her heel upon my hand, grinding my fingers with her shoe. With a cry, I yanked it back. Red oozed about the knuckles as my fingers roared in pain.

"You little bitch!" I shouted, clutching my wound. "Damn you both to hell and may your wombs shrivel and fall out."

I turned from them for the door to see Regis before me, scowling with face red.

CHAPTER NINETEEN

Regis grabbed me by the shirt collar and dragged me from the room. He took for the stairs in haste, and I barely managed to stay upright as he hauled me down them. As he shoved me out the kitchen door, I retreated from him backwards, hands raised in supplication.

"I am so sorry, sir. I lost my temper. It will never happen again."

Regis fist slammed against my cheek, and I stumbled, my back striking a fence post behind me. The second blow brought me to my knees, and the kick to the stomach that followed took me to the earth. He raised up his boot for my face, and I covered it with my arms, but the blow did not come.

Shaking, I looked up to see Sebastian clutching Regis's arm. The words "valuable" and "bleeding hand" were spoken, but I did not catch the rest. Instead, I studied the muck upon which I lay, still damp from the rain of last night.

I had to get out of here. It could not wait.

With a glare, Regis turned from us and walked back into the house. Sebastian took my arm, and I clutched my stomach as I stood. "What the hell, weaver? I thought we had a deal."

"I am sorry," I said. "Your sisters are skilled in the art of annoyance."

"Father wants you flogged. I convinced him to have you staked instead."

"Staked?" I said, not at all assured by the title.

Sebastian led me away from the house to an area cleared of trees. At the middle of the clearing, drilled into the ground, was a metal stake with the top bent over on itself. "Take off your shirt," he ordered, and I looked at him in question. "Just do it."

I pulled the shirt over my head and handed it to him.

"Sit," he said, and I tentatively knelt before the metal rod. Using rope from his back pocket, he tied my hands to the stake.

"This is staked?"

"Don't count yourself too lucky," said Sebastian. "And keep in mind we do this in the winter as well. Let me see your hand."

None of the bones appeared to be broken, and the cut was not as large as the blood made it seem. It still ached, but Sebastian would not be losing money from the injury as he had feared.

"If you try to escape, I'll beat you and put you right back for double the time."

Then he walked away leaving me sitting like a wayward tot.

It was boring, sitting there tied to the earth. But no one dies of boredom. I took the time to study the architecture of the house, the way the shale roof glinted. Occasionally a cloud would pass and the shadows would darken the sheen. The trees rocked in the breeze, and the men journeyed back from the fields for supper.

I also took time to contemplate my escape. I could not delay much longer here. As well as things had been going, a trip to town could have been gained by requesting to pick out the material for the next dress. But I had spoiled that opportunity with my quick tongue. Regaining my master's trust and forgiveness could take months now, which would lead into winter. Trips to town would be fewer if not non-existent.

The magistrate of Burganne would grow impatient and possibly enslave Etienne out of spite. Even if I did escape at that point, returning to Burganne to fetch him would be suicide. No. I had to accelerate my timetable and make a run for it.

Not tonight, for Sebastian would be most suspicious of me right now. I would wait for a waxing gibbous to full moon. I risked being caught that way, but I could not go running deaf and blind through the forest and hope to live.

As the day dragged on, my thoughts returned to Marta and that day inside the booth after Etienne was taken. When finally, I had collected my breath and my wits, we sat together and watched the crowds pass by, each seeing to their own business as necessary then returning to sit in silence side-by-side.

Business did well for me that week, although I believe many purchases were made out of sympathy. The expectancy of the child had been well-known, as had its sale to foreign traders. What was done by the surgeon remained a secret except for in our house. As I had already managed to make my master a small fortune, he threatened to flog for anyone in the household who spoke of it outside.

"A man needs control of his destiny," I told Marta once the crowds dispersed for the day, and she looked at me curiously. "People need freedom, Marta."

She squeezed my hand tight, and I could see a plan formulating behind her eyes as to how to smuggle me away.

"I will help others reach their freedom in whatever way I can."

"But what of your own freedom?" Marta asked.

"My son has already been taken. I believe others may benefit from freedom more than I at this point."

"Your life is not lost, Zayim. You can have other children, build a new family—"

"Please!" I closed my fist and placed it on my knee. "Please, do not push me further at this time."

"Alright, but what do you have in mind?"

I looked to my loom once more, an idea forming but not yet fully developed. Once the idea was conceived, I set to work like a half-crazed man. And perhaps I was. But I weaved piece after piece, map after map. They started out as orders from Marta's contacts, but others saw my work and requested their own as well. Soon the roster of my clients acquired a gilded edge.

Master was able to purchase a shop for me instead of the booth on the street. He assigned other slaves to run the shop as I wove. I requested to stay at night and work by lamplight when the others went home, and soon the shop became a hub for runaways to hide before being smuggled out of the city.

For five years this went on until Master stopped by on an unexpected visit. The child hiding in the hidden room beneath the floor had taken ill and was crying most of the day. The slaves working the shop, all of whom knew but had until then turned a blind eye, alerted me of this, but there was nothing for me to do. The child and his mother could not be moved in the middle of the day.

In all likelihood, everything would have been fine had he not stopped by. When customers complained, we merely told them it was coming from next door. Within minutes of his arrival, however, the hiding place was revealed.

"What have you done, Zayim? You have ruined me! I am ruined!" Gabor, my master, paced the floor, running his hands through his hair.

I, however, took a bottle of wine from my cupboard and poured us both a drink.

"You may wish to send the others home," I said, and he dismissed them with a wave of his hand. "Sit, drink. We shall talk."

He downed the goblet and set it back on the table. "Why have you done this? It is illegal!"

I sipped on my drink. "It is a fine."

"That's not the point! My reputation will be destroyed by this!" Then he leaned across the table. "Is that what you want? Are you that unhappy?"

"I do not wish to bring you trouble."

"Then what is it that you want, Zayim? You have made me a wealthy man. Ask and I will give it. A better shop? Better clothes? A wife?"

I nearly spat out my drink. "A wife, are you joking?"

"You will not have children, but I left what is important…"

My mouth fell open, amazed by his ignorance. Then I clamped it shut, poured another goblet for him, and slid it across the counter. "When this is found out, it can be said one of two things: You, Gabor, have done this, or the free man Zayim has."

"They will hang you, Zayim!"

"Then I will die a free man."

Before the day was out, my papers were signed and handed over to me. As I had no money to start out, Gabor allowed me to rent his shop and equipment for some time. Once I had enough funds to buy the tools myself, I saved the rest of my money for Sloan and Etienne. Beyond that, I had no plans as I did not expect to not get caught for that long. But for ten years after that, I stayed in business, sending money to my son, buying vineyards, smuggling out families.

I did not know how many people came through my shop on their way to freedom. Marta told me I was one of their most reliable members. Perhaps this was so. Until a single mishap, a single indiscretion brought down the whole operation.

As the sun sank behind the trees, I kept waiting for Sebastian to return and release me for sleep. Missing dinner was a given, but I did not expect to stay out for the night. When he did finally step out the back door of the house, I straightened and practically held my hands out to him. He ignored me, however, and mounted stairs at the base of a tree that led to a wooden platform built in the limbs.

And that's when I grew nervous. The slave watcher usually took his place once the rest of the house was asleep, and anyone who stepped out after dark risked being speared as a runaway.

The shifting shadows of the trees turned into phantoms lurking in the darkness. I prayed for a full moon, but darkness was all I received. Without my eyes, the world was quiet and void. Movement caught the corner of my eye, and I turned to face it only to see nothing there. My eyes burned as they bore into the darkness. Tightness rushed across my chest and I struggled to find my breath.

Damn the beating, I could not stay here. But as I tugged against my restraints, they did not budge. Even with the use of my teeth, I got nowhere. Something shifted in my peripheral vision, and I spun in a circle to face it. The wind blew, kicking up leaves, and I retreated from them.

You're acting like a child, I chided myself, but the childlike part didn't care. I sat huddled on the ground shaking. I did not notice when the temperature dropped, as I was shaking with fear before I knew I was cold, but the wind crashed against me, chilling my bare flesh.

For hours, I carried on shivering and shaking, until I collapsed in the grass, drawing my knees to my chest, staring wide-eyed into the darkness. I entered a state halfway between sleep and consciousness as if hypnotized by the dark.

Then light flashed from the base of the tree where Sebastian had perched. A flame from a torch caught and advanced on me quickly. Behind the flame, Sebastian shouted and jumped. Was he shouting at me?

But something shifted on my left, and I turned to see the fangs of a wolf snarling in the firelight.

CHAPTER TWENTY

White fangs and yellow eyes caught the torchlight. The monstrous body dipped low, ready to pounce. As I jerked away, the wolf launched at me, snapping at my neck. The beast's paws struck me on the shoulders, knocking me to my back. Jaws open, it lunged at me again.

The weight of the wolf collapsed onto my chest, rending breath from my lungs. I pulled away, but my arms were immobilized by the stake and rope. Warm moisture spread against my chest and neck, and I cried out as my lifeblood soaked into my shirt.

But Sebastian grabbed the wolf by the scruff and a leg and tossed it off of me. A spear protruded from its side. I touched my neck, finding it warm and moist, but no cut was present.

Using his knife, Sebastian sawed through my bindings and pulled me to my feet. Just outside the light of the torch, another wolf darted across our path. Sebastian ripped his spear from the wolf and held it at the ready. Together, we backed our way toward the tree as two more beasts entered the circle of light. They barred their teeth, showing their fangs. One launched, only to receive a jab to the eye from Sebastian's spear. He limped off, but the others lingered.

Once we reached the tree, Sebastian pushed me toward the ladder, and I climbed without delay. He tossed the torch to me, then joined me, barely evading the fangs of the nearest wolf.

The wolves circled the tree, pawing at it and jumping occasionally. I counted four. The injured one bled as he swiped at his face.

Sebastian looked down the ladder at them and laughed, pounding his feet on the platform floor. Then he cocked his head back in a howl. "Damn, that was something else, wasn't it, Zayim?" He howled again.

I extracted my fingernails from the wooden floor.

"You should have seen your face!" he said. "I hollered at you, hoping you'd be able to scare it off, but of course, you couldn't hear me."

I rubbed my hand over my eyes, then pulled it away to find it covered in wolf blood.

"You're actually speechless!" Sebastian said. "Didn't think there was anything in the world that could make you speechless." He took the torch and slid it into a holder on the platform.

He was right. I had no words for the occasion, just eternal gratitude for the flame of the torch. The wolves circled for a time but finally wandered off in search of different prey. I glanced in the direction of the stake, fearing Sebastian would put me back. The platform was barely big enough for one man, but he made no move to do so.

As I calmed down, the sweat generated from the run chilled me once more, and I started shaking again. Even the heat of the torch barely touched it. Sebastian tossed a blanket to me, and I looked at him in confusion.

"I won't tell if you won't," he said, and I wrapped the blanket around my shoulders. He'd have no complaint from me.

"Since you're feeling generous, could you just beat me next time and be done with it?"

Sebastian grinned as he leaned against the trunk of the tree. "I would have preferred that, but Father likes to make his punishments memorable."

He had certainly done that.

"He once saw a cage made of metal hanging on posts outside a castle," Sebastian continued. "The lord would cage his prisoners and leave them to starve. Father has talked of constructing a cage, but until then, we have the stake."

"That is a cruel way to kill somebody," I said.

Sebastian shrugged. "He's not interested in killing anyone, just punishing. And it would have kept the wolves away."

"How long is my punishment to go on?" I asked.

"Just until tomorrow evening. Once the sun comes up, I'll put you back."

I pinched the bridge of my nose until it ached.

Sebastian put out the torch flame a few minutes later, stifling any possible conversation. I stared once more into the darkness and at the dangers lurking there. The presence of the wolves complicated my plans of escape. A deaf man running from such monsters would not have a chance. The face of Etienne appeared before my mind's eyes, blurry as if fading.

I dozed off a couple of times throughout the night but never really slept. Things were better being off the ground, but I still feared I'd topple off the narrow platform if I tried to sleep. When the sun finally crept up from behind the trees, my back ached, my head pounded, and my throat cried out from thirst. At Sebastian's command, I took the ladder. My legs wobbled and threatened to give.

All that remained of the body of the wolf were bones and tufts of fur. Blotches of blood coated the grass next to the stake, and I swallowed hard as I considered how close it had come to being my blood.

Sebastian nudged the corpse with his foot. "Drag that off into the woods, will ya?"

I opened my mouth with a spiteful comment, then sealed it back shut. Regis's punishment was working.

I grabbed the wolf by the tail, wincing as my fingers closed around the wet, exposed bone, and hauled it to the tree line. The thing really should be buried, but Sebastian ordered me back. No wonder they had a wolf problem if this was how they took care of dead animals.

Sebastian waited for me above the stake, and I glanced at the woods once more. But Sebastian was younger than me and fitter. If I ran, he would catch me for sure.

So, I knelt beside the bloodstained grass and submitted my hands for tying. Once I was secure, he stood, dusted the dirt from his hands, and trudged to the house. Not long after, the property buzzed with activity as each man went to work. Several passed by me, pointing to the blood while speaking to their companions about "the wolf." A couple even ventured to the woods to inspect the thing. None, however, attempted a greeting or conversation with me, probably fearing punishment for interfering. The feeling of loneliness deep in my gut increased.

As did my hunger. The smell from the kitchen rose, taunting me from afar. I had been provided no water since yesterday, and my tongue stuck to the roof of my mouth. As morning turned to afternoon, the intense heat of the day dried up my sweat, and I practically panted for breath. The day felt hotter than normal and my head grew woozy.

The sun burnt my flesh, making it red and warm. There was no way I could lay where my skin would not be exposed with my hands tied low before me. I sat cross-legged in the grass and my body rocked back and forth. Everything became a blur of arid heat.

My memories became mingled with my present. Before me sat an unfinished tapestry. Water beaded upon the threads of green, reflecting the light of the sun. On the other side of the loom sat Alonya, smiling at me through the warp. Blood lay upon the ground around her.

The loom and green threads dissolved into grass dotted with rain. The blood of the wolf remained, and the water felt as a balm for my burnt skin. But the shower quickly fled, leaving the grass to steam and the scent of rain to linger. Sebastian had said this punishment was doled out in winter. The heat was bad. The cold would be worse.

Escape.

Escape.

The word echoed in my mind. I would steal cloth to hide my brand and silver to pay the way. Could I forge papers and procure my master's seal?

When a trio of horses entered the yard, I barely noticed them as everything passed before me like a fog. Upon reaching the house, one of the riders dismounted and rushed to me, but it appeared that a round blob of shadow rode to me on the wind. Hands clasped behind my head, steadying my neck, and I frowned at Marta's face. I knew I must be dreaming.

Her gentle hand caressed my cheek as worry creased her brow. "Zayim," she said as if through a tunnel. "It's going to be alright. You're safe now."

Sebastian exited from the kitchen and crossed the yard to us. "Lady, if you would walk away from him, I would appreciate that. He's under punishment."

I flinched at his words. Did we share the same vision?

Marta tore a cloth from her underskirt and wet it with a pouch from her waist. She dabbed my face and neck with it, and I felt the moisture. This was no vision.

"You're alright, Zayim. We're taking you home."

Home? What home?

Sebastian placed a hand on her shoulder, and she smacked it away. He moved to grab her, but a man clutched his arm, drawing him back. Vernard pulled him toward the horses. "Excuse me, sir, but if I might have a word about the slave." Soon Regis joined them from the house.

Marta pressed her hands to my face. "Where are you hurt?"

I blinked up at her, still unsure of how she came to be here. "I am unhurt, just thirsty."

"You have blood on you, Zayim—"

I shook my head. "Not my blood. It's – it's a long story."

She fetched the water pouch from her hip and pressed it to my lips. I gulped it down. Within seconds, it resurfaced and I grew woozier. Marta called over her shoulder, and Kai trotted over.

"Hey, Zayim, I must say you've looked better." He pressed a hand to my forehead. "Give him water, but do so slowly," he told Marta, then he took my hands and cut through the ropes with his blade.

"What of Regis?" I asked.

"Vernard will take care of it." Kai draped one of my arms over his broad shoulders and helped me rise. Although my legs shook, I could still walk, and he brought me into the shade of a tree and leaned my back against the trunk. "What's that smell?" he asked.

"Dead wolf." I pointed to the corpse surrounded by flies. Then I gestured to the old blood on my chest.

Kai patted Marta on the shoulder. "I'm going to see how Vernard is getting along."

Marta continued to dab my face with the wet cloth and drizzle water into my mouth. Regis and Sebastian kept turning to look at me, and soon, Kai brought out a tapestry from his horse's saddle bag.

The article was a failed project, a disaster created during an overzealous afternoon. It had been hidden beneath my bed for months. I never intended to sell it. The distance was not too far to read lips from, and I watched as Kai attempted a negotiation with the rag.

"What are they saying?" Marta asked, and I repeated what was said.

Regis examined the fabric with a smile. "This is extraordinary work! The colors, it's like waves of the sea." He looked over to me and said, "Your friends really think you're worth this much, eh, Eunuch?"

I winced at the title and omitted it from my repetition, but he must have said this part loud enough for Marta to hear because she did not meet my eye.

"I can castrate three of my men and afford the loss of labor with this," Regis said.

Kai slammed his fist into Regis's face, and the man crumbled to the ground. Kai straddled him, pinning him to the ground with a knife pressed against his neck. Sebastian lunged at him, but Vernard drew his sword and smacked him in the head with the pommel.

I shouted, "Stop! Kai! Vernard!"

Kai jammed his knife between Regis's legs. The man screamed and flailed beneath Kai, but the blade stuck into nothing but earth.

I gripped the tree trunk behind me and forced myself to stand. Marta took my arm to steady me.

Kai spat in the man's face. "I should make you eat them!"

"He didn't do it, Kai," I said.

Kai's brow crinkled in confusion. "But Zayim—"

Clutching Marta's arm, I took shaking steps forward. "We have business elsewhere, or did you find the man already?"

Kai looked between me and the man beneath him.

"We have not found him yet," Vernard said.

"Then we should go," I said. "Payment has been made. There is no further reason for us to stay."

Vernard re-sheathed his blade. Sebastian, however, stayed kneeling on the ground as he clutched his head. Blood trickled down his forehead from the wound. I offered my hand to Sebastian. "I am sorry. Truly."

Ignoring the hand, Sebastian straightened his collar and stood. He snatched the woven fabric from the ground and sneered at me. Kai let up Regis, and the man scurried away from him, shaking as he did.

Sebastian crumpled the fabric in his hands. He was not a stupid lad and knew he had been cheated in his price by possessing a work of the creator rather than the creator himself. But Vernard kept his hand upon his sword and Kai his knife, so he uttered, "Enjoy your freedom, weaver. It's clear your friends believe you deserve it."

CHAPTER TWENTY-ONE

I continued to take sips of water as I rode in front of Kai on the newly purchased brown colt. One of his great arms wrapped around my middle while the other flicked the reins, leading us from that awful place. All the while, I felt strangely without appetite even though I had not eaten since yesterday.

Marta and Vernard rode upon their horses flanking us, but they did not speak. I could not raise my eyes to Marta. Although I tried to hold my head as high as before, I found it drooping nonetheless. What did my friends think of me now? If only I had hung upon the gallows of Burganne. Then at least I would have died with dignity.

We had traveled a couple of miles from the estate when Kai turned our horse from the road and halted beneath a copse of trees. He slid down from the saddle, and the others dismounted as well.

"Why are we stopping?" I asked as I dropped to the ground. "There are wolves in these woods. It's not a good place to camp."

"You are in no shape for a long ride," Kai said.

My chest, back, arms, and face were burnt to be sure, and some places blistered, but Kai had provided me with an oversized, airy tunic with long sleeves, and my hat shielded me from the worst of the sun damage. Besides, I had delayed them enough and did not desire to be of further trouble. "I'll be alright."

"Weaver," said Vernard, "I do not wish to violate your privacy, but with your injury, the last thing you should be doing is riding."

It felt as if all the air had been purged from me.

"Vernard—" Marta started, but I spoke over her.

"The injury is not new."

"Even if a full month had passed—" Vernard said.

"Seventeen years have passed," I said. Kai's mouth dropped. I did not look at Marta but studied the ground as I continued, "After the birth of my son, my master feared I would contaminate his stock with my deafness. So, Etienne was sold to a foreigner who did not know about his deaf father, and I was castrated."

I raised my head to find my companions speechless and unable to meet my face. I found the nerve to look at Marta. "I'm sorry," she said. I looked away again.

"If the issue has been addressed to your satisfaction," I said, "I'd like to create as much distance between us and Regis as possible before they seek retribution for your actions."

Without waiting for a reply, I swung into the saddle once more. My head grew woozy from the action, and I clung to the saddle pommel to stay upright. Kai mounted the horse as well, took the reins, and prodded the horse onward.

***

As sunset neared, we reined in the horses for the night and set up camp in a clearing. Our supplies were limited to bed rolls and food, so there would be no sleeping in tents. At least there would be a fire and company, but that did not stop fear from rising at the prospect of sleeping outside for a second night. I shoved it down with a gulp of water and announced, "I'm going to fetch firewood," before marching to the woods.

Kai grabbed my arm, turning me back to himself. "I will fetch firewood. You stay in camp."

"There is nothing left to do but cook, and I am terrible at that."

"Then you will rest," he insisted. "You are not yet recovered."

My lip curled at his insistence. "You forget who employs you."

He took a great sigh. Releasing my arm, he said, "It is clear I have overstepped. I am sorry, Zayim." Kai returned to the horses, and I pinched the bridge of my nose.

"Kai," I called, and he turned back to me, but I had no way to express what I felt. I walked into the woods in search of broken branches, letting camp dissolve into the space behind me. I did not venture far, just far enough so they would not pursue me or see me cry.

All the while I berated myself for the treatment of my companions. They had saved my life, but had I yet to thank them? They should have left me to rot.

I dripped of sweat when I returned to camp with a load of sticks half the size we'd need to make it through the night. Vernard was busy with the horses while Marta cut up potatoes for a stew. Kai arranged rocks in a circle to create the firepit. As I stood from surrendering my load beside Marta, a wave of dizziness swept through me. Before I fell, Marta grabbed my arm and had me sit on a log, and I hung my head between my legs. Without a word, Kai stood and finished collecting the firewood, bringing back three times as much wood as I could carry on a good day.

"I'm sorry," I said to him as he stacked the firewood.

The logs slid off each other as Kai's face pinched in sorrow. "Sorry? Zayim, if anyone should apologize, it's me. It's my fault you were taken."

"They snuck up on you, Kai! Someone bashed your head in with a club! They could have killed you!"

"I should have been more aware. I was supposed to be on guard, after all. You have been so good to me, Zayim, but when you needed me most, I failed you."

I swallowed hard, attempting to dislodge the tightness in my throat, but to no avail. "I do not blame you, Kai. I didn't then, and I don't now. I have very little family, and you are closer to me than they. In truth, I am just glad you're alive."

"But it is my fault!"

"And even if it is," I said with a shrug, "whatever wounds I've gotten I will recover from. It is my pride that has been most damaged after all."

He pursed his lips, knowing that I minimized the truth of my time of enslavement. More had been fractured than pride, but I would not see him carry the blame for this as well. Whatever had happened on the estate was now my secret to keep.

Marta, who had been cutting up potatoes in silence, opened her mouth to speak, but Vernard wandered over from the horses and sat on a log beside me. He removed his boot and inspected a worn place on the sole, oblivious to the weighty conversation he had interrupted. Kai restacked the wood and lit a handful of pine needles with his flint. Soon a fire warmed us, and Marta positioned her stew over the coals. The sun set behind the trees, and the only light present was from the fire.

"There has been something neglected that I wish to address," I said as the pot boiled, and each turned to me in question. "I have yet to say thank you. I could not have gotten out of there alone."

"Bah," said Vernard. "Had we been further delayed, I have no doubt you would have led the slaves to mutiny and seized control of the estate."

I allowed a feeble smile.

"We bought you back with your weaving," Kai said. "I don't think we fully deserve the credit for that one."

"You mean the horse blanket?" I asked with a wicked grin.

"Horse blanket? I thought that was one of your finest works! That's why you kept it for yourself after all."

"I kept it hidden under my bed. Not for myself."

Marta giggled, and even Vernard smiled. "He's a bit of a perfectionist, isn't he?"

"Always," Marta replied, but I dipped my head before she had time to say much else. Still, I could not look at Marta for more than seconds at a time. If I had been whole, I would have married her and started a life with her. As it was, I felt I had cheated her out of the best years of her life with unspoken promises. I should have told her years ago so she could move on and find another instead of holding out hope for me. What a loathsome man was I.

I cleared my thoughts with a shake of my head. "How did you find me?"

"Let's just say it's not as hard to track a talking deaf man as a man with brown hair and brown eyes," Kai said.

"We sold most of your works for new horses and supplies," said Vernard. "Kai sent a letter to Marta, and I sent one to my father requesting funds."

"Marta arrived first," Kai said.

"I was already planning a trip," she said, "so I was able to leave at once."

"A trip to smuggle Zayim's son and his mother out, no doubt." Vernard crossed his arms and stretched his legs out before him. "Word came from my father regarding this as well as the silver."

"Marta was not involved," I said. "I requested another friend to—"

Vernard raised his hand. "I have no plans of reporting her to the magistrate. You have led me further than I could have gone on my own, so, as far as I am concerned, you have kept your end of the bargain."

I churned the fire with my stick. He may not report us, but that did not mean it would be safe for Marta to return. Now that Etienne was out of the country, perhaps we didn't need to. Perhaps it was time to seek a new home.

Vernard nudged my arm, and I looked back up to him in question. "I have not forgotten, weaver, that you saved my life from the bandits. They would have killed me if you had not spoken. Not only will I not report you or your friends to my father, but if you wish to be released from this mission, I will not pursue you."

I glanced at my companions on either side of me. From their expressions, I could tell they would have no objections to what I said next. "We will see the thing done. We have but one final destination anyway."

"Are you sure? But—"

"When your father first recruited me, he told me it was 'up the liberationist's alley.' This is true, Vernard. I would have taken this job regardless of the leverage your father had over my son. But you also understand why I had to get Etienne out of Burganne?"

"I – yes," he said. "Of course."

"Then, I suppose, the one I really have to thank most is you, Marta." And I met her eye for the first time that evening. "Thank you, from the depths of my heart. For everything."

She smiled softly at me. "Always."

My heart seized. Did she truly have no hatred against me? No lingering spite? But her face was true, her eyes soft upon me.

"Excuse me," I said as I rose from the little group. "I would like a moment of peace."

No one objected, and I stepped away from the fire. I did not go far, especially after last night, but there was a small stream a stone's throw from our camp, and I sat on a rock beside it, watching the stars dance in the water. Then the water caught the reflection of a flame, and I turned to see Marta join me with a torch.

"I will go if you wish," she said.

I shook my head and patted the rock beside me. She sat, wedging the torch between two rocks. We watched the water for a time in comfortable silence, although I was keenly aware of her presence. I could have reached out my finger and touched her and imagined her warmth mingling with my own.

"How are Sloan and Etienne doing with all this?" I asked.

"They are adjusting," she said. "The Abbess will help them, and I believe Etienne will do just fine in Candorlan, as young as he is. We sold the vineyard, so he will have enough to support himself and his mother for now."

"And Sloan?"

Marta bit her lip. "She sends her blessings."

I tilted my head.

"Alright," she said, "she sends her curses, but I will not repeat them."

"That sounds more like her," I said, and she laughed.

Things had not gone smoothly for Etienne when he returned with me. I purchased a house in a hamlet outside Burganne, intent on settling there and establishing my family. As I spent most of my days in the back of the house weaving, my encounters with the townsfolk were few. Instead, it was Sloan who endured the sneers and whispers because of her status as a former slave and my failure to marry her. Etienne was called a bastard and none of the children were permitted to play with him. Both of them blamed and hated me for their lives. Things became so intolerable that I returned to Burganne and continued my work there.

Things did get better for both of them upon my leaving. Now, since I was not present, Sloan was permitted to slander me in any way she deemed fit. I doubt anyone in the town would believe me to be a eunuch, they were so convinced I had abandoned my family for Marta. According to Sloan, because I was a favorite of my master, I was permitted to use her as I deemed fit. And now, after fathering a bastard with her, I had abandoned them to poverty while I made riches in Burganne.

When I did visit, Etienne ignored me, and Sloan scowled during my entire stay. My trips to the hamlet became less and less frequent. If any business needed to be conducted, I usually sent Kai.

Marta scooped a rogue strand of hair behind her ear. "I swear Etienne has grown six inches since the last time I saw him. He's also become quite the musician, did you know? He serenaded us with his lyre along the journey."

"I knew he had a lyre but am not one to judge the quality. His fingers moved in a fast, complicated pattern, however." I mimicked the motion and she smiled.

"He's very good," she said. "Gabor was unfounded in his fears about the boy's hearing."

I looked out to the creek where the fire swirled and tumbled in the reflection. Then a soft wind rippled over us mixed with the scent of pine and coming rain. I turned back to her. "I'm sorry I did not tell you, Marta."

She shrugged. "It was not my business to know.

"I am not blind, Marta. I know you had hoped someday that I would look at you with affection. And although I love you, I do not have the ability to give you what you would hope."

Her face softened as she stared off across the creek. "I am an old maid, Zayim—"

My shoulders fell. "I am sorry you waited, but you have years left that can be spent with another. You can have children and a family and—"

"What I was going to say," she broke in, "is I am an old maid because of my work. I cannot do what is required of me and tend to children as well. If I had wanted children and a family, I would have sought them, Zayim."

"You say that now, but you have just found out. If you take time to think of it—"

"I have known for years."

I stared at her, jaw slack, seeing what she said but not perceiving it fully. "You…you knew? What do you mean?"

She shrugged once more. "Sloan told me. She curses you with many names behind your back, Zayim. I used to pay her no mind, and neither did Kai, but one day I challenged her about them while you and Kai were out of the house."

"So, Etienne also knows?"

"I don't know what Etienne knows," she said. "Like I said, she calls you many things and not all of them are true."

I shook my head. All these years of keeping secrets and Sloan had been wagging her tongue behind me. "Why didn't you tell me?"

"Perhaps I should have brought up the subject, but I was afraid of how you would respond to my knowledge." She studied her hands upon her lap. "There are times, Zayim, that sadness falls on you like a great fog. It is all Kai and I can do to reach you when it happens, and I was afraid this would bring on one of those times. In truth, I still am."

I knew the fog she spoke of. On these days, I would force myself from bed and run my hands mechanically over the threads. My memories from such days were few. Day and night mixed until finally it ended. If Kai had not been watching over me during those times, I do not know if I would have survived. It was he who reminded me to eat, shave, dress, and sleep. I had never experienced such days prior to Etienne's birth, and I was quite certain the castration was the cause of my illness.

She was right to be concerned. Even now, I could feel the weight of my mind descending on my shoulders, but there was enough going on to keep it at bay for now.

"I hoped you would eventually trust me enough to tell," said Marta with another shrug. "But after everything that has happened in your life, I understand that is hard to do."

"I was afraid of what you would think of me," I breathed.

Her brow furrowed as she turned her whole body to me. "Did you imagine I would think less of you? The world seems to rage against you, yet you are the most compassionate and courageous man I know. You are my greatest friend, and I will never think less of you."

I felt as if all my breath had been snatched from me. Disbelief at this moment reigned and then dissolved into an ocean of emotions that flooded within my core. I could not think, let alone speak.

"I certainly think less of your former master," she sneered. "Father continues to do business with him, but I cannot be in the same room as Gabor."

"He was only doing what was right for his business."

Her eyes flashed. "He was cruel. What he did was wrong."

I bit the corner of my lip and breathed deeply. "Yes, it was."

Marta slid her hand into mine and warmth spread across my palm. They were as soft as I imagined, gentle and kind. She pressed her hand against my cheek, drawing me into her words. "I do not wish for a different life, Zayim. I just wish to spend it with you."

A sob erupted from my throat, but the tear that followed slid from her eye. Firelight glistened upon that tear. I pulled her near and kissed her, and she kissed me in return. Then I closed my eyes and pressed my forehead against hers.

Marta slid her arm around my back and leaned against my chest. Things would never be as I wanted them, or perhaps she wanted them, but as I held her that night and she held me, I felt a missing piece slip into place.

CHAPTER TWENTY-TWO

My eyes flickered open as the sun penetrated the tree branches the next morning. One arm lay cold and numb, tucked beneath Marta's side. With care, I tugged on my sleeve, attempting to extract my arm without her notice. She shifted in her sleep, and her lips pursed together. Then she rolled over and laid her head upon her own arm.

I pressed against my arm, coaxing the blood back to my fingertips. Kai, who had been keeping watch, grinned at me from where he sat on a log poking at the fire.

After gathering supplies from our bags, I set out to make biscuits and dried beef. As I sat on the log beside Kai, however, he nudged me in the side and nodded to Marta. "About bloody time."

"Shut up," I returned, and his cheeky grin expanded. I could not refrain from smiling either, and he nudged me in the ribs once more.

It was not long before the smell of breakfast woke our companions, and they sat up, rubbing the sleep from their eyes. Once everyone had a plate and ate heartily, I asked, "Where the hell are we anyway?"

"We are on the road to Nostria," said Vernard. "Our last town is three miles north of there."

"I had some customers in that town," I said. "We are near the country of Soren." And the town of Candorlan.

"Nearly just," said Vernard and wiped his hands clean of the meal. "If we leave soon, we can reach Nostria by nightfall and be at the estate tomorrow."

And with that, we doused the fire and loaded our saddlebags once more. Before we mounted up, however, Kai drew me aside and pressed a sheathed knife into my hand.

"What am I supposed to do with this? I am not a man of war."

"It does not take a man of war to stick a pig," said Kai. "I will, as always, do my best to defend you, but in case I fail again…"

Running my thumb against the leather sheath, I said, "I doubt you will fail again."

"Keep it," he insisted, patting me on the shoulder. "Just in case."

As he stepped away to his horse, I slid the knife deep into my pocket. I doubted I would ever use it. I was more likely to hurt myself than anyone else, but I did feel a bit safer having it.

Since I was better after having eaten and rested, I rode behind Marta. Kai's horse rejoiced. I, too, enjoyed the closeness of the lady against my chest, my arms around her middle. It was as if my soul were being revived by the touch. The lack of physical embrace had contributed to my emptiness more than I had known.

Although I was weary from our travels and quite ready to rest my head on a bed of my own, I enjoyed this part of the trip. The weather was fair and the terrain was quite lovely. And I was free once more.

We reached Nostria with only a few hours of daylight left and spurred our horses onward before the gates of the city closed. Compared to Nostria, Burganne was a hamlet.

Nostria sprawled across both sides of the river and massive stone walls encompassed the town. We entered through the south gates, in pursuit of an inn.

"There should be one a few streets over," I told my companions.

"Have you been to Nostria, Zayim?" asked Vernard.

"No, but I have woven a tapestry of this town before. I know the streets well enough to be trusted." And I coaxed my horse forward without awaiting a reply. Sure enough, three streets over sat an inn. A shingle with a daisy painted on it swung in the breeze.

Since our inquiries were not in Nostria, I rolled up my sleeve upon entering the inn and placed it on the counter. "We are merchants all. And this is my wife."

The second part of the statement tumbled out of my mouth on its own, and heat rushed to my cheeks. I turned to Marta to apologize, but the corners of her mouth rose. I slid my hand into hers and she squeezed it back. Neither Vernard nor Kai said anything, although they appeared more than a little surprised. It was a lie and a possible sin, but I merely desired to be close to her.

"Two rooms then," said the woman, sliding across the keys. "Supper will be served in about an hour, and we have a minstrel staying with us tonight."

After the luggage was brought in, Marta and I entered the streets of Nostria, walking hand in hand as we perused the shops. I kept running my thumb over her hand, still in disbelief that I actually held it. That she could accept me as I was.

We found a spot by the river to watch boats roll into port and leaned against an elm tree as the sun danced upon the waters. "I hope I did not speak presumptuously at the inn," I said. "If you wish to have a separate room, that would be fine."

"Not at all," she said, squeezing my hand. "I asked at the start of your journey if I was going to be disguised as a merchant's wife or not."

I brushed back the hair on her shoulder and caressed her cheek. She was indeed beautiful as the sun shone through her chestnut hair. And although I did not yearn for her as I would have in my youth, I savored the touch of her as well as her company. "I love you, Marta."

"And I you. With all my heart."

I brought my lips near her soft ones and kissed her. How precious was that kiss and the closeness that came with it. I placed an arm about her shoulders and we watched as the colors of the sun shifted and descended behind the hills.

***

We returned to the inn to find a warm plate of dinner waiting for us across from Kai and Vernard. Seating was scarce, as members of the town had come to hear the minstrel play. I watched with interest as his fingers ran across the strings as he tapped his foot upon the floor. Others clapped and stomped along, and Marta's foot bounced with the rhythm. Vibrations shot through my shoes. Ale flowed freely as did laughter, and all through the evening, Marta held tight to my hand.

"I saw something interesting today when I was purchasing a horse for you and Dorsey," said Vernard as he returned to our table with pints of ale. "One of your tapestries is hanging in a livery."

I wrapped my hand around the tankard and downed a sip of the frothy brew. "Someone else thinks my work to be a horse blanket too, I see."

"It was a piece like my father purchased," said Vernard. "A map of the city of Nostria. If they paid close to what he paid, that is a strange use of silver indeed."

"Sometimes work gets handed down to ungrateful children," said Marta. "Or those who do not see its worth. They sell it in the market and someone with a few extra coins picks it up."

I looked between her and the Captain. It was a weak excuse indeed, and I did not know if he would accept it.

Someone bumped my arm as they wedged a chair between Marta and me. A man plopped into it and reached for a pint. "This is not your table, sir," I said, drawing the pint from his grasp.

"You are the merchants searching for the slave boy, am I right?" I think he said, although I had to study his lips with care to discern his words, as they hung limp, and his speech garbled together. "I have information. That earns me a free drink."

"We shall see," said Vernard. "What's the information?"

"Archer is the name of the man running the mines. He came through here a month ago leading five men into the hills. They haven't come back. They never do."

"The mines?" said Vernard. "I thought it was an estate."

"No, they are mines," said the man. "Deep, dark mines. Pits to hell if you ask me. The Romans dug them and now Archer sends his men into the earth to bring up copper. The greedy son of a bitch uses fires to bring out the metals too."

"I do not understand," I said. "Uses fires?"

"You burn the rock. It weakens it to allow the men to dig out the copper more easily, but it can collapse the tunnels too. Nearly five trips a year, Archer takes to get more slaves."

A pit opened in my stomach as I looked to each of my companions. Color had left their faces as well as we gazed at each other in stunned silence. Vernard stood, his chair banging into the back of the patron seated behind him, and trudged to the stairs.

The man reached for the pint once more. "Now about that ale?"

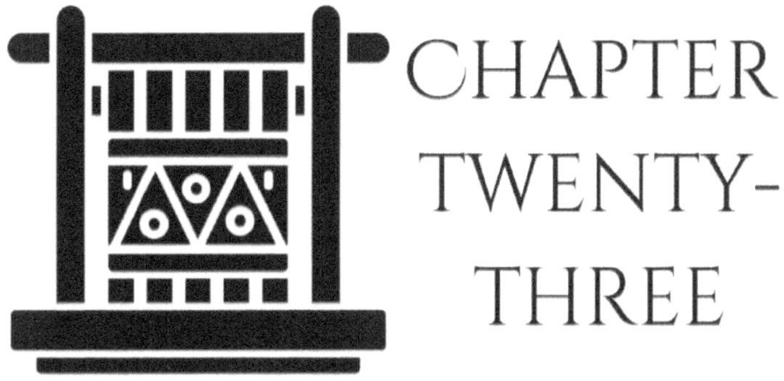

CHAPTER TWENTY-THREE

For the rest of the night, there was no further foot-tapping from our table. Marta and I dismissed ourselves shortly thereafter and followed Vernard's path upstairs.

When the door closed behind me, a knot gripped my gut. It came on as sudden as a wave, as did a shiver up my spine. The face of Jeanette passed before my mind's eye. Sweat gathered on my brow as I held tight to the door handle, but it was Marta who stood before me, undoing the braids in her hair.

"When we get to Candorlan," she said, "we will need to get you a loom. A shop too, if that is possible."

"You will need a shop as well." I released the door handle and forced myself to take slow, even breaths.

She waved her hand. "I can sew anywhere."

I felt against the pockets of my pants, finding the parchment from Regis's home. "I copied one of your designs. I hope you don't mind." I extended the dress pattern to her and a coy smile danced across her lips.

"This is the dress I made for the Duchess of Willowford, although the dip in the bodice is a bit more pronounced. How did yours turn out?"

"Pretty well. I didn't finish hemming it, but it was on the right track." I sat upon the bed and took off my shoes. "I was hoping to impress them and earn a trip to town."

"Ah." Marta bent low, scooped up my shoes, and inspected the rabbit-skinned husks bound with leather cord. "These are terrible!" she said with a giggle.

"A gift from Regis."

"It's a wonder they are still together. What happened to your other pair?"

With a sigh, I leaned my shoulder against the wall. "I don't know why, but people seem determined to steal my shoes. First the jailers in Burganne and then the slavers."

"You always did have good taste in shoes." She tossed them to the floor. "We will get you a new pair tomorrow. Can't have you tromping across all of Gaul in these horrid things."

The mattress shifted as she took a seat on the bed beside me, and the knot in my gut increased. What expectations did she have of me now?

Marta slid her hand into mine, but I dropped it and stood, moving to the window. The street below was illuminated by the lights from the inn as people exited, making their way to their homes. Some walked alone while others walked arm in arm. One man weaved as he made his way down the street.

Marta placed her hand upon my shoulder. "What is wrong?"

"Nothing. I am just tired."

"Are you sure? You haven't seemed quite right since we retrieved you. What other cruel things did they do to you?" She brushed her fingers against the bruised place above my eye where Regis had struck me.

I flinched. "I was not struck that much. It was more…" Searching for the words to describe what it had been, I chewed on my bottom lip. "I forgot what it was like to have no say over what happens to you."

"That sounds frightening."

I shrugged and took a seat on the bed once more. "As a boy, I didn't think much of it. In fact, in some ways, it was easier. I didn't have to figure out what I did each day, what I was to eat, or how to live my life. I didn't question my master about anything. At least until Etienne was born."

She took my hand once more, and I did not pull away as I continued. "At the beginning, I thought, since I had been a slave before, I could bear it once more."

"You know now that you are safe, don't you, Zayim?"

I squeezed her hand. "Yes, my love. I do know this, but forgive me if I forget now and again."

"Always." She squeezed my hand in return. "I wonder how Vernard is doing as it relates to his brother. Did he say much to you?"

"He is worried, that is clear. And he should be. Especially if Dorsey's been in the mines all this time. Our masters always threatened to sell us to the mines if we did not behave. With my deafness, it is a wonder I didn't end up there."

"They would have taken a deaf man into darkness like that? How could they have communicated with you?"

I shrugged. "For the basic things, there is not much to communicate other than 'dig there.' If your hands work, they don't care if you're deaf. To live in such a place would have been the depths of hell. In a way, perhaps it is a blessing my other – insufficiencies – left me more suitable for the house."

I looked down to see my hands shaking, and the tremor spread through my arms as well.

"Perhaps we should speak of something else," Marta said. "Or better yet, get some rest."

I cleared my throat and rubbed my hands together. "Yes, I believe you're right. Some rest would do me good." I put on my best smile as we prepared for bed, but when it came time to lay down for sleep, it refused to come. For hours, I lay holding Marta in my arms with the only thing keeping me from panic being the scent of lavender upon her hair.

* * *

The following morning, I rose bleary-eyed and tired as soon as the sun crept over the window sill. Marta continued to sleep, looking beautiful as the rays of light rested upon her hair. From the travel bag the bandits had left behind, I pulled out two sets of clothes. In hopes that we would eventually find the boy, I had brought a set of my normal clothes consisting of a woolen tunic, a leather jerkin, and breeches. On the other hand, I had a wool shirt of poor weave and stockings to take up my role as a slave once more. I laid out both then sat by the window and watched the still quiet streets.

Several minutes later, a gentle hand slid over my shoulder, and I looked up to see Marta beside me. With a smile, I kissed her, tasting her soft lips. "Good morning."

She caressed my cheek and the patchy growth of stubble I had not yet shaved. "Good morning, Zayim." Taking my hand, she sat in the chair across from me, and we watched the merchants set up their stalls for the morning. A drizzle set in upon them, and they quickly raised tarps above their wares.

"Vernard will be itching to get moving. I suppose we should get dressed." I ran my thumb over the slave tunic.

"You don't have to wear that, Zayim," she said, and I ran my hands over my face. She tugged at my sleeve. "It's far too dangerous."

"It is unlikely that we shall see any more bandits. If I go as a slave, I can mingle—"

"With men in a dark mine?"

I ran my thumb over the garments once more, liking her reasoning better and better. Pretending to be a slave before had been interesting at first, but she was right, it had turned quite dangerous. "So who should I go as then?" I asked with a sigh. "Zayim the weaver, the merchant, or the eunuch?"

She clasped my hand with both of hers. "How about Zayim the Free Man?"

"Yes, I can be that."

*　*　*

We descended the stairs of the inn hand in hand and found Kai sitting at the table in the taproom, eating a sop in wine. The door swung open, and rain entered with Vernard. His cloak was soaked, and as he threw his hood back, it was clear the clothing had not helped him fare well against the elements.

"Horses are packed and ready," he said. "We should be there by mid-morning."

I stepped to the windows and pushed back the shutter. Rain splattered my face as it blew horizontally. "You wish to leave in this weather?"

"This is nothing but a late summer storm," said Vernard. "It will pass before we are out of town." Vernard rubbed his eyes with this first finger and thumb, and I noticed the red about them. If he had slept, it had been little. Our greatest delay was for my benefit, however, and I could not refuse him further.

The rain did not pass.

Although I am sure the horse was grateful to be carrying only one person, I almost wished Marta and I still shared. Her warm body pressed against mine would have calmed both of our teeth's chattering. Three miles felt as ten.

Most of the journey was uphill, but I was still surprised when giant white cliffs sprouted from the ground before us, the road veering right to follow them. Our trail deposited us before a wattle and daub house next to a cliff overhang. On the ground within the shelter of the mountain lay nearly twenty men, half-naked, all branded with a lily on their temples. Dirt and grime covered them, causing their races to be indeterminable. A couple of them raised their heads as we passed before dropping back onto their stone beds in exhausted sleep.

A well-fed man dressed in blue linen filled the doorway of the house. On his brow crunched a question, and Vernard dropped to the earth to answer it. We were waved inside and out of the weather in short order with no detectable ill will.

The house had wooden floors and decent furniture. Our host had us sit on benches covered in animal furs around a cheery fire.

A stooped man with an ancient brand received our cloaks and soon provided us with a warm drink. Vernard, however, refused his and handed out the portrait of Dorsey to our host instead. Upon receiving the portrait, the man looked repeatedly from it to Vernard.

"If the man is yours," said Vernard, "we will handsomely compensate you for his return."

The master scratched his chin and looked again from the portrait to Vernard. "He is here."

"He is?" Vernard scooted to the edge of his seat. "Thank God."

The master called an attendant from the other room and showed him the portrait. The two exchanged a knowing look. I looked to Vernard to see if he had caught the exchange, but his hands were pressed upon his face as his shoulder raised and lowered. "Fetch him," said the master, and the attendant left at once. The wind blew from the door as it opened and rain splattered the side of my head.

"Allow us just a moment and he will be brought to you," said the master.

"And you are sure it is him?" said Vernard. "Dorsey?"

"To be honest, I do not know his name." The master picked up a dry quill from his desk and passed it from one hand to the next. "But I know that face. It is him. I am sure." The quill spun between his fingers like a tormented flag.

"What are you not telling us?" I said, and my companions looked at me in question. The master, however, bit his lip.

"I treat my slaves well. They are fed plenty, allowed breaks, watered. But this is a dangerous business."

Vernard clutched the arm of the chair until his fingers turned white. Judging from the state of the men outside, I believed he greatly inflated his 'care.'

"There was a cave-in," he continued. "A portion of the roof previously thought stable collapsed and—" He shrugged.

"He is wounded and still you make him work?" Vernard seethed.

"He is not wounded," said the master. "Well – not outwardly."

Vernard's nails dug into the wood. "What happened to my brother?"

"You said you were merchants hired by the family—"

"They are hired." He gestured to us. "I am his kin. What happened?"

The door opened, blasting us with cold rain once more. The attendant returned, clutching the arm of a man so filthy, he appeared to be made of mud with eyes set in among the dirt. The man shuffled as he walked, limping on his right leg while his right arm hung at his side. His gaze remained downcast, away from the light of the fire as if the flames hurt his eyes.

Vernard stepped around his chair. His hands froze reaching halfway out to the man, as if unsure whether or not to gather him to himself. "Dorsey?" he said, and the man's brow creased. With great hesitancy, his head raised, although recognition did not pass before his eyes.

For a moment at least.

Then his eyes lit, and he pulled from the grasp of the attendant, wrapping his left arm around the neck of Vernard. Vernard clutched the man close, holding him as if he might slip away.

After a moment, Vernard held him out from himself. "I didn't understand that, Dorsey."

Dorsey jammed his good hand into his hair, and his lip curled. He forced a single word from his lips: "Four."

Vernard cocked his head to the side. "Four? Four what?"

Dorsey gritted his teeth and repeated the word. "Four."

CHAPTER TWENTY-FOUR

I looked at Marta and Kai, but they, too, seemed just as baffled by the stated "four." They turned back to the master, who had started speaking.

"That's all he's said since the accident: four. I think he took a hit to the head. Hasn't been the same since."

Dorsey gestured wildly, but his right arm hung lower than the left. He stumbled as he shuffled forward, and Vernard's eyes wide, his face scrawled in horror at the state of his brother, clutched his arm to keep him from falling. Then Vernard pulled him close, enveloping him in another embrace.

"When did this happened?" asked Vernard. His gaze flickered to me, and a lump formed in my throat. Would he have been fine if they had not delayed by searching for me?

"The second day he arrived," said the master.

I stifled a release of breath.

"He slept for a week," the master continued, "and we feared he would not wake. Since then, he has not said a word of sense. We've had him doing simple jobs, fetching water for the men mostly." The master stood and rounded his desk. "I am sorry. It is a sad thing to happen to anyone, especially someone young. I could not in good conscience charge you what I paid since he is now an imbecile—"

Vernard grabbed a handful of coins from the purse and threw them at the man. "Then that should suffice." The man blinked in surprise as coins scattered about, falling to the floor, a couple set to spinning. Taking his brother by the arm, Vernard led him from the house.

After a moment of stunned silence, the rest of us rose and followed as well. When we reached them outside, the rain had turned to drizzle, and Vernard was busy fetching a cloak from his saddlebag. Dorsey wrapped the cloak close to himself but continued to shiver.

"We'll get you back to our inn with a cheery fire," said Vernard, rubbing vigorously on his back. "It's not far from here." Dorsey nodded, and Vernard tousled his hair as he attempted the faintest smile I had seen yet.

When we tried to sit Dorsey on a horse, a few of the men beneath the outcropping rose from where they slept to watch. The poor boy could not stand steady enough on his right leg to hook his left foot into the stirrups, so Vernard took him by the middle, and I flipped the right leg over the saddle. Upon being released from around the middle, however, he floundered and slid off the horse back into Vernard's arms.

I looked to the slaves beneath the overhang expecting to find them laughing, but although they watched with interest, they did not so much as chuckle.

For our second attempt, Kai held Dorsey in the saddle while Vernard climbed on behind him. He wrapped his arms around his younger brother and prodded the horse forward with his knees. Kai tied the remaining horse to his own, and the rest of us mounted and followed. Although the rain let up, our journey continued without conversation back to the inn.

When we reached town, heads turned and gazes followed us as we went past. It was a strange sight indeed, a branded and filthy man sharing a horse with a man in a nice cape. Upon reaching the inn, Kai dropped from his horse and moved to help Dorsey down.

Vernard tried to ease him down slowly, but the poor boy collapsed into Kai's arms. Once on stable ground, Dorsey limped forward to the door of the inn, but Vernard scooped him up like a child and carried him inside.

Marta pressed a hand to her mouth as she observed the two, then she dabbed at the moisture gathering around her eye. With a sigh, I dismounted my horse and handed the reins to Kai. "Can you see to them? Marta and I will see if we can help in any way."

"Sure, Zayim." Kai sighed. "Damn, this is bad. Not that we found him. It's just – it would have almost been better to have found him…" He didn't say dead, but I guessed the word nonetheless.

I clamped my hand upon his shoulder. "Perhaps, but we will take in stride what we are given."

Marta and I entered the mostly deserted taproom to find the innkeeper bringing ale to Vernard and Dorsey. Vernard had sat his brother at a table near the fire and draped his arm protectively around his shoulders. As the ale was set upon the table, Dorsey licked his lips. He drew it in with his left arm. A single draught set him to coughing, and Vernard tried to take the pint from him.

Dorsey grasped the handle with his strong arm and slid it away. "Four!" he said and drank some more. Coughing followed, and Vernard tried again to take the tankard, but Dorsey turned his back on him, bringing the pint to his mouth with both hands.

Vernard reached for it again, and Dorsey erected his middle finger, took another drink, and stifled the coughs that followed.

"You are choking!" said Vernard. "You must drink slower. Let me help you."

The young man slammed his fist upon the table and shouted "Four!" at Vernard.

"Dorsey, please, you aren't making any sense," said Vernard. "And I know I'm probably not making much sense to you either, but I'm only trying to help."

Dorsey stood, pressing his good hand against the table for support. His face contorted in rage. He opened his mouth, only to clamp his teeth together in a snarl. "Four," he repeated, his face turning crimson.

"Captain," I said, but Vernard did not turn to me. "Captain!" I said louder.

Vernard lip twitched as he turned. "Not now, weaver!"

"Yes, now." I stepped forward to the young man, but Dorsey retreated from me, bumping into the table behind him.

"You are frightening him!" cried Vernard.

"Look at me, Dorsey," I said. "I'm the type of man you would brag about beating with your left hand tied behind your back, aren't I?"

Dorsey's brow furrowed, and for several seconds said nothing. Then a laugh came from his chest as he clutched and unclutched the fist of the right arm hanging at his side. Vernard glanced at me sideways.

I leaned against the neighboring table and crossed my arms. "Your brother is under the impression you are confused, but I disagree. Am I wrong?"

He swallowed hard before looking between me, Marta, and Vernard. Then he shook his head.

"Then let us prove it. Raise three fingers."

He did so.

"Now four."

Again.

"Now what is the sum of those numbers?"

He looked at his hands as if seeking the answer, then jammed them into his hair once more.

"Okay, okay," I said with placating motion. "You can't show me, but you know it. Is it eight?"

He shook his head vehemently.

"Six?"

Another shake.

"Seven?" To this, he nodded emphatically, and I turned to Vernard. It was clear from his baffled expression, however, that he did not fully grasp what had been demonstrated.

"In the same way my ears do not work, he cannot speak," I said.

"So, he is mute?" said Vernard.

Dorsey nodded with enthusiasm once more.

"I've never heard of such a thing," said Vernard.

I gestured to Dorsey. "I know what it looks like when a man understands but can't speak, and your brother understands you, Vernard. To me, that much is obvious."

Dorsey grasped my hand with both of his. I flinched, surprised at the gesture and the gratitude written upon his face. Had no one else ascertained his ability to understand?

This should not have surprised me, given my own experience with people. I clasped his hand in return, meeting his eyes as I nodded firmly. "Your brother is no imbecile, Vernard, so give the man his damn ale."

A grin rose across Dorsey's face, the white of his teeth accentuated against the grime upon his skin. At the sight of the grin, the disbelief written across Vernard's face fractured. Grabbing hold of his brother's shirt, Vernard drew him close, cupping the base of his head with his calloused hands. "I'm sorry," he said. "My God, am I sorry."

***

There was no further need for pretenses regarding our identities since Dorsey had joined our group, so once he had bathed and his clothes changed, he looked like a wealthy noble once more – except for the raised red burn on his temple in the shape of a lily marking him as a former slave.

He touched the brand a couple of times throughout the meal, wincing as he did. Other than the brand, however, he appeared to be an attractive young man. I guess his age to be around twenty, if not younger.

The similarities between Dorsey and his older brother were uncanny, and not just physically. They had the same facial expressions, the same way of laughing. Besides age and a slight reddish tint to Dorsey's hair, I could have mistaken them for the same person.

After the meal, Vernard insisted on inspecting Dorsey's weak arm as we gathered in chairs about the fire, sipping on ale. The younger brother's lip curled as Vernard straightened out each of his fingers. He was able to make a fist and raise the hand off his leg, but not as high as the other.

"It's alright," Vernard said and tousled his hair. Dorsey smacked his ruffled hair back into place with a scowl, but Vernard grinned.

"You should still try to use it," said Marta. "If you don't, it will only get weaker."

Dorsey looked to us in turn, his brow fiercely creased. His tongue perched upon his lips, but then he shook his head and collapsed back into his seat.

I stood and took Dorsey's empty ale tankard to the bar. After receiving a refill from the innkeeper, I handed it back to him. "Perhaps you are trying too hard. Or perhaps you need to start from the beginning."

"From the beginning?" said Vernard. "What do you mean?"

"I learned to speak by watching how others formed words with their mouth and copying them. If I learned without hearing, I think Dorsey may be able to re-learn if we help him. Start with ale. Watch my lips. Aa—"

Vernard touched my arm. "No offense, Zayim, but perhaps someone who speaks – well – clearer—"

"You say I speak poorly, Vernard?" I pulled my arm away. "You seem to have no trouble understanding me."

"I don't have trouble understanding you. You speak quite well for a deaf man."

"For a deaf man?" I stood. "I have crossed the country to find your brother and have helped him considerably, and now you insult me?"

"I…uh…I do not mean—" Sweat beaded upon his brow.

Then I grinned and glanced at Marta who hid her smile beneath her hand. "I am teasing you, Vernard." It was about time someone broke the tension of our interactions and I had seized upon the moment.

As the color returned to his brother's face, Dorsey cocked back his head and laughed. The others laughed as well, but Vernard shook his head. "I should strangle you for that, weaver," he said, but as he raised his tankard to drink, a smile betrayed him.

"So try it, Dorsey," I said. "Listen to your brother speak and copy him."

"Ale," Vernard said, then elongated the sounds for him. Dorsey formed the word with his mouth and reproduced it to the satisfactory nod of his brother.

"Good," said Vernard. "So you are capable of forming the words. They're just stuck in your head somewhere."

"Four," said Dorsey and swung his head low.

"It will take time," I said, "a lot of time, but you will get there."

He tipped up his tankard and downed it to half before a coughing spell caught him. He leaned back against his seat.

The door to the inn flew open, and Kai darted inside, slamming it closed behind him. "Regis and Sebastian are in the town square with ten guards."

CHAPTER TWENTY-FIVE

"We paid them!" Vernard jumped from his seat, knocked his chair over backwards, and rushed to the window. Turning back, he asked, "What charge could they—?"

"Regis knew of my skills as a weaver," I said. "He will say you cheated him into underselling with your sword. Innkeeper!" The man stepped in from the back, and I met him at the counter. "I…uh…don't know how to ask this, but will you hide us?"

"Certainly, Master Zayim," he said, waving to the back. "Come this way."

I frowned at his eagerness. "You know who I am?"

"You have a reputation and are hard to miss, sir. And I doubt you chose my inn on a whim."

Of course, he was not mistaken. The yellow daisy on the inn's shingle corresponded to the map in the livery Vernard had found the day before. The innkeeper was one of us.

Vernard clutched his brother's arm as we followed the innkeeper, and Marta took my hand. In the kitchen were stairs leading into the cellar lighted by torches. Here, barrels of ale and wine were kept cool. With Kai's help, the innkeeper rolled a massive vat away from the wall, revealing a hiding place carved into the wall.

Upon seeing the dark hole, Dorsey retreated against the opposite wall, his hands splayed against the vat upon which he leaned. He shook his head wildly.

"Dorsey," said Vernard, "it is okay. It will be only for a few moments, not forever. But if we are to make it home, we must hide."

The poor boy trembled against the far wall as he stared into the darkness. Then my companions gazed to the ceiling.

"Someone is knocking," said Marta.

"Dorsey, we have no time."

Still, Dorsey shook his head. "Four."

"Here," the innkeeper grabbed a broom from the corner. "He has just arrived. Those seeking you will not know his face. I will say he is my slave."

Vernard removed Dorsey's cape from his neck and tousled his hair again. "If there's any sign of trouble, run, Dorsey. Find a way to get home." Into his pocket he shoved the remaining silver.

The rest of us retreated into the carved-out space in the wall, and the innkeeper rolled the vat back over us. Through a crack, I watched as the innkeeper climbed back up the stairs leaving Dorsey standing in the middle of the room with the broom.

The poor boy stared wide-eyed at the stairs as he tossed the broom back and forth between his hands. The weaker one faltered, however, and he dropped it. We had not had time yet to tell him all that occurred on our journey to fetch him, so he was undoubtedly confused as to why we were hiding.

As he retrieved the broom from the floor, three guards barreled down the stairs in a rush of shadows. Dorsey startled as they surrounded him, and he drew the broom close to his chest. Movement rippled on the other side of Marta from Vernard, and I imagined him gathering his sword.

Dorsey glanced once to the vat then peeled his gaze away. The soldier before him was tall and wide in the shoulders. A broadsword hung sheathed upon his back and a dagger dangled from his side. He wore a cape similar to Vernard's, although his broach was of different design. A captain of the magistrate.

He spoke to Dorsey, and the boy bit his lip. "Four," he replied.

"Yes, four people," said the Captain. "Three men and a woman. One deaf and branded."

"F-four," answered Dorsey.

Anger creased the brow of the soldier, and he raised his hand. Dorsey cringed, waiting on the blow, but then they both turned toward the stairs to where the innkeeper descended with Sebastian and another guard. I did not catch what was said, but the innkeeper placed a hand upon Dorsey's shoulder then tapped a finger to his head. The Captain of the Magistrate rolled his eyes and motioned for his men to check the room.

A scowl remained fixed upon Sebastian's face as he rounded the cellar with a torch, and I reflected on the half-finished dress and the sister that owned it. I could not go back now. If I did, I would die at that house, either by the hand of his father during punishment or by a wolf trying to escape. I knew nothing about fighting, but if the vat rolled away, I would charge Sebastian first and try to rend his head from his shoulders with the knife Kai had given me.

They rounded the cellar, pounding on walls, stomping on the floor, searching everywhere with their eyes and ears. The crack I peered through was no more than a slit, but as they neared me, I turned my head, fearing the light might reflect in my eyes.

After several more attempts at finding hidden passageways or smuggler's holes, they ascended the stairs once more, leaving Dorsey and his broom behind. The boy sank onto a crate and scraped his brow with the back of his sleeve. He looked to our hiding place and gave a stiff nod. I, too, let out a sigh of relief.

Now we just had to hope they would leave the inn entirely. Unfortunately, our arrival at the inn this afternoon had not gone unnoticed. What story had the innkeeper concocted? Would it send them away, or would they watch the house?

With a look of alarm, Dorsey turned his head to the stairs once more, and the innkeeper descended. He gestured for Dorsey to leave the cellar with him and took the torch as well. The entrance to the stairs was covered, plunging us into darkness.

Seconds turned to minutes turned to hours and still we waited for some sign of activity from the inn. If my companions heard anything, there was no way for them to relay the information to me. Tremors started in my own arms as anxiety threatened to overtake me, but if Dorsey had managed to keep it together, so could I. So, I bit my knuckle to distract me from the sensation, holding in my wavering breaths. This nothingness, this foreboding silence, felt like a curtain resting upon me.

Never before had I been on this side of things, and I began to reflect on what I should have done to make the hole in my floor more comfortable. Some straw, perhaps. A candle for when the darkness took hold of one's nerves. A candle here, however, would have given away our position.

More than anything, I should have given updates to those in my care. My days went by as normal with one foot upon the trapdoor that concealed my charges. I never considered whispering to them, telling them everything was fine. But at least they were not alone as I weaved above them.

Marta pressed a flask of water into my hand, and I drank a few sips of it. Were we to stay here the whole of the night? Was it night already?

A light flashed from the stairs once more as someone descended into the cellar: the innkeeper's wife. Through the slit she wiggled bits of cheese and bread that I passed to Marta behind me. Then she pressed her face into the crack, and I felt her breath upon me. Marta's chest vibrated as she replied back to the woman. I suppose this was the update I was hoping for. Too bad I missed it.

Once the woman left, the others knelt crouching in the bottom of the hiding hole. I crouched with them and settled in, assuming it was for the night. It would have been nice to have performed some personal business beforehand, however. The space was tight, and each movement was a shared experience.

After a few hours of unpleasant dozing, another flash of light came from the stairs. I looked out, hoping to see the innkeeper. Instead, it was a young lad and Dorsey. Kai moved the vat, and I nearly tumbled out of the hiding place. Upon standing, I arched my back, stretched my arms, then hopped in place to return blood to my legs.

"Come with me!" The boy waved us to the stairs, and I took Marta's hand as we followed him out of the cellar.

It was dark outside when we entered the main floor, and the lad led all of us to a backdoor where a cart sat waiting. Two strangers lifted up hay, and we hid ourselves within the load. Once we were all seated, a tarp was spread above the straw, and the cart lurched forward but only went a few blocks. When it stopped, I began to rise up, but Marta pressed her hand against my chest.

We sat together, hidden among the hay, until the sun rose, streaming gray light in through the tarp. The light was enough for me to see Marta's face and mouth, and I desperately wished to ask her what was going on, but feared being heard. She must have seen the discomfort upon my face, however, and mouthed, "Everything is fine. We are getting out."

I nodded fervently, and she squeezed my hand tighter.

Near what I guessed by the light to be nine in the morning, the cart lurched forward once more, bumping along the cobbles. Then it came to another stop. Through the tarp, I saw the silhouette of a pike above us.

Were we being stopped by soldiers? Or were we at the gate?

Finally, the cart moved again, and the driver continued for another hour. Suddenly, the light above us dimmed, and the cart lurched to a stop. The tarp was pulled back, and the others sat up, cueing me to do so as well.

Wood aged gray surrounded us on all sides, and behind a stall door, a tan cow ground hay between her teeth. A couple of chickens strutted about the place, pecking at odd intervals. Our guide, a man I had never met with a scraggly beard, smiled at us and told us we were safe.

"You will stay here for the night," he said. "Your next guide will be here in the morning."

From the hay in the loft, the farmer formed beds, and his wife brought in quilts. Within the hay beds we found traces of others who had stayed before us: a lost doll, a few buttons, an old chicken bone. Hidden beneath an old board, Kai pulled out a game of backgammon. Although several acres of property surrounded the homestead on all sides and chances of being seen were unlikely, we stayed inside the barn and waited.

Vernard knew how to play backgammon, and soon we set to compete in tournament fashion. Dorsey and I alternated for champion, but he would have beaten me every time had he not been irritated by his weak hand.

Thankfully, Dorsey's affected arm was stronger than his leg, but his movements were awkward and haphazard. More than once, he swiped the board clean of checkeres while trying to move his across the way. He tried switching to his stronger left hand, but we, his companions, prodded him to switch back. Both Vernard and Kai had seen a few head wounds during their time as soldiers, but none knew how best to treat them. It seemed proper, however, not to neglect the hand. It was slow and awkward to go about this way, but we were patient. I believe the others' time with me aided in this.

The most impatient of us all was Dorsey, however. Often, he shouted at his own hand, and the frustration regarding his speech was obvious. I had no answer for him in this. If I had not been born deaf, the injury occurred so soon after that it might as well have occurred at birth. This was my world, and I knew no better.

We stayed the night in the barn and were preparing for another night when Kai alerted us to a rider approaching the house. As I peered through the slats of the barn, I smiled in recognition of the young man in the saddle. "It's a friend," I said and made for the ladder.

A smile broke across Faustin's face as I emerged from the barn, and he dropped from the saddle to embrace me. "Zayim! Father was worried about you when we hadn't heard anything from you or Marta. Are you all well?"

"Better than we should be," I said, reflecting on our misadventures.

"We should get out of sight, sir."

Once we were inside the barn and the usual introductions were completed, Faustin explained his concern about our being seen in the middle of nowhere. "Reward is being offered for information regarding your whereabouts," said Faustin. "Spies, they are calling you."

"That's a bit drastic," said Kai.

The boy shrugged. "But no matter. If we can get you to Candorlan, the Abbess will know what to do."

Vernard pulled at his chin. "The Abbess of Candorlan. I should have guessed your people would be in league with an outspoken liberationist like her."

I opened my mouth to reply to this statement, but the farmer entered the barn. He took in Faustin, then he extended an item wrapped in cloth. "From the wife."

Wrapped inside the cloth were some pieces of cheese and dried beef. "Thank you." I smiled graciously at him.

The farmer scratched his head and nodded sheepishly. "My wife's grandfather was a slave. Anyone who helps people with such a fate is more than deserving."

Vernard jammed his foot into the earth, causing a small hill to form. With a sigh, he reached into his purse and removed several coins. "I would like this to be split between you and the innkeeper," he said as he pressed the coins into the farmer's hand.

The farmer's eyes grew huge as he looked between the coins and Vernard. "Sir, I cannot."

"You have saved my and my brother's lives," he said. "It is the least I can do."

The farmer's face grew crimson, but he nodded and took the coins. "I will pass on the innkeeper's share. You have my word."

Vernard nodded. "And you, my trust."

I forced my mouth closed as I observed the exchange. Had this journey grown the man's soul? But as I looked to Dorsey, he did not seem surprised by the expression of gratitude coming from his brother. Perhaps I had misjudged Vernard's black-and-white view of the world. Or perhaps a personal favor outweighed his loyalty to the office of the magistrate.

Without further ado, we loaded up in the farmer's cart once more, and a tarp was laid over our heads. Straw was placed on top of this, but light still passed enough for me to see Marta's face beside me. Soon the wagon jerked forward and I let out a long sigh. One more day until we reached Candorlan and safety.

The first time I met the Abbess of Candorlan, she was a novitiate only months from taking her final vows. Three months into Kai's employment, he expressed concern regarding his family and if they had received news of his enslavement. More than anything, he feared they thought he was dead. I had not once considered his relations as I had none of my own. It was a daft oversight, and I felt like a simpleton for not having thought of it sooner.

"Are you referring to your wife and children?" I asked, holding my breath and praying for a no.

"My mother and sisters," he said. "I have no wife and my father passed on a year ago."

"Ah," I said and released a subtle exhale. A wife and child would draw him home. A mother and sister less so. "You can write to them if you wish, and I will send the letter under my name."

"My mother does not know how to read, sir. Although my sister might. She is a nun after all. They teach nuns to read, do they not?"

In truth, I did not know either. But we sent a letter to Sister Marie of the nunnery in Candorlan nonetheless. Kai and I worded the letter carefully so as not to reveal his freedom if it were intercepted, and I signed it. Once the letter was sent, I forgot about it, until the gray habit of the nun darkened my door.

Kai was out purchasing supplies in the market when the metal flap above the door caught my attention. I recognized her immediately as Kai's sister as their facial features are similar. "I wish to see your master," she said.

"I am a freeman. My name is Zayim."

"Zayim the weaver?" she asked, peering past me into my shop.

"I am."

The nun stood silent for a moment as her eyes bore into my brand. Then she cleared her voice and said, "If you are Zayim the weaver, then it was you who purchased my brother, Hezekiah. I wish to purchase him back." From her satchel, she removed a silver candelabra.

My eyes grew wide at the object, taking in the woolen habit and wooden cross about her neck. I pulled her inside, closed the door, and locked it. "A nun could not afford such a thing. Did you steal this?"

"What does it matter to you?" she asked, pulling away from me. "Will it suffice for payment? If not, I have gold as well." She reached into her pocket, but I clasped my hand about her wrist to find it shaking. How many vows had she broken to be standing at my door?

"Be still," I said. "If your brother is the man I call Kai, then yes, I purchased him. But I do not keep him against his will."

Marie snatched back her hand. "I do not understand. You wrote to me saying he was your slave. What do you want from me if not money for his return?"

"He was a slave, but—" Then his face passed before the shop window. "Ask him yourself, Sister."

The door opened, and Kai stepped inside, arms laden with wares. He stopped short upon seeing his sister, and in haste, he set the parcels on the ground and drew her into an embrace. Kai pressed his hand to her cheek, swiping away the tears gliding down her face. Warmth flooded my cheeks as I looked about the room, embarrassed by my intrusion on the emotional reunification.

After a moment, Kai motioned to me. "You have met my employer, Zayim."

"Employer?"

Kai relayed the story of the auction house from his point of view. The way he told it, I had beaten down three of the auctioneer's men to place my bid then thrown the shackles at the feet of the slavers. Warmth grew over my face at the startling heroics.

"It was not as dramatic as all that," I told the nun, but she considered me with parted lips.

"You saved my brother," she breathed. "A man you did not know. But why?"

And for that, I could not find an answer. There were pragmatic reasons for purchasing him, yes. But I did not have to free Kai. In fact, I had risked a great deal in doing so. So, I answered her, "Because I wished to make a friend instead of an enemy."

And by doing so, I gained two friends.

Marie, like Kai, had never been a liberationist or had even taken a second glance at the laws of our nations as they regarded slavery. Until that day. After this, however, a passion seized her and she devoted her life to the freedom of the enslaved.

Due to this passion, she gained many enemies, but also friends. Some of those friends were prominent members of the church in Rome. It was not long before she gained the title of Abbess and took over the nunnery in Candorlan. Now the nunnery was synonymous with freedom for my people. A New Jerusalem for those in bondage.

Morning woke me as light streamed through the tarp, and as usual, my peers were still sleeping. I guessed sounds woke them rather than light, but had never pondered enough to ask. The cart continued to rock along the road, but I noticed Faustin lying among us instead of Kai. If the sun was up, however, we would need to switch soon. And within a few minutes, just as I predicted, Kai pulled off the road and raised the corner of the tarp.

After a brief breakfast of beer and bread, we set to the road once more with Faustin driving. Per Kai, a town was coming up. Faustin was going to circumvent the town, but we kept the chatter to a minimum in case we passed anyone else upon the road. Beneath the tarp, I twiddled my thumbs and wished Marta knew how to read lips so at least we could better pass the time conversing. Never had I been away from home for so long, and I was quite ready to be done with this journey.

Suddenly, Marta went rigid against the floor of the cart, and her eyes grew wide with fear. Kai, on the other side of me, stiffened as well and I knew they heard something. I, too, froze, afraid my very breath would give us away.

The cart shuddered to a stop and lingered there for some time, waiting. Had we been ordered to halt by a guard? Damn that it be Faustin at the reins and not someone with more experience! Would the boy's façade fracture when put to the test? He was so young for such a lie!

A weight pressed against the tarp, and I jumped at the sudden sensation. The pressure reduced as suddenly as it had descended, then came down once more. This time, Dorsey sat up, clutching his leg. His face contorted in pain, and the hand came away bloody.

CHAPTER TWENTY-SIX

Vernard ripped back the tarp and the brilliant light blinded me. It took a moment for my vision to focus, and then I saw Vernard warring with a soldier for the shaft of a pitchfork. The cart was surrounded by fifteen men, all armed and angry. Knife in hand, Kai leaped upon the soldier nearest the wagon, tackling him to the earth.

Vernard wrestled the pitchfork free and struck the man over the head with the shaft of the weapon before stabbing another with the prongs. A man grabbed him from the back, however, toppling him from the cart. It took three to subdue Kai, but soon, he lay kneeling upon the road with a sword to his throat. The remaining soldiers turned their weapons on us: the youth, the mute, the woman, and the deaf man.

A man with a scar across his forehead, clearly the leader, stepped forward, glaring at the two fighters in our group before ordering, "Get out of the cart."

Having no way to battle these men-of-arms, Marta and I scooted to the edge of the cart and dropped down. Faustin and I aided Dorsey down as he clutched his bleeding leg. Only one of the prongs had caught him, but the wound looked deep and turned his pant leg red.

Two men emerged from the trees on the side of the road on horseback. I recognized one of the riders as Sebastian and the broach on the other man marked him as the Captain of the Magistrate we had seen in the wine cellar. "Are these them?" the Captain asked Sebastian.

"I do not recognize those two." Sebastian pointed to Dorsey and Faustin. "But the others, yes. They are them."

Attention turned to Vernard, who spoke from where he knelt upon the ground, his hands lashed behind him. "I demand an audience with the magistrate!"

"I am of the magistrate," said the Captain. "I speak on his behalf."

"Not as it concerns matters of the state," said Vernard. "I have in my pocket an agreement signed by the Marquis of Halfshire giving me status as a diplomat in your country. It will be honored and I shall receive my audience."

The Captain nodded to a soldier, and the paper was extracted from Vernard's pocket and passed to him. He glanced over the page and then eyed Vernard with a curled lip. "You are of Burganne?"

"Yes," said Vernard. "You witness there the seal of my king and the Marquis of Halfshire. The document is binding."

"This document is impressive," said the Captain. "And would be helpful if the treaties between our country had held. As it is, we are now at war. All diplomatic statuses have been rescinded and those remaining in the country with them are to be marked as spies."

"What?" blurted Vernard.

The Captain folded over the paper. "Hang them."

"No!" I cried, stepping toward him. A blow struck my head, and I fell to my knees. The soldier behind me grabbed my arms and the coarse feeling of rope wrapped around my wrists. Terror etched across Marta's face as her hands were secured as well. "No!" I cried louder, standing. "You cannot! We are not spies!"

"Sir," said Sebastian, "do as you must, but my slave there—"

"Right," said the Captain, then nodded to my soldier. "Bring him here."

I was dragged by my arm away from the others and shoved to the ground at Sebastian's feet. Sebastian's nostrils flared as he looked down upon me.

"Sir, my friends have done nothing. You must plead for their freedom," I said to him.

"And why the hell would I care about your friends?" he sneered.

I pressed my forehead against Sebastian's feet. "Please, Master. You cannot allow this!"

He shook me off. "I would not help you even if I had a say."

My vision blurred. "Please!" I cried, bending toward his feet once more, but he took a step back.

Kai lowered his shoulder and charged at the soldiers and received a blow to the head for his efforts. Vernard continued to snarl complaints at the Captain while Dorsey shouted his word. Faustin cried. Marta shoved and kicked against the man who held her, and he brought her to the ground, pressing her face into the dirt. Through tears, she gazed at me, pleading.

A soldier tossed a noose over a tree branch and secured it.

Sebastian watched with his arms crossed, cool and silent, his attention no longer upon me. Like others before him, he viewed me without fear, and rightly so. I had no fight in me, before or after what was taken. Not for my own freedom at least, but for my friends?

For Marta?

Stretching as far as the ropes would allow, I slid my hand into my pocket and took hold of the knife Kai had given me. With a flip of my wrist, the blade was unsheathed and I cut through my ropes. Still, Sebastian continued to watch the others, a smile of triumph rising upon his lips.

The soldiers took hold of Kai first, the bane of this mission, leading him to the noose. Another rope was hung from a nearby tree, and the guards took hold of Vernard next.

Clutching the knife tight, I rose from the ground, wrapped my arm around Sebastian's neck, and jammed the knife against his ribs.

CHAPTER TWENTY-SEVEN

"Captain!" I called, and the man of the magistrate turned to me. His hand reached for the broadsword upon his back but kept it sheathed upon seeing the blade against the young noble's ribs.

Sebastian shifted, trying to pull away from my grasp, and I jammed the knife into his skin, piercing the flesh but not deeply. He retreated against the pain, but I kept my hold about his neck.

"Do not try that again or I will kill you," I said, surprised by the calmness of my own words. His chest rumbled against mine as he spoke. "I can't hear you, remember? Now nod if you understand me, Sebastian."

His head bobbed up and down.

"What do you hope to gain, slave?" said the Captain. "A noose for yourself?"

"I wish for what most men do: peace, love, security. And I would rather die than live without them. Now drop your weapons and release my friends."

Marta flipped her hair about, gaining my attention. "Behind you!" she mouthed.

Keeping the knife pressed into Sebastian, I turned to see the man approaching with sword drawn. "Do you wish him dead? Join the others where I can see you!" I ordered.

With a sneer, the man re-sheathed his sword and obeyed.

"Now," I said, turning back to them, "you will begin releasing my friends or I will press this dagger inwards, an inch per minute of your delay." I increased the pressure on the blade, and Sebastian's chest vibrated with his cry.

The Captain's lip rose in a snarl as he unsheathed his sword and tossed it from him. The weapons of his men came next. "You will regret this, slave. I will see your entire family killed."

"That's a rather short list," I muttered then nodded to Kai. "You will untie that one first."

Upon the Captain's order, Kai's bonds were removed. After rounding up the weapons and tossing them into the woods, Kai asked, "Would you like to switch, Zayim?"

"Absolutely," I said, and Kai took control of Sebastian while the soldiers released Marta and the others. "What should we do with them, Vernard?"

"Hang them," he said with a sneer.

"Uh, no," I said. "Something less final."

"We should tie them up," said Marta. "A patrol will come by and release them in due time."

"They will follow us," said Vernard. "If we kill them, there will be no witnesses to what has happened here. No one will know we came through here."

Kai looked around the woods and then up at the sky. "I think we can make it, Zayim."

The Captain of the Nostria Magistrate laughed. "You wish to reach the nunnery, don't you? You think a silly nun can save you?"

I looked to Kai and Marta, weighing the risks of such a journey. Rumors of the Abbess's influence had reached me, but I had never seen it for myself. There was no chance we would be able to make it to the country border before we were pursued, at least not while the soldiers were alive.

"We go for the Abbess," I said. "Tie them up and get ready to run."

CHAPTER TWENTY-EIGHT

As we bounced along the road, Marta tore bandages from the hem of her dress and wrapped Dorsey's leg as best she could. His face had turned a dangerous shade of pale, and his hands were cold to the touch. Vernard wrapped his arm around the young man and helped him sip water from his flask.

Faustin remained silent as a stone as he stared at the walls of the cart. Occasionally his hand would reach for his throat and he would swallow hard.

"Not as fun as anticipated, Faustin?" I asked and immediately regretted my words as his terror-filled gaze rose to mine.

"I'm sorry," he said as moisture filled his eyes once more.

I moved to sit beside him and draped my arm over his shoulders. "It was not a critique, and I am the one who should be sorry. This was not a good mission for you to have been involved with." I pulled him into my chest, and tears tumbled from his eyes. I shielded him as he cried and looked at Marta who bit her lip.

Kai's estimations were correct, and, within an hour's time, we rounded a bend to find the white stone walls of the abbey on the horizon before us. A square tower stood in the left corner of the walls where a man-at-arms watched us. A bow rested in his hand, strung and ready. Behind the great walls stood the keep, also a structure made of stone with a smaller rotunda in front and a larger one rising above it in back. Two massive doors made of wood with iron brackets stood closed upon the walls.

I had not realized just how close we were to the abbey, and now that we were here, everything became clear. As the Abbess held no secrets regarding her views on slavery, Sebastian and the Captain had doubtlessly set their trap close to the nunnery in case we were to flee there. We should have anticipated this, and I chided myself for not having done so.

"The flag," said Faustin to Kai. "It's under the buckboard. You must raise it to gain entry."

Kai reined in the horses and found the flag as described. Once a golden flores de lis on a background of black rose above us, the massive doors swung open. As we entered, heads swiveled to us, curious about the new arrivals.

"State your business here," said a man with a spear beside the gate. His head was covered with a helmet, but part of a brand hid beneath it.

"I am Hezekiah, brother of the Abbess," said Kai. "She is expecting us."

To this announcement, Vernard's mouth popped open as he looked from me to Kai. "Of course," he said to no one in particular. Had he heard of the brother of the Abbess? It was not unlikely as she spoke of him and his 'adventures' publicly when arguing for the freedom of slaves.

The spearman nodded in acknowledgment to Kai's statement and sent a lad to fetch her. As we entered further into the courtyard, the gates swung closed once more.

Faustin slid out from beneath my arm and stood. "Ranae!" he cried then leaped over the edge of the cart.

Ranae, who wore the dress I had made for her, descended the steps of the keep, her smile wide. Faustin embraced her, spinning her in a circle. Then he pressed her against himself, pinching his eyes closed.

Kai looked over his shoulder to me. "Well, that is something no one foresaw."

I chuckled despite our circumstances and dropped from the cart as well. A gurney was brought for Dorsey, as well as a trio of nuns. They swept him up upon the litter and carried him inside, Vernard fast on their heels. The rest of us unloaded and were offered seating, food, and water outside the guardroom. As Marta and I sat beside each other, I slid my hand into hers. A great wave of exhaustion flowed over me. Marta pressed her hand against my arm. "Are you alright, Zayim?"

"I shall be, my love. I am just – how close I came to losing you again after only recently finding you. What if they try to take us once more?"

"The Abbess will know what to do."

"The Abbess is but a nun."

Kai folded his arms and leaned back in his seat. "Do not sell the Abbess so short. She has great influence."

"We are fighting amongst kings."

"Have you forgotten God?" asked Kai.

I closed my eyes and pressed my hands against them once more. We had fallen into bad times for sure, but I could not blame God for this. It was the sins of man that brought us to this point. "Of course not."

The doors to the main building opened once more, and a woman, tall and broad in the shoulders, descended the stone steps. With the wimple hiding most of her other features, it was as if a softer version of Kai approached us.

Kai stood and opened his arms wide, and the nun disappeared inside them for a moment. Marta and I stood as well.

"It has been too long, Kai!" she said, holding him at arm's length. "You should have visited me sooner than now!"

"You will have to blame my Zayim for that," he said with a wink in my direction.

The Abbess's grin grew as she took me in and wrapped her arms around me then Marta. "It is good to see you safe, Zayim. You have given us many scares of late."

"Yes," I said. "Far too many scares for a lifetime, I would say. Unfortunately, it is not over, and I fear my actions may bring repercussions upon you and your convent."

"Oh?" She pressed a hand to her cheek in mock horror. "Heaven forbid the arrival of conflict."

"Abbess, I do not believe you understand the extent of the trouble about to arrive on your doorstep—"

Her smile filled with gentleness. "Whatever trouble has entered here, it will be dealt with in due time. Until then, there are those to whom you need to attend. Namely your son and Sloan. They are awaiting your visit in the house three doors down."

I bit my lip, not wanting to leave without fully discussing the oncoming struggle, but she turned from me to speak with Kai, dismissing me from the conversation. I opened my mouth to speak further, but Marta tugged on my hand, nodding in the direction of the house.

"That was a bit rude, wasn't it?" I asked once we were out of earshot. "Turning from me like that to speak to Kai? We have known each other for a long time. She knows how I have to communicate. And the way she dismissed my concerns—"

"There was a tone of urgency in her voice, Zayim," said Marta. "I do not think your concerns were dismissed, but I believe she has much to do now that members of the magistrate are involved and in pursuit of a spy."

"So, her tone was filled with urgency but spoken with flippancy," I said. "Is that a good thing or a bad thing?"

Marta shrugged. "How should I know?"

The nunnery in Candorlan was now lauded as a sanctuary for runaway slaves and defended by many figures of high authority in the church. But the nunnery still sat within the borders of Aquilla, and not even their high walls could keep out the king if he wished to enter.

As I entered the indicated house behind Marta, I glanced over my shoulder as if expecting the Captain and his men to be leaping over the walls at this moment. When arms wrapped around my shoulders, I jerked back in fright, nearly toppling backward through the door.

"Sorry, Father," Etienne said, his hands raised in apology. "I did not mean to startle you."

But startled me he had, not just by his touch but by the sheer attempt at an embrace on his part. I cleared my throat. "It is nothing. Just distraction."

He opened his arms wide once more, and I allowed him the gesture of affection, but not without passing a look of bewilderment to Marta standing beside me. She shrugged, as if not knowing what had changed that earned me such endearment.

Etienne's hair was brown and curly like my own, but his face was that of his mother. An old scar sat upon his temple: a triskelion from the forge of his former master. And the source of my greatest regret. The house was cozy and simple with a table and chairs in the center; the sleeping quarters were divided from the rest of the space by a thatch partition. Sloan stood beside the fire, spoon suspended above a steaming kettle, glaring at me and Marta as we entered. If she was still capable of a friendly expression, I had not witnessed it in years.

Etienne released me with a final squeeze of the shoulder and motioned us to sit at the table. With a grin, he removed a bottle of wine from the cupboard and set this and three goblets out for us. "This is from the vineyard, father. It's an excellent beverage."

"Thank you, Etienne," said Marta with a smile as she took the drink.

I, however, swirled it about the cup, suspicious about the warmth I was receiving as I sat with my back to Sloan. Etienne sat across from me, biting his lip, waiting for me to take a sip. I, however, set the cup on the table and folded my hands. His face fell at my rejection of the drink, but he looked to Marta next. "It's good to see you, Marta. I'm glad you both are well. Although I must say, you do look tired."

"It's been a long trip," I said.

"Yes, the Abbess said you had quite a bit of trouble. You found the man though? The son of the magistrate?"

"No one should be after you on my account any longer," I said, leaning back in my chair. Etienne and Marta looked beyond me to where Sloan stood. A hue of pink rose upon Etienne's cheeks and Marta bit her lip.

"She's doing it, isn't she?" I asked Marta. "Speaking about me behind my back." I peered over my shoulder, and Sloan snapped her jaw shut. With a final glare, she turned back to a basket of linens which she folded in sharp, abrupt movements. I turned back to Marta and Etienne and asked, "What did she say about me this time?"

"It matters not, Father," said Etienne. "I know she spouts lies."

I took a sip of wine, determined to forget her and her half-truth slanders. "If you wish, I will have the Captain accompanying us write you a guarantee of safe travel and you can return home."

"Thank you, Father. I will consider that, but…" He shook his head slowly. "I may wish to stay in Aquilla. I find the people here agreeable."

"I would hope so. They are primarily nuns." Has he fallen in love with one of them?

"Actually, they are not," said Etienne. "They are primarily former slaves. Like us."

"Are they? Hmm, I suppose that might be possible."

"Yes, and what's more, they all seem to know of you."

I scratched my cheek, unsure about the statement and if anything was insinuated by it. "I have been a liberationist for a long time. Since you were born, in fact."

"Father," he said, then covered his hand with his mouth. His face contorted, pinched as if in pain. Once under control, he dropped his hand. "By the time news of your planned execution reached us, the intended date had already passed. I did not even know you were involved in such things or at risk, and suddenly…" Tears collected around his eyes. "And suddenly you were gone. Father, I thought you died."

My mouth formed an O. Not in surprise from what he thought, but that he had cared. "I'm – I'm sorry, Etienne." I glanced at Marta to see if she was as surprised as I was, but her eyes were filled with sympathy instead. "It was not my intention to cause you worry."

"When word reached us," he continued, "I don't know, Father. It was like I saw you for the first time. And I realized how unfair I had been to you. I had blamed you for my being sold in the first place, then for being so miserable when I came home to Mother. But when I learned what you were doing for other slaves, what you were risking… Father, I am sorry for how I treated you. You were only trying to do what was best for me."

As I sat before my son, taking in his words, I felt warmth drain from my face. I was stupefied, unable to believe this moment was real. Words I had been craving to hear for years were being spoken to me by the son I loved more than life itself. And I had no speech to give in return.

"I'm sorry," said Etienne, glancing to Marta. "Did I speak too fast or—"

"I understood your words, Etienne," I said, then cleared my throat. "I am just—" Emotion caught in my throat, and Marta slid her hand into mine beneath the table and squeezed. I cleared my throat once more. "I am glad to hear this, Etienne. And I do accept your apology. I am sorry as well. I regret that you were pulled into any of this business with the magistrate, and I regret that I did not send word to you myself regarding my fate. I never wished this life for you."

"Father, I have a good life. I am free, and I have wanted for nothing. The people here at the nunnery…" Etienne shook his head. "The things they witnessed, what they fled. I have no right to complain. I never knew how much you saved me until I spoke with them and learned what it was that you suffered. How you and Mother both suffered from the loss of a child. I think about that often, especially now."

I cocked my head to the side. "Especially now?"

"I…uh…" Redness rose to Etienne's cheeks as a smile played on his lips. "Father, there is someone I would like you to meet."

From behind the partition entered a beautiful girl with hair the color and shine of silk. She possessed a womanly shape and a bump gathered on her abdomen. My eyes grew wide as I stared at the bump, and for the second time in my visit, I sat in shocked silence. Finally, I turned to Marta in question.

"You kept this from me?"

"It was not my secret to tell," she said with a wink.

"My name is Chloe," said the girl, stepping forward with an outstretched hand. "It is a pleasure to meet you, sir."

Numbly, I took the hand, surprised by the callouses along the tips of her fingers. These were a working woman's hands.

"Etienne tells me that if I speak plainly, you will understand me."

"Yes, lady. As long as you are facing me." I turned to Etienne. "And just what are your intentions here, Etienne? I see she has no ring upon her finger."

"We were waiting on you. I did not wish to marry without your blessing."

"My blessing? You have my insistence! It will be done at once! We are in a nunnery after all. It will not be hard to find a priest."

"The Abbess has already sent for one," said Etienne. "Father, please do not be angry. I know what we did was not proper, but—"

I sneered at the lad. "Not proper? Dammit, Etienne, do you lack all self-control?" Etienne's shoulders slumped, his face falling like a curtain. Still, I continued, "You have shamed yourself, this girl, and your mother. How could you—?"

Marta gripped my arm, turning me to herself. "Zayim, a word please."

"Why did you say nothing?" I snarled.

"If I had known you would act so poorly, I would have said something. Now step outside with me, please." Without waiting for a reply, she turned for the door. After a final sneer in Etienne's direction, I followed her out.

"What?" I grumbled with arms spread wide.

"What happened to the sweet, compassionate man I entered the house with?" she asked. "For the first time in his life, Etienne has spoken to you with kindness, offering you grace for the circumstances surrounding his birth. Now he has made a similar mistake and you get angry with him?"

"He should know better because of my mistakes!" My hands shook as I spoke.

"No, that is not it. You are not just angry. You act afraid. Why are you afraid?"

I scoffed. "Afraid? Why in hell would I not be afraid with the whole damn army of Aquilla bearing down on us, and now my son's whore is with child."

"You think her a whore?" asked Marta. "You have barely met her, Zayim. She's quite nice, from a decent home, and an excellent cook."

"He's too young!" I cried.

"He's near the same age as you when you fathered him."

"And look how well that turned out!"

Marta paused. "Zayim, Etienne is not you. He is not a slave. He is not deaf. And the child will not be taken. What happened to you will not happen to him."

I ground my teeth. She was right, and I knew it, but—

I had been with Sloan one night when she conceived. It was an impulsive mistake on both of our parts. In sincerity, I could not be angry with Etienne for making the same mistake as his father, especially since I had not been there to guide him as I should have. But the fire in my chest did not easily abate. "He has sinned."

"Yes, but he is doing the right thing now, Zayim. He will not leave her destitute. And I have already seen him with her. He is quite attentive. The child would be looked after, and they shall be married."

I stared at the dirt, seeing her words, but not willing to accept them. But slowly, reason whittled into my conscience. Like a creek after being cleared of debris, my anger slipped through.

"Have you considered, my love, what this makes you? You will be a grandfather." With a look of glee, Marta slipped her hand into the bag on her shoulder. From within, she drew out a green blanket edged in white. I ran my fingers across the soft woolen fibers, and the tightness in my throat intensified.

"This was not in the crate," I said. "I thought it was lost."

"No, it wasn't lost. I just did not wish to risk something so precious on a journey and—"

I drew Marta in, planting a kiss on her cheek. "You are wonderful. Thank you."

Redness rose to her cheeks, but I did not care. The praise was well-deserved. With a deep breath, I reached for the door once more. As we entered, Sloan's eyes locked onto the blanket in my hand.

"Etienne," I said, extending the blanket to him and Chloe, "I weaved this for you before you were born. Unfortunately, we never had occasion to wrap you in it. I would like you to have it for this child."

"It is beautiful," said Chloe, her gaze shifting between me and the cloth.

"And to you, lady," I said, taking a new seat facing Sloan this time, "I owe an apology. Please, tell me about yourself. I would like to know more about the woman my son will marry."

Sloan turned back to the kitchen, tossing bowls about.

"Thank you," Etienne said to Marta, and I squeezed her hand once more.

CHAPTER TWENTY-NINE

A gust of wind struck my back, and those seated at the table turned to look behind me. I turned as well to see Kai standing in the doorway, clutching the doorframe as he leaned in. "Excuse the intrusion, but they are here. Zayim, you're needed at the gate."

The peace that had settled over me from being with my small family retreated, and dread took up residence once more. "Keep the women inside," I said, standing. "Lock the doors and let no one through."

Marta clutched my forearm. "I'm coming with you."

I opened my mouth to protest, but the steadfast look in her eyes showed me it would be no use. Etienne would cave to her demands in a moment if I left her.

"Lock the doors," I emphasized to Etienne once more before following Kai back out. In the courtyard, people bustled about, gathering children and belongings to be taken inside. By the time we made it to the gate, hardly anyone not armed still remained in the open. The guards eyed us closely as we approached the closed gates where Vernard stood waiting, his sword about his waist and a shirt of mail over his chest.

"How is Dorsey?" I asked.

"He has lost some measure of blood," said Vernard, "but the nuns are optimistic. At the moment I am more concerned about what is going on out there. There are many more men outside than ambushed us. They must have sent word to their magistrate."

"We were not far from town when we were ambushed," said Kai, inspecting his knife as he spoke. "The Abbess says we are to be courageous and trust God."

"Does that mean she has a plan?" asked Marta.

"I bloody well hope so."

"I should turn myself in," I said. "This is between Sebastian and I—"

Vernard shook his head. "That will solve nothing, weaver."

A hand rested on my elbow, and I turned to see the Abbess standing beside me. She smiled softly, as if containing a secret. "Zayim, did you meet Chloe?"

I did not expect this to be the topic. "Yes, Abbess."

"She's such a sweet girl. I'm sure she'll be a great daughter to you."

I dug my toe into the dirt as a chuckle escaped my chest. Vernard cocked his head in question, and Marta did the service of explaining the situation to him.

"Well, congratulations then, Grandfather," said Vernard with a friendly slap to my shoulder.

"Yes, well, let us hope I get to see the babe." I raked my forearm against my brow, smearing the gathering sweat into my hair.

"Everything will turn out fine," said the Abbess with that enigmatic smile still upon her face. I wished she'd reveal whatever was in that look of hers and still the pounding in my heart.

"Do you know something I don't?" I asked.

"Nothing I can think of, but I have faith. And so should you. Things work out when we leave them in His hands."

I tried to muster a smile, but I believe it turned into more of a sneer. She patted me on the shoulder, as if the gesture would add to my courage, and stepped past us to the gate to speak with the guards.

"We can get a better look at them on the battlements," Kai said, and we followed him up a nearby spiral staircase. We stopped midway down the battlements and squeezed between a pair of branded archers.

Forty horsemen gathered before the door, five abreast in eight rows. A man in the front middle stepped forward and called up to those upon the battlements as his horse, a black giant with a rippling mane, pranced with excitement. It was not the Captain we had met before, as he stood in the line behind this man with Sebastian beside him.

Sebastian gazed up at the wall, his eyes locking with mine. I looked away as my stomach rolled with nausea. "What are they saying?" I asked Kai.

"The man in front has identified himself as the Duke of Orleans, the magistrate over this district. He states that if we are not brought out, he will bring the issue before the king and return with an army to seize the nunnery."

Vernard leaned past Kai's shoulder and asked, "Will that not be declaring war on the Church?"

"If the Church backs up the Abbess, then perhaps," he said, still facing me, knowing his voice would carry behind him as well. "She has many friends in the Church, but several enemies too. I suppose it will depend on how high in office her contacts go as compared to this man's."

The gates swung open a fraction, and the Abbess slipped between the massive doors.

"What the devil is she doing?" cried Kai.

The horse pranced back a few paces as the Abbess approached, looking like a child from up high on the battlements. Her veil trailed upon her shoulders, and she stepped to the man's horse. The beast jerked back, but then dipped his head, pressing it against her chest as she stroked the head and mane.

The Abbess spoke to the man, but the others said they could not hear her. I would never learn the words she spoke, but soon, the man dipped his head, clutching and twisting his reins. Abbess Marie continued to stroke the horse with gentle movements, petting his nose and cheek as she spoke with the master. The horse nudged her side, and she removed an apple for it to munch, then she turned to the wall and called to the men there.

"What did she say?" I demanded.

"She…uh—" Kai muttered. "She ordered the men to open the gates."

"She is giving us up?"

Vernard grabbed Kai's tunic, spinning him to himself. I did not catch the words, but his face was scrawled with anger and confusion. Kai spread his arms wide, expressing his mutual lack of understanding.

Marta slipped her hands around my arm. "The Abbess has been our friend and ally for years. We need to trust her."

But my gut bubbled with uncertainty. There was very little capacity for trust left in me. Marta, reading my fears, wrapped her arms around me and pulled me into an embrace. I returned it, closing my eyes as I did so.

The embrace was interrupted by a tap on the shoulder as a man-at-arms approached our small group. "They want us to join them in the courtyard," said Kai. "We are getting that audience before the magistrate."

"Not that it will do much good, after raising arms against them," muttered Vernard. He walked past us to the stairs, stiff-legged and straight of face. With a deep inhale, Kai mirrored the straight-backed posture and walk, but I followed with shoulders slumped, my hand intertwined once more with Marta's. Perhaps for the last time.

As we re-entered the courtyard, I felt Sebastian's eyes boring into me from where he stood beside his horse. My hand slid to the knife at my belt as I noted the torn place on his tunic and the white of a bandage showing beneath it. The wound had been enough to draw blood, but not big enough to do serious damage. In other words: enough to anger but not maim. I imagined the taste of his whip striking my back and flinched. Marta squeezed my hand tight, bringing me back to our present reality.

The Abbess mounted the steps of the keep and had the Magistrate join her while Sebastian and the Captain also came forward. We drew near, staying in our clump as one.

Faustin stood by the gates, eyes wide as he clutched Ranae's hand. He gestured in question whether or not to come forward, but I motioned for him to stay with as subtle a movement as possible. He was not the instigator of trouble. Hopefully, the Captain had forgotten him entirely.

"Abbess," said the Magistrate, "I would like to seek a more private venue for these proceedings."

"No," said the Abbess with a shake of her head. "These things will be spoken of in public for all to hear." She nodded to the growing crowd now bordering the forty men. Some held weapons, but most were common folk. More than half wore brands.

"With an audience such as this, I fear a dispute may break out," reasoned the Magistrate.

She raised her head high as she looked over her people once more. "Only if you strike first," she said, and a ripple flowed through the crowd as if stilled by her orders.

The lip of the Magistrate rose, but he said, "Very well. I hereby charge these four with espionage, which, during times of war, is punishable by death."

"And I charge that one—" the Captain pointed at me. "—The slave with rebellion against his master, also punishable by death."

I frowned at the specific hostility against me. Dead was dead, was it not? What did an additional charge matter?

"If you hand them over to us," said the Magistrate, "we will leave with no further trouble."

"You will not take them without hearing their case," said the Abbess.

"They are not citizens of this country," said the Magistrate. "We are not required to do any such thing."

Kai stepped forward from our group, jamming a thumb against his chest. "I am a citizen."

The Captain laughed aloud. "Such audacious lies! They are from Burganne, all."

"My name is Hezekiah son of Marcelin; Marcelin the blacksmith who ran a shop in Orleans for nearly thirty years," said Kai. "You know of whom I speak, Your Honor. You patronized his shop on more than one occasion. I remember your face."

For a fraction of a second, the Magistrate's brow retreated into his hairline, then he looked to the near glee-filled face of the Abbess. With a sigh, he asked, "He's your brother?"

"Yes," said the Abbess, her smile growing contagiously broader. "Hezekiah is a dutiful man who served his country in battle on more than one occasion."

"I recall," said the Magistrate. "But you disappeared for a long time. And now you return alive and unharmed, having lived in Burganne for some time."

"I was captured at the Battle of Kingsman Hill," said Kai. "Upon my release, I was employed by my master, here, Zayim."

"The slave is your master?"

"I am free." I stepped forward showing the brand on my wrist. "While journeying in Aquilla, I was captured by bandits and my papers were destroyed. I was then taken to an auction house and sold."

The Magistrate cast an eye upon his Captain. "So, your slavery was illegitimate making your escape not a crime, but an act of free will."

"Now hold on," said the Captain. "This all due to the word of some strangers—"

"A stranger whose word is backed up by the reputation of an Abbess no one in Aquilla will dispute!" The Magistrate clenched tight his fist.

"But they are spies!" cried the Captain. "That one bears the mark of Burganne!"

"I entered the country legally!" said Vernard. "I had papers signed by my king and the Marquis of Halfshire granting me permission to enter Aquilla to find my brother. I had no knowledge of the failure of peace between our nations!" He jammed his hand into his jerkin and removed the papers, handing them to the Magistrate.

Upon scanning the documents, the Magistrate handed them back and scratched long at his chin. "And you found your brother?"

"Yes!"

"Where is he? Have him brought forth."

"He has been wounded," said Vernard. "One of your men stabbed him with a pitchfork in the leg. And besides this, he sustained a blow to the head during his time enslaved and cannot speak."

"I must confirm all parts of this tale. Have him brought forth!"

A group of men entered the keep and brought out Dorsey upon a litter. His pale face would have sufficed for my investigation, but only after a long period of questioning followed by the consistent answer of "Four," did the Magistrate appear satisfied and Dorsey sent away.

"What are your intentions now?" asked the Magistrate of Nostria.

"I wish to take my brother home to my father's estate where he can heal," said Vernard. "That is my only wish. I have no further orders from my king or motives otherwise hidden."

"I cannot say your journey back will occur soon," said the Magistrate. "But I will see what can be done."

"You Honor!" cried the Captain. "Tell me you do not believe this nonsense! They raised weapons against us!"

"Captain, you allowed your men to be overwhelmed by a deaf eunuch and his friends. Not only this, but you conspired to execute a citizen of Aquilla and a war veteran without trial. I suggest you fall silent before you otherwise embarrass yourself."

"Excuse me, Your Honor," said Sebastian with a bow, "But what of my family's loss of a slave? We paid good money for him—"

"The slavery was illegitimate. Nothing is owed to you."

"I beg to differ, sir! We had no knowledge of the illegitimacy, and my family paid quite a large sum for him! My father is a very powerful man and a close friend of our king. If you do not handle this—"

"Oh, Blessed Mother!" cried the Magistrate before growing red as his gaze fell upon the gathered nuns. "Abbess, this is a nunnery. Do you have some trinkets or something to give the man so he will be silent?"

"I...uh..." the Abbess looked at me apologetically. "This is a poor nunnery, supporting many mouths. We have no trinkets."

My soul dropped to my feet.

Then a tug came upon the sleeve of the Sebastian. He turned with a bewildered look to see the beautiful Ranae.

"Sir," said Ranae, "if money is your concern, I do not have much, but I do have this." From around her neck, she removed a cross made of silver and held it out to him.

Sebastian's brow contorted as he stared at the object, then his gaze flitted to me.

"Please sir," said Ranae. "Zayim saved me from an existence too unbearable for words. At the least, I can offer something in exchange for his freedom."

A man with raven black hair and olive skin approached from the crowd, clutching a bag in his hand. "I have very little, sir," said Maccario, "but it is yours if you release him."

Another man approached; one I did not recognize. "This man, Zayim the weaver, showed me the way to freedom. Now I have a wife, a family, and a future. Please, take what I have. It is not much, but—"

"Sir! Take this!" another said, shoving a bag forward.

Faces, bodies, and purses blurred before my eyes as my knees shook. Marta tightened her grasp around my hand, adding her strength to mine so I could stand. A few faces I recognized as they approached from their time spent in the hole in my floor, but most I did not know. Each had similar stories – he showed me to freedom.

Emotion welled up inside my chest, escaping with a groaning cry, and I clamped my hand upon my mouth. Tears dropped from my eyes, but I did not care who saw. Purses, jewelry, and trinkets piled up before the feet of Sebastian as he gazed upon me with wonder as if seeing me – truly seeing me – for the first time.

And the Abbess beamed at me, those mysterious, secret eyes glowing with mirth over the outcome none of us had seen. When the outpouring of love from my fellow former slaves had ceased, the collection about Sebastian's feet tallied to a small fortune, perhaps more than what I could have ever made for him. Wordlessly, the men gathered the money onto their saddles, loaded up, and left.

And I was free once more.

CHAPTER THIRTY

Nuns, I discovered, love a celebration, and by the end of the day, we had two causes for it. During the commotion following the leaving of the magistrate, the priest promised for Chloe and Etienne arrived.

I noticed the priest the moment he arrived in the courtyard, brow depressed as he observed the jubilant clapping and spontaneous dancing. The joy only known to those familiar with oppression once that oppression is removed. Etienne had fetched his lyre and – per Marta's description – played a cheery tune.

The priest's habitus was a dark brown girded by a white cord with three knots. A rosary with massive beads hung on the opposite side of the cord. As he walked about in his bewildered state, no one else seemed to notice him, so I approached him through the crowd. "Can I help you, sir?"

"What?" he cried, pointing to his ear. "I cannot hear you."

I smiled at the irony of the moment. "Come with me," I beckoned, leading him to the steps of the keep to where the Abbess stood.

Once his song was completed, Etienne bowed before the crowd of dancers who clapped at his performance. "Excuse me fine people!" he said, "I must go get married!"

Laughter poured from the merry group as they waved him a fond farewell. Gathering Chloe on his way, they joined us: Sloan, Kai, Marta, and I, upon the steps and we entered the keep. Shut off from the boisterous crowds, the inside of the keep felt almost too still. Unlike the monastery where we collected Ranae, the convent had a warmer feel to it. Perhaps it was a higher prevalence of torches, or perhaps it was the love and life of those who lived here. Imperfect people with imperfect lives pursing love in the shelter of steadfast stone.

Inside the chapel, several stone arches stood on either side of the aisle leading to the altar. Above them were windows from which sunlight streamed through causing squares of light to rest upon the stones. Wooden benches carved with ornate designs sat in rows. At the front stood the altar with massive pewter candle stands the height of a man with twenty candles each.

Etienne and Chloe joined the priest at the altar as the rest of us took a seat in the second row. As I sat beside Sloan, she turned her hips from me as if afraid I may brush against her. I pretended not to notice the constant ice surrounding her, but it bothered me more than I allowed her to see.

"Since the circumstances surrounding this union are more than noticeable," said the priest, nodding to Chloe's abdomen, "I would like to emphasize the importance of marriage concerning the future. We do not dwell now upon mistakes of the past, but instead look forward to the future for the sake of this family and child. If there are any grievances left to be had, now would be the time to express them."

I glanced at Sloan who continued to show me her shoulder. I had not spoken to the woman in years. If there were objections, they were not spoken to me.

"Very well then," said the priest as he opened a well-worn book, "we shall continue."

I did not understand the words read from the priest's book, so my attention wandered to the couple standing side-by-side, holding hands. I thought of Sloan and how close we once had been.

Surrounding us on all sides was this dark, long-lasting grievance that I had no ability to address. Her suffering was not my fault, and this hatred for me had ceased to be rational a long time ago. Still, it hurt to think of where our friendship had started and how it had ended.

My heart was an open wound when I came to live at my new master's house after witnessing the death of Alonya. For nearly a month, I pretended not to be able to read lips or speak, but Sloan overheard me talking to Alonya's ghost when I thought I was alone.

Words were something Alonya and I had shared, and I did not wish to share them with anyone else. Sloan did not tell our master I knew how to speak, but eventually, with her encouragement, I revealed my ability to him.

"You lying welp!" Gabor raised his hand to smack me, but Sloan protested.

"Please!" she cried. "Please, it was a mistake, Master, but his heart was broken. You understand, don't you sir?"

"I saved you because I thought you were harmless and helpless," said Gabor. "Now I find you can speak? How do I know you were not plotting with the man who killed my brother?"

"If I would have known, I would have killed him, sir," I had said as tears sprang into my eyes. "I have no family, sir. They were the only people I ever knew. My world was that estate. I would not have destroyed my world for such as Eglis."

His lip twisted as he considered me, hand still raised. But then he lowered it again. "You will not lie to me again, boy. Or you will face the consequences."

And I obeyed this order – up until the day he betrayed me.

Etienne slid a ring over his bride's finger and she glowed with pride. And as they made their vows, I made one too: to ensure they received a better chance at this than Sloan and I had been allowed.

***

By the time the ceremony was completed, the celebration was in full swing, and the newly-weds entered the hall with applause. Chloe and Etienne were drawn into the crowd by the shaking of hands, pats on the back, and well-wishes.

Massive plates of food and copious amounts of wine flowed throughout the dining hall, and the room rippled with activity I could feel through my chest. Marta took my hand as I entered the space, and I beamed at her soft face. I, who was generally not overly fond of large groups due to the quick back and forth of flapping jowls, caught on well to this merriment. Especially considering the joyous events of the day.

We pushed through the crowd to a spare seat near the corner, and only upon sitting did we realize the space across the way was occupied by Vernard and Dorsey. Half of Dorsey's plate lay untouched while the other was a scattered mess as he tried to eat with his right hand. He sat propped up in the corner with his leg upon the bench, wrapped in clean bandages. His face was still a bit pale, but had improved some in color.

"Good evening, both of you," I said. Vernard returned the greeting, but Dorsey offered a half-sneer in return.

"I've already said it once, but congratulations, Zayim," said Vernard. "This has been an interesting day, no?"

I looked over my shoulder to see the man and his new bride, still shaking hands with well-wishers. Etienne glanced at the door, and his plastered smile cracked momentarily. He nodded toward the exit, and Chloe took a step in that direction, but a nun intercepted their path, leading them to the food. Interesting that women destined to live lives of celibacy were so eager to celebrate the married couple.

Dorsey attempted another shuddering bite, spilled half, and slammed the spoon onto the table. He picked it up with his left hand, but Vernard pressed his palm against his brother's forearm. "I know you are frustrated, but this is for the best."

Dorsey patted his stomach emphatically.

"Perhaps every other bite?" I suggested. "We don't want the man to starve after all."

Vernard bit his lip as he considered this proposal, but Dorsey shook his hand free and plopped a bite into his mouth before returning the spoon to the weaker hand.

"Keep in mind that Dorsey wishes to get better too," I said.

Dorsey extended his hand to me with a nod then pointed to my tankard. He raised his fist up vertically then turned it horizontally.

"Excuse me!" I called to a servant. "Would you mind getting this man some ale?"

Dorsey nodded at me once more with a giant smile.

Vernard, however, frowned. "You have been making that motion to me for the past half-hour and I never understood it. Was that your meaning the entire time?"

"He was mimicking a pitcher being poured." I reproduced the action, and Dorsey nodded emphatically.

Vernard shook his head. "I swear, weaver, you understand my brother better than I do."

"I doubt for long," I said. "You two will develop an understanding between yourselves no one can beat given time."

Dorsey rolled his eyes.

"You will," I insisted. "But with everything, it will take time."

Vernard looked over his brother, still unsure and uncomforted by my words.

Marta tapped me on the shoulder, and I turned to a young woman who had stopped at our table. "I'm sorry," she said, "but my mother and I came through your shop when I was nine years old. I did not get a chance to thank you earlier, but you brought me to freedom, sir." She clutched my hand and brought it to her lips, kissing it. "Thank you, sir. You do not know the blessing you gave."

My cheeks flushed as the maiden disappeared into the crowd, and I cleared my throat and took a sip of ale. Marta tapped me on the shoulder, and I nearly choked to see a motherly woman past her forties with two children at her side approaching now to give thanks. Dear God, was this to be a continual event?

"You have quite the fame here, weaver," Vernard noted when they were gone. "It seems you helped half the country find their freedom."

I took a drink in response to this statement. Had I been in Burganne, this would have meant I deserved death several times over. Thankfully, since my crimes were in Burganne, Candorlan could not give a damn.

Vernard stood and said, "Would you mind staying with Dorsey for a moment while I speak with the Abbess? I wish to discuss plans for our return trip home."

"That's fine," I said, and he smiled thinly.

Dorsey's lip turned up as his brother left and he dropped his head to his chest.

"He's bothering you that much?" I asked, and he nodded emphatically once more. "Your brother cares for you, that's all."

"Brothers like that are rare," said Marta. "I wouldn't take him for granted."

Dorsey pointed to Vernard, now sitting beside the Abbess then circled us and pointed to himself again. I read this as 'I'm fine. I don't need you two babysitting me.'

"Would you like us to leave you alone, Dorsey?" I asked. "We could step away for a moment and you could wave if you needed help."

His shoulders heaved in a sigh, and he shook his head, gesturing to our plates as if to say, 'You're here now. Go ahead and eat.' But another former slave approached, and I was soon caught up in conversation with them as well leaving my plate untouched.

A rhythmic vibration shot through the floor, and I looked across the way to see Etienne with his lyre upon his lap. People swayed, clapped, and bounced their legs to the beat. Marta's heel started to tap and a few even got up to dance. I did not know the words to the song, but it must have been catchy as many sang along with Etienne, his bride included.

So that is how he captured such a fine maid.

I slipped my hand into Marta's, feeling the vibration of her heel tapping through her body. It was pleasant, being surrounded by such a merry company, even if I could not hear the music itself. Even the nuns joined in on the tune, clapping as they sang. I did not think nuns sang much beside their prayers.

Only one conversation continued through the celebration: Vernard's and the Abbess's. They were too far away for me to clearly make out what was being discussed, but the expression on both of their faces was grave. Then Vernard pressed his hands against his eyes, shaking his head with a look nearing distress. What was it they discussed? Because I doubted travel plans would be that concerning.

Marta tapped me on the shoulder once more, and I cringed as I turned to her, expecting more well-wishers, but she pointed to Dorsey instead. His mouth was open and words poured forth from it. I looked at the others about him, they were the same words formed to the lyrics of the song – elongated in such a way that I could not understand them, but the same nonetheless.

"Is he?" I asked Marta.

"Yes!" she cried as a tear breached her eye. "He's singing with us!"

A smile erupted upon the lad's face as he sang. What was this magic of music and lyre that caused the mute to break forth in song?

I did not know, but I clasped his hand across the table, joyous in his moment of speech.

Vernard, hearing his brother's voice from across the room, raced to him, grabbing him by the shoulders. Then he joined into the song as well.

CHAPTER THIRTY-ONE

A thick mist covered the ground, preventing any view beyond the nunnery walls from those within them. The beginnings of sunrise penetrated the fog causing the air to have an ethereal sheen. In the center of the courtyard stood two saddled bay mares, packed and ready to leave.

Peace would not come between Aquilla and Burganne for over a year, but the Abbess used her contacts to secure passage for Vernard and Dorsey with an envoy of priests bound for Burganne a few weeks later.

I did not expect to feel much emotion upon the leaving of Vernard and Dorsey, and was surprised to find sadness gathering in my belly. I told myself it was due to the leaving of Dorsey. The boy had, after all, manifested a sort of charm while within the convent walls. More than one maiden had been wooed by his singing, and his speech had expanded daily.

Most of his speech was reserved to objects rather than actions, but combined with his gestures, he was learning how to make himself known. Vernard, although he understood his brother better than most now, continued to push Dorsey to speak. If Dorsey gestured for a pitcher, Vernard would prompt "W—" and wait until Dorsey at least attempted to produce the word "water." It was slow, and both brothers were often frustrated, but the boy was much further along than he had been.

Besides gaining in speech, Dorsey had gained in wallet-size as well. The nuns did not approve of gambling, but turned a blind-eye when anyone sat across from Dorsey, hoping to gain money from a win at backgammon. Due to his speech and weak arm, they assumed him to be without sense as well.

Vernard added to the game by dispelling any qualms of competing with an 'imbecile' by shaking his head and uttering, "He must learn not to bet all his money. How will he learn if he does not lose?"

Within a few moves, the gambler would learn of his mistake, then another would sit down behind him, thinking himself more clever than the first. Watching the exchange and loss of money had become a favorite pastime of mine. Things would be quite boring after they left.

When time came for Vernard to assist Dorsey into the saddle, Kai stood on the side opposite, ready to catch the man if he fell. But once seated, Dorsey held his back straight, although he did have to clutch the saddle more than once for balance. Vernard would be sure to make the journey slow, and the man would be in the best of hands.

Besides the Abbess, only Kai, Marta, and I had come out to say farewell on that cool morning. Everyone else who cared to had said their goodbyes the night before. Faustin had already returned to Lasen with promises to write Ranae. I suspected his main reason for returning was to gain permission from his father for engagement to the maiden, as they had become inseparable since arriving in Candorlan. It was either that or he left to escape an accrual of gambling debts from Dorsey on the backgammon game.

Before mounting his horse, Vernard shook my companion's hands, meeting their eyes as if equal. I tried to resist it, but a twang of doubt lingered in my gut. Sure, he had learned to respect us during this journey, but would he return to his previously black and white view of the world once he returned? Once the pain of his missing brother dissolved?

But it was not my place to determine man's fate, so, when he came to me, I took the hand and shook it firmly, resolved to hold no lingering resentment toward him or the system he had pledged fealty to.

"Thank you, weaver, for all you have done," he said. "I will not forget your help."

"You're welcome, Vernard," I said. "May God give you a safe journey free of further trouble."

Vernard lingered with my hand pinned between his as he dropped his gaze to the ground. "I fear my journey may just be starting once I reach my father's house. I have learned much over this time, and things cannot be as they were for me."

I did not understand his meaning.

"You once created a tapestry for my father's estate," said Vernard. "I wish to commission another of your works, the funds for which I will send as soon as I return. Instead of the flower being positioned over your home, I wish it to be over mine."

My jaw fell open. Surely, I had seen incorrectly, but Vernard patted my hand a final time then reached for his saddle. Once upon the beast, he confirmed his statement saying, "I shall send you a map of the area. And, at the price I shall be paying, I expect it to be your finest work."

"As soon as I find a loom, I will begin it," I replied.

With a nod, he tugged upon the reins, turning for the gate. Dorsey nodded to us as well before following his brother and the priests through the archway and down the road.

My friends stood slack-jawed as well as we watched them leave – all but the Abbess that is, who continued to wear her sly smile.

"He knows of the maps?" said Kai. "My God, we shall have to send word to have them burned or—"

The Abbess smacked her brother's arm. "The man meant as he said, Hezekiah! He wishes to help us, not hinder us."

"Are you sure?" said Marta. "He is, after all, the man who arrested Zayim. His father sentenced Zayim to death!"

"He had me flogged!" cried Kai.

The Abbess folded her hands into her large sleeves. "And did not Saul of Tarsus persecute the church before he became Saint Paul? Just as Paul saw the Savior on the road to Damascus, your Captain saw the Savior on this road. He witnessed the suffering of his brother and of you, Zayim." She pressed a warm hand upon my cheek. "He saw his hand in the midst of these evil deeds and repented of it. I have spoken with him often these past several days and am sure of his devotion."

"Forgive me, Abbess, but what did he say?" I replied. "Since it is my work he wishes to procure, I would like some assurance of my own before I trust any of my people into his hands."

"I understand, Zayim. We first spoke the night of Etienne's wedding, the night when Dorsey first sang…"

"I am the son of the Magistrate," Vernard had said to the Abbess. Around him others danced and made merry, celebrating the victory won for Zayim against those who would see him enslaved once more. Victory against someone like himself. "I have a duty to my father and to my country. Part of my responsibility includes returning stolen property and punishing those who would take it."

"And by property, you mean people," said the Abbess.

Vernard stammered, taken aback by the correction. "Yes, that is correct. Nobody would deny that they are men and women. But they are tools of a business as well. The people of Burganne who own slaves are not evil men. Most of them are God-fearing people who provide for their families and care for their livestock and slaves. But…"

"But what, Vernard? What causes you to pause?"

"I…I know Zayim's former master, Gabor. In fact, he has eaten at my table more than once. Gabor is one of the God-fearing men I would have referenced if I did not know what he did to Zayim. Something so unnecessary and violent against one of the kindest men I've ever known. And worst of all, it was an act I could see myself doing."

"It was in his right to do it," said the Abbess.

"Which is the root of the problem, I suppose." He straightened in his seat as if replenished by a new truth. "Zayim is right. A man should be in charge of his own destiny." Then he pressed his hands to his face as if seeing the conflict of his own revelation was too much for his eyes to bear. "But I am the son of the magistrate. I have sworn fealty to the crown. I cannot recant such oaths."

"Who is your highest master, Vernard?" she asked him. "The king or God?"

"I swore fealty to the king and God."

"There are times when it cannot be both," said the Abbess.

Vernard sat frozen, his gaze boring into the table as a bead of sweat gathered on his brow. "God, of course," he breathed.

"And when God brings you to stand before his throne and asks you why you did not turn away those being led to slaughter, what will you say to him? That you did not know?"

"No," he whispered. "I could not say that. Not any longer."

"Then I think, Vernard, you know what to do," said the Abbess.

"But how can I approach my father? How can I tell my wife what I intend to do?"

"We are not called to do what is easy, but what is right."

And with this statement, a grim resolve settled over Vernard and he set his face as stone. He gazed across the room as if seeing the future road ahead. But then a melodious voice floated to their table, and the whole room stilled, turning to hear the song. Upon recognizing his brother as the singer, Vernard leapt from the table, crossed the room, and slung his arms around Dorsey. Weeping, the brother sang, joining in the celebration.

Upon hearing the testimony of the Abbess, I too became resolved. The first tapestry woven on my new loom was designed for his household. To my knowledge, it still hangs in his hall to this day.

EPILOGUE

"And that, young Adeline, is where you come in." I smiled down at the infant set upon my lap as I cupped her between my arms. Her mouth opened, creating an 'O' and a bubble formed upon her lips. As it burst, her little body shook with her giggles.

Movement caught my attention as the door to the church opened. Marta smiled at me as she descended the stone steps and crossed the courtyard to where I sat upon the bench beside the gates. "Is the service over?" I asked.

"Nearly just," she said, taking the seat beside me and running her hand over Adeline's downy hair. "Not much longer and I think she'll be asleep."

"You say this," I said, "but I have spent the past hour telling her how we got to Candorlan, and she has yet to yield."

"Would you like me to take her for a moment?"

I considered the option, as my bottom had grown numb from sitting, but Adeline smiled up at me, kicked a foot free from her blanket, and played with her toes. "No, I don't mind holding her," I said.

Marta looked to the tower where the brass bell rocked. Soon, the church doors opened once more and a crowd of people stepped out. They parted the way, however, for Ranae and Faustin to pass. Ranae wore the dress I had sewn for her, although Marta had taken it and modified it to make it more presentable for a bride.

Faustin clutched the hand of his love as they made their way through the crowd, and I smiled as I slid my hand into my own love's hand. According to Church law, I might not be able to marry her, but we had decided to live as a family nonetheless. It caused a bit of a scandal, but there would have been a scandal regardless of what we did.

A hand rested on my shoulder, and I looked up to see Etienne and Chloe standing beside me. "Father," said Chloe, "would you like me to take her back?"

"I do not mind holding her," I said. "I'll watch her until she becomes fussy, hmm?"

With grins as large as their faces, the two merged into the crowd, hand-in-hand. "You spoil them, watching the baby as much as you do," Marta said, nudging me in the side with her elbow.

Adeline gripped my finger and I swayed her fist back and forth. "This little one spoils me."

"Well, I am going to go get food."

While she was gone, I continued to hold the little bundle, talking to her, ignoring the crowd around us. When a shadow fell across me, I expected to see Marta return, but it was Sloan. With a smile, she caressed the baby's cheek.

A pang of jealousy stole at my chest. Sloan was my greatest competition for holding the child, but I also knew I could not deny the grandmother from her turn. "Would you like to hold her?" I asked, attempting to hide the grumbles in my voice.

Gathering her skirts around her, Sloan took the seat upon the bench beside me, and I passed Adeline to her. With smiles and words I could not understand, Sloan bent over the child and spoke to her. Adeline giggled and squirmed as her grandmother ran her fingers up her ribs, tickling her.

I frowned at this. Afterall, I had spent the greater hour trying to coax the child to sleep, and now she had awoken her. But I held my tongue, knowing that my words would do no good. Soon, however,

Adeline yawned and stretched, nestled against the bosom of her grandmother and fell asleep sucking on her thumb.

I continued to watch the child as her chest rose and fell with ease, no fear or burden weighing in her sleep. When I raised my gaze to Sloan, I was surprised to see her watching me. Smiling at me.

"She's beautiful, isn't she?" Sloan asked.

I cocked my head to the side, startled by the break in years of silence. "Yes," I said. "She is."

Then Sloan returned her gaze to Adeline, rocking and cooing at her once more.

Acknowledgments

To all those who had a direct hand in making this dream a reality, I offer my love and sincere thanks. To my beta readers and critique partners: Connie Swann, Bertha Hague, Andrew Rucker Jones, Marcel Stipetic, and Zoltandeak of Critique Circle. Thanks also to Miracle Blakenship, Zenko, Belle Moon, Christine Erikson, Sara Erickson, and Devon Erickson who publicly supported me during the "X" controversy that should never have been. Comments regarding this not-even remotely controversial book were the catalyst to all the drama. The internet is weird, but y'all are awesome!

With all my heart, I thank my family, especially my husband for listening patiently to twenty different versions of the same chapter without spontaneously combusting or walking away from my nonsense. Thanks to my mom for watching the newborn so that I could actually finishing putting the book together, and to my sister for cheering me on, even when things got rough. Thanks also to Nana, who has now read more of my books than anyone else!

And thanks to Igor Dunaev, who painted the cover!

Did You Enjoy The Freedom Weaver?

Consider Leaving A Review!

The Freedom Weaver is not just an entertaining tale, but a story that demonstrates the real-world psychological effects that slavery has on those who have suffered from it. Unlike what we would wish to believe, slavery is far from ended. People daily experience the horrors of slavery through human trafficking. Their experiences are different and most of society does not accept this treatment as they did in former years, but it is far from over. If nothing else, this book is written as a way to acknowledge these victims and to bring awareness to their plight. Also, my hope is that those who have suffered trauma will find comfort and strength from seeing their experiences reflected in others. But the impact of this story will only be felt if they know that these books are out there for them. Leaving reviews does not just let others know you liked this work, it incentivizes platforms such as Amazon to advertise it to others. It does not take much time to leave a review, but the help that it brings to the series cannot be understated!

Go to linktre.ee/rwhague to let people know how much you enjoyed the read!

9 789898 927057 6